THE KILLER WHO LOST HIS MIND

THE KILLER WHO LOST HIS MIND

MATTHEW A. KNORPP

Copyright © 2023 Matthew A. Knorpp.

All rights reserved. No part of this book may be used or reproduced by any means,
graphic, electronic, or mechanical, including photocopying, recording, taping or by
any information storage retrieval system without the written permission of the author
except in the case of brief quotations embodied in critical articles and reviews.

This is a work of fiction. All of the characters, names, incidents,
organizations, and dialogue in this novel are either the products
of the author's imagination or are used fictitiously.

Archway Publishing books may be ordered through booksellers or by contacting:

Archway Publishing
1663 Liberty Drive
Bloomington, IN 47403
www.archwaypublishing.com
844-669-3957

Because of the dynamic nature of the Internet, any web addresses or links contained in
this book may have changed since publication and may no longer be valid. The views
expressed in this work are solely those of the author and do not necessarily reflect the
views of the publisher, and the publisher hereby disclaims any responsibility for them.

Any people depicted in stock imagery provided by Getty Images are
models, and such images are being used for illustrative purposes only.
Certain stock imagery © Getty Images.

ISBN: 978-1-6657-4495-9 (sc)
ISBN: 978-1-6657-4497-3 (hc)
ISBN: 978-1-6657-4496-6 (e)

Library of Congress Control Number: 2023909866

Print information available on the last page.

Archway Publishing rev. date: 8/10/2023

PROLOGUE

Some people work for money or for enjoyment or even just to work with their friends. Those kinds of people want their sacrifices to be justified. I totally understand. It makes sense. Why work somewhere where you will be unhappy? Why work with people you don't like? I mean, sure, you might get paid good enough money. But some people value their minds. They don't want stress. They don't want to grow old and tired from hard work and be weak-minded because they didn't get to work with their childhood friend. Sure, they'd be richer if they made a different choice. But then they'd just be more unhappy in retirement.

I said I understood it. But do I? I mean, it's just the way life goes.

That's what I hate in life however, having to work hard and then be unhappy. This is not a ploy to convince people against capitalism. No. Most of the time, in any part of the world, the agony of retirement and loneliness is unavoidable. Might as well die young and happy, rather than live old and sad.

Then again, who's to say retirement is sad? You get to spend time with your family.

I was worried about something that wouldn't affect me. Why had it been on my mind recently?

My work, on the other hand, is simple. I'm a gang member—a paid killer. I'm a monster to some, a crook to many and a hard worker by income standards.

Most of the time, I'm more of the courier sort. I get paid to watch and report like some stalker or private investigator.

It's illegal work and frowned upon by those same people who live unhappily. Were they jealous? Was I in denial? No. They just knew it was wrong, and I couldn't justify what I do. In truth, sometimes I was told to do things even I didn't agree with. But I didn't care. I was just content with the whole thing. I was completely emotionally detached. It worried me from time to time. But I wouldn't be that good at my job if I were all sympathetic.

As to my backstory, I started off my younger years as a decent and well-mannered kid in the streets of Los Angeles. I was young and careless. I didn't understand life, and I didn't listen to politics or adults. It was adolescence. I was just another kid being a kid. As a teenager, the other kids and I partied and tested the boundaries of the law. We all thought we were special and unique and lucky just because we were having fun. It was just the way us kids thought. To live without fear, to be wild and never regret—it was what we valued.

Some things stuck with me from that time. That regret itself would drag me down with sadness; it would show weakness. One guiding principle had stuck with me this whole time—a strong mind gives you a strong will. Mental prowess was something I'd always strived for, and that remained true to this day. Mental strength was important for me. It kept me calm in times when I needed to be.

When I was done partying, I simply joined the military, as dropouts often do. It was one of those random decisions fueled by no thought or planning. I just woke up and flipped a coin pretty much. I was in the Marines for a good couple of years. They taught me structure, discipline, and everything else I would need to know in my future with and without them. The corps itself taught me I should've gone to college, and those people were always on my side.

Within my first six months overseas, I acquired my first confirmed kill.

A local Iraqi ran up to me with a knife in his hand.

Everything changed after that. I wasn't the same person I had been an hour earlier. When something like that happens, you tend to go through many stages of emotions over the course of a couple days depending on the situation. I was different. I didn't want to be, but I was. I was completely emotionless about the whole thing. No remorse. Was there something wrong with me? Or was I just glad I'd survived?

Looking back, it's almost like he wanted to die, running at me with an open chest and closed eyes. An investigation was started, as he'd been one of local contractors helping out on base with ethical work. Everyone was very surprised. No one could make sense of it.

He was forced to retire at the age of sixty-seven—no family, no children, no next of kin, nothing. All he enjoyed doing was working on base. It's all he had, and we took that away from him. We turned into the bad guys.

I saw his reasoning while no one else could.

I was consumed by the fear of loneliness. I was still young, so there was no reason to be. Still, it was a scary thought. What about all these other people? These Marines, Sailors, Airmen, civilians—whoever. Could their sadness be prevented? And why did I think that was my problem?

Maybe if I was so set on this idea of sympathy toward the lonely, I could do something about it. Right?

These thoughts first came up after the incident with the Iraqi, and they kept coming back. Over and over in my head, these migraines of constant thinking about this one subject played out.

If you were wondering, I didn't enjoy killing this man—especially as he was someone who could have been helped. Regardless of how I felt with all these contradictions in my head, I never chose to regret what I did.

My service flew by after many years of grunt work and good conduct. The ending itself, however, was more of an unfortunate circumstance. The more I thought about it, the angrier it made me. It was unfair to have been cheated and framed for brutalities such as those assigned to me. I hadn't wanted to talk about it afterward. And I didn't want to now. Not yet.

Those thoughts came back, though, and stronger than ever. What caused loneliness? In a sense mostly of what could be prevented, I concluded it was violence. Violence drew apart families and countries. War and killing separated us. I wanted to prevent that. But how could I, fresh out of service with a dishonorable discharge?

Many options came to mind—how to help. How would I be allowed to do anything with my kind of record, though? Looking back on how I'd tried to do the right thing while in the military, I saw that one thing had always gotten in the way. The law.

Even saying that out loud made me think I was some sort of vigilante. It didn't really steer me away though. I was still dead set on the idea of being some hero—especially when I thought about how I hadn't deserved a terrible ending to such good military service.

I couldn't even show my face in my hometown after everybody had heard. I had to relocate. I put thirteen states between me and them— from Los Angeles to New York City. With the scenery change, I started a new life—a life of crime. I became a gangbanger with the goal of the betterment of society. Even when my morals started to slip and fade, I could always turn back to the thought in the back of my head. *Give back to the community*. But how could I after the government had treated me so wrongly?

For a long time, I couldn't. For a long time, I was selfish and harsh. I wasn't a vigilante. I was a goddamn criminal. Or at least that's how it started.

Andrew Carter McGraw

1

The banker called me in after some time sitting patiently in the waiting room. I followed him into his office and sat down as he shut the door behind me.

BANKER. So, give me the rundown, Carter.

The "banker's" name was Todd. He was my immediate supervisor and a close friend. The whole bank was a sort of cover to run our meetings and money laundering. I would come by to give him updates and to collect payment.

CARTER. Well, the husband actually turned out to be cheating on her. And as she requested, I broke one of his legs.

TODD. I don't care. Was she happy?

CARTER. No. She couldn't believe I did it, so she paid me half.

It was a sad aspect of any person's career to know they weren't doing at all what they'd signed up for. Save the world? No! Go be a couple's therapist. Bullshit.

TODD, *practically ignoring me, as if the statement had bored him.* I'm sorry to hear that.

Anyway, I have something different for you. None of the normal stuff.

CARTER. If it's getting a cat out of a tree, I swear to God.

TODD. Ha. You know you're really not funny.

He was being a real asshole today. It was starting to frustrate me.

TODD. A client wants you to protect a jewelry store.

CARTER. You're kidding.

TODD. No.

He seemed confused at my tone. I leaned forward over his desk.

CARTER. Todd, that sounds fucking stupid. I'm not a goddamn bouncer.

TODD. Why are you complaining? It's only like one fucking day. Besides, you said you wanted to do more shit. So just take the job.

CARTER. I mean, I'll take it, don't get me wrong. But you should still know my opinion on it.

TODD. Carter, I've had a long morning, and I'm not trying to hear any of your jokes. If you're gonna accept it, then fuck off.

There was this saying I heard a while ago when I was still in the military—overreact at the simple things so, when something that requires extreme focus comes along, you'll remain calm. You'll have considerably less stress. I was skeptical about it. It was based on psychology or something or other. Wasn't my expertise, so I never really worried, but it was always a thought.

The meeting went as normal after that. We bickered back and forth. We were friends, so we could handle it without getting upset at each other. Todd slid a file over the desk that contained the information for the job, and it was time to go home.

I admired the sights of the city on my way back to Tremont in the Bronx. The run-down businesses and overrun homeless alleys were always upsetting. But by this time, I was used to it. I didn't want to be, but it was so common and rooted in every class of wealth's home turf that you could never escape them. I was always curious about them, though. Each of them had their own lives, their own stories, but it all went wrong. I didn't care enough to fight it or learn more.

My apartment itself was nothing special—a bedroom, office, living room, and kitchen. The balcony cost extra, and I thought it was worth it. The fridge was constantly stocked with beer and expired food, so I usually ate out. Tap water may have been too dangerous for consumption in the city, but it was the best I could get here, so I made do.

I didn't consider my lifestyle healthy, but I took pride in my work, and I considered myself to be somewhat happy. It was rare that plumbing or electricity were a problem, so I was lucky in that sense.

I lived on the fourth floor, so I could get a decent view of an identical complex across the street, where hardworking single mothers smoked on the terrace on the same level as me. I could even hear the yells of their multiple children from my balcony. It was almost like looking at a different world. A state of poverty and hidden kindness, and all just across the street. Even smiling at them couldn't make them smile back. Sad.

Across the hall, there was a similar story. But this woman smiled through it, and I actually believed she might be happy. She must have had an easy job that paid well. No double shifts and no double jobs. Her name was Sandy. She had two kids—one girl and one boy, both around six or seven. I usually passed by as she was struggling to open her door with her hands full of groceries and her kids arguing at knee level. I would smile and greet her, as she's my neighbor after all, and I wasn't going to avoid communication. I wasn't rude.

I'd even attended her son's sixth birthday celebration a couple of weeks ago. I'd had a stupid little party hat and everything. I'd thought about buying him a little toy gun, but Sandy had decided against it. So I just bought him a toy car.

My apartment could get messy at times, so I just pushed debris and clothes out of the walking lane with my feet. I wasn't really the cleaning type—it wasn't in my genes. I'd get around to cleaning though. Just not as often as I should.

When I was home, my free time varied from watching movies to playing video games or just sleeping. It was somewhat boring. I'd get out one of these days; just not today.

This night in particular, I sat out on my terrace listening to the distant gunshots and sirens for an hour or two. Then I went to bed half-drunk. Love this town.

Waking up could be a struggle for some people. It was hard sometimes, I understand. For me and probably for many others, it didn't matter what time they went to bed the night before. Waking up in the early hours of five or six, you'd never be fully rested; you'd just be tired and sluggish.

I didn't like coffee. It gave me the shits. So on the rare occasion I decided to eat breakfast before going to work, I made tea. Usually, I'd fill up on snacks or get breakfast on the job, which could lead to distractions sometimes. One time, I hadn't had breakfast, so I got Subway and was eating on a park bench while I was supposed to be tailing someone. I got lost in my food, and then he was gone.

I had to be more careful.

This time, I just ate some gas station precooked garbage in the car and was finished before I arrived. The jewelry store opened at 7:30 a.m., and I arrived at 6:45, but not even the manager was there. I just had to wait. It started to rain, so I took some shelter underneath the overhead above the door.

Luckily, the manager arrived a mere fifteen minutes later. He was a nice person, but I was in no mood for civil conversation. My day was already off to a bitter start. He opened the glass doors, and we both walked inside while introducing each other.

JEWELER. You must be my help for today.

CARTER. Uh-huh.

JEWELER. Well, there's no need for much of a tour, I suppose. The bathroom is connected to the break room in the back next to the office.

CARTER. If you don't mind me asking, what exactly do you need me for?

JEWELER. Protection.

CARTER. Why don't you just call the police department and get one of them to do it? I'm sure it's a lot cheaper. I'm not complaining; I'm just curious.

JEWELER. You needn't worry about that. Just act like a customer and keep an eye on people. No trouble, no problem.

He said it with a smile and a nervous look. He was hiding something—I knew it—something he didn't want the cops to deal with. Or someone. He was expecting a situation.

It was basically a retail job at this point—a horrible occupation meant for teenagers and retirees. I'd had this job before; it was unbearable, borderline psychological torture for me. I couldn't understand it. Risking your sanity for money. Some people enjoyed this, in which case they'd lost their sanity already.

I did as I was told and walked around for the first couple of hours, acting like some sort of customer. I grew frustrated when employees kept asking me if I needed assistance, at which point I told the manager to make them fuck off. He understood.

Either this manager had been threatened by teenage punks yesterday, or he expected a robbery so large it required help from a crime syndicate. I didn't know. I might have been overthinking my predicament. The jewelry looked high-end, though, so I supposed the manager made a decent living. Especially with a location in lower Manhattan, a couple of blocks from Times Square.

Around twelve thirty or so, after I finished my lunch from the break room's vending machine, I went back out onto the floor. Two guys in flashy suits walked through the front door and immediately up to the register, asking for the manager. This was definitely something I could be here for. I was certain.

The girl at the register looked petrified and pointed toward the back rooms. I turned myself around and went directly to the manager's office. I walked in and closed the door behind me.

CARTER. There're some suits here for you. Should we be concerned or cautious for any reason?

He fumbled with the papers on his desk for a moment.

JEWELER. Don't let them touch me, OK? We're gonna let them in. And we're just gonna talk. Maybe let them know your armed; just don't let them do anything rec—

There was furious knocking at the door. How did he know I was armed? Some things still didn't make sense.

We looked at each other for a moment. He was pale. He looked terrible. I was unfazed. I pointed at the door and asked if he wanted me to open it. He nervously nodded.

I opened the door of course, and as the gentleman I am, I attempted to shake hands with the men. They obliged and responded politely. To be honest, I was surprised. But obviously, they weren't here for me. They were gangsters, after all.

GANGSTER. Who's this, Saul? Your new bodyguard?

SAUL THE JEWELER. I'm entitled to protection from thugs. I know my rights.

GANGSTER. Oh, thugs? Is that what you think we are? A couple of fucking low-life thugs who take pleasure in fucking over old men in their jewelry stores, huh, Saul?

The man's accent was some cliché Italian fucking mobster accent. It made me smile.

But there was no fucking way. Right? The mob was dead. After the '80s, the whole business had crumbled. The Mafia had died out as crime syndicates and gangs took their place long ago, and the remaining stragglers of the crime families had been forced to run away and hide.

SAUL. I don't have your money, OK. I'm asked to pay an unfair amount, which even you can agree. So I can't do it. It just can't be done. It's unfair, and you know it.

GANGSTER. I don't get paid to argue with my own fucking boss, OK. I get paid to get him paid. So you've gotta give me something to go back with, or we're gonna have to ruin your day.

At this point, the man started to become physical, whilst the other assumed I would intervene so he stepped in front of me all tough like.

The first man slammed Saul's head on the desk and pressed him there.

GANGSTER. I swear to God, Saul, I'm not here to fuck around anymore. You're starting to get on her nerves.

Her? I thought. Definitely not a Mafia. They didn't hire women. It was just their tradition. These were definitely some sort of syndicate thugs who liked to play dress-up.

SAUL, *starting to cry in fear.* Please don't—

GANGSTER. Saul!

Well, at this point, I kinda figured it was my time to intervene. I knew the man guarding me wouldn't expect it. I had been unfazed throughout the whole altercation thus far. So, he'd assumed I couldn't be a threat and had turned his head to view the entertainment.

I was being paid for this anyway.

I intervened.

I took the head of the guy in front of me and slammed it into the wall next to me. But that wouldn't be enough. So, I grabbed a nice, thick book off the bookshelf behind me and ensured it made contact with the entirety of his face. Then I delivered a nice uppercut to his stomach while simultaneously swiping his knee, so he would lose his balance.

This was all done within seconds keep in mind. It needed to be quick, especially with his partner at high tension.

At this point the apparent main man of this duo had noticed my violence. So, he began to look up but not before my hand was already cocked back to launch the book at his head. The point of this was to cause a distraction, as I was too far away to do the kind of damage I had done to the other guy. I knew this, and I couldn't just keep launching shit at him like a fucking monkey.

He was stunned and confused for a second, which gave me an opportunity to put my left hand on his face, my right hand physically threatening to pull his arm out of its socket, all while I swiped his legs so he, too, would lose his balance.

And I wasn't even out of breath.

GANGSTER. What the fuck do you think you're doing? What's wrong with you? Do you even have any idea—

At this point, the other guy got up, sluggish and out of breath to reach for what I assumed was a gun out of his holster.

So I drew my attention to him.

CARTER. No, buddy. Sit the fuck down. You do anything dumb, I'll pull your friend's arm right out, right now.

I increased my tension on the arm of the man I was holding just enough for him to yell in pain and to further illustrate my point.

This entire choice of intervening wasn't smart. But that wouldn't cross my mind till after. Why the fuck had I just done this? I must've been only thinking about my responsibilities, rather than how powerful these men could be.

It may have been a little too late. But at any rate, I tried to deescalate the situation.

CARTER. Now here's what's gonna happen. We are all gonna fucking calm down and settle this like civilized men. Isn't that what we want? To be civilized? Now, I agree that Saul—(*directs attention to the still terrified jeweler*)—shouldn't let you fine gentlemen leave without considerable compensation for your good work here today. So, I'm gonna let you go, and you're not gonna try anything, because if you do, I just might break your arm instead of bruise it. Do we understand each other?

He wasn't responding, which promptly required a good tug on his arm.

GANGSTER. Fuck. Yeah, fine. Sure, pal.

This was risky but I had no choice if I wanted to get out of this situation. I first got him to stand up and then pushed him over to his buddy.

We stood there, still snapping back from what had just happened.

GANGSTER. Where did you find this guy, huh, Saul?

His mood had changed, and my stress was lifted. This man believed I could do it again. Good.

CARTER. Pay them, Saul.

Saul sat there, still grasping reality.

CARTER. *Pay them!*

He snapped back and fumbled to a safe under his desk to pull out what looked like a decently concerning amount of cash to put in a trash bag, of all things to hand over.

CARTER. Are we happy?

GANGSTER. You know, I'm a little sore. But I got what I came here for. So, how can I complain?

He was being sarcastic. He wanted me dead. I could see it in his fake smile. They both did. I was gonna have to deal with them at some point. I knew it.

Shit.

They got their bearings back and left calmly. They didn't want a handshake, so I didn't try.

SAUL. You were supposed to help me.

I became frustrated.

CARTER. And you told me I was just standing guard. You didn't tell me shit, all right. Even when I asked, you kept me in the dark. So, tell me now. Who were those fuckos? And what did you do?

SAUL. They're fucking punks. I paid for protection. And after a while, I stopped paying. But they kept showing up. I told them not to, but they still expected money.

I was done with this. Fuck this place and fuck Saul.

CARTER. Well, fuck you, Saul. I'm going home.

SAUL. Don't you want your money?

CARTER. No. Keep it. They'll come back for more. And besides, I need to save my own ass now.

I left quickly. I needed to get out of there. I needed to protect myself from a fucking self-inflicted gang war. Maybe I wasn't being calm. Maybe I was overreacting. All these thoughts rushed back and forth.

Was I scared?

Shit.

I couldn't help constantly looking in my rearview mirror and memorizing license plates of cars that had been behind me for miles at a time. It was habit and a good one in my profession.

I even tried doing unnecessary shortcuts and detours just as a safety precaution. I ended up going in circles for some time.

I was being followed.

Shit. I knew I fucked up. Damn my boredom. I had wanted action. Well, I guess I got what I asked for.

This may have seemed like minor problem. But with my overthinking, I think ahead as if everything is a domino effect.

Eventually, I stopped at a red light with my tail a mere two cars behind me. I couldn't get a decent look at the driver, seeing as the windows were tinted. I realized I may need to break a few traffic laws for this one. But I wouldn't dare run a red light in lower Manhattan.

The light turned green, and I just put it to the fucking floor swerving in and out of slower vehicles I caught up to. I took a turn a little too fast and almost pissed myself but got back on track and drove into an alley, breaking off my driver's-side mirror and scraping my old paint job.

I stopped the car at the dead end and got out armed and ready to defend. I knew a dead end would leave me at a disadvantage. But I did it for a lack of witnesses, not my own safety. I wasn't worried about that.

The car never showed and after five minutes or so. I was in the clear.

I might have been too cautious to leave car in Bowery and get a cab. But I needed to be careful. I would pick it up later before the fucking residents stripped it for parts. It was a shitty situation, but I had to make tough decisions for the safety of myself and my employers. I didn't want some sort of war. *But it might be too late.* There I went, overthinking again.

The cab took me a block or two away and behind the bank. I gave the driver a normal fare and no tip. Too careful? Nah, I'm cheap anyway.

Walking a couple blocks trying to look as casual as possible, I even stopped at a hot dog stand to survey a bit. I was OK. But I wasn't safe.

2

I just barged into the office without consideration for the bank tellers who tried to stop me. Todd already had a customer sitting in front of the desk.

TODD. Can't you see I'm busy, Carter? What the fuck.

The way he vulgarly addressed me told me how upset he was that I'd disregarded protocol and showed up unannounced. I didn't care. There was danger on its way, I was sure of it.

CARTER. Hey, pal. You here for like a mortgage or loan or something?

I couldn't help making a joke.

MAN AT THE DESK. Well, I—

CARTER. Don't care. Get up. Get out.

TODD. Carter!?

CARTER. Now.

He got up and left, confused. He might not have been here for anything of the sort. Maybe he was even here for the same line of work as me.

TODD. Carter, you can't just—

CARTER. Todd, shut up, OK. Fucking I just had to beat up two fucking gangsters of what I think may have been a rival syndicate. Then I was followed.

TODD. Slow down. What are you going on about?

CARTER. Do we know any rival gangs with a female boss?

TODD. What?

CARTER. Damn it, Todd. Do we or do we not?

TODD. Yeah. The fucking Russian Mafia has some bitch in charge. And that's all I know.

CARTER. Todd, they weren't fucking Russian, you retard. They were Italian.

TODD. Look. What happened at the fucking jewelry store?

I explained to him verbatim the entire event and my thoughts on what it could mean.

TODD. You're overthinking it, Carter.

At this point, I almost beat the shit out of Todd. I was frustrated and aggravated. I might've been scared. I had good reason to be.

TODD. Maybe it's some small thing we haven't picked up. Or it's a joke, as in they're so small they're no one.

A joke? Was he serious. He was a just so clueless. He didn't know how to act, so the best course of action for him was just assume it was nothing. Completely useless.

I shook my head. I told him about the car and asked him to have someone pick it up for me and take it home. I was being cautious. I took a cab home from there.

Was I overthinking it? Better safe than sorry. The drive home made me think through all possible outcomes and all solutions. It made me more on edge. I didn't like it.

Out in the foyer, Sandy was screaming on the phone about court dates and divorce proceedings. I just nodded and headed inside. I was starting to calm down at this point, but there were still some thoughts in the back of my head that worried me.

My apartment hadn't been broken into. But I checked the rooms to be sure it was free of any unwanted guests.

I grabbed a beer and sat down, reminiscing on my poor choices.

To be clear, I don't work for some fucking gang, like some fucking Albanian or street rat crew killing people of different-colored clothing. I'm not scum. I work for a motorcycle crew. Big difference.

Hypocritical, I know, but not entirely.

Over the last decade or so, the Outlaws motorcycle club had split into different sections after internal conflict. Our section was more professional and bureaucratic. We didn't rape women or beat up fags. We left that to the riders—who I don't associate myself with. I just did my job and got paid. I was like a businessman with no affiliation with the bikes. In fact, I couldn't even ride a bicycle. I mean, I knew how it worked. I just was no good at it.

The cops didn't even know our section existed. As far as I was concerned we weren't strength in numbers but, rather, strength in power. We were few, but individually, we were as efficient as many. God, that sounded selfish. But I didn't care. I knew I had training others never even got the opportunity to hear about. I was lucky, and I knew it. And I was grateful. Even in my service, I was given time to train with more special warfare types. There are a lot more people who are mentally unstable then most think; it made me a little uncomfortable at times. To see an operator burn out cigarettes on his biceps before slamming a bottle of whiskey is entertaining at times but concerning often.

Some people in my work asked me why on earth I would give up the opportunity of a lifetime and turn to a life of crime. I never told them my story. They would never understand. I had been unlucky in a sense. But still, it was none of their business. I surprised myself sometimes with my overconfidence on matters I knew nothing about. Maybe it was ego. Maybe it was selfishness.

I was lost in thought at this point, not realizing my beer hadn't been sipped in minutes. I didn't even want it anymore.

Todd called me moments later to inform me that my precious, shitty used Ford Corolla had been vandalized. I was surprised it had happened so quickly. But then I found out the car had been incinerated, just set ablaze, and that doesn't happen in Bowery. What had happened to my car? It wasn't locals. It was competition.

I slept early on my thoughts after a useless day with no money. I always keep a gun under my pillow. But this time, it had one in the chamber.

I got up at a decent hour with no place to be except wanting to get a new job from Todd. I got ready and looked for my car keys and got frustrated. Eventually, I remembered what had happened. I said good morning to Sandy on my way out.

SANDY. Hey, Carter. Good morning.

Oh, Carter. Can I ask you something?

This struck me by surprise. I stopped and turned around slowly to stare for a second before responding, unsure of what could follow.

CARTER. Sure. What's up?

SANDY. My car is at the shop, and Timmy has a soccer game at five. Do you think it would be a burden if you could help drive him there later if you're not busy of course.

I felt heartbroken. What bad timing. Well shit. Now what?

CARTER. Sandy, I'm really sorry. I have a meeting at four down at the police academy. I'm so sorry. I could lend you money for a cab.

SANDY. Oh no. It's fine.

CARTER. Are you sure?

SANDY. Yes. Thank you though.

SANDY. Have a good day, Carter.

CARTER. You too, Sandy.

In all situations when asked my occupation, I tell people I train cops in New York City. It helps explain some things like long hours or law enforcement experience. I still felt bad of Sandy's predicament though. I'd make it up to her.

I caught a cab to the bank, with breakfast just down the street from it, where I requested to be dropped off. Gas stations make really good omelets—proven fact.

I walked in and sat down patiently, unlike yesterday. I was sure to behave this time around. I must've startled workers and civilians in here. I already recognized some faces from before. Todd's door opened, and he waved me in for a another always fair contract opportunity.

TODD. I got a fucking grade A one here for you today.

CARTER. Better not be another joke.

TODD. No. You just have to go to a psychologist.

CARTER. Do you think there's something wrong with me?

TODD. No. Apparently, this doctor has been giving his patients illegal drugs and manipulating them into taking their own lives.

And don't worry. I already booked an appointment for you under the name Jeffrey.

Was yesterday meaningless? Was I being punished? I hadn't even accepted the job, yet I was already undercover.

CARTER. OK. That's kinda fucked. What am I supposed to do?

TODD. Go in there and kill the son of a bitch.

Murder but seemingly justified. I didn't refuse but, rather, graciously accepted. More often than not, our side of the Outlaws did good deeds that cops turned a blind eye to. It was our way of giving back to the community, I guess.

Todd, having a gentle heart and being a good friend, let me borrow his car. I was, of course, thankful and wished to repay him. But he assured me there was no need. I'd fill up his tank anyway and buy him a case of beer later.

This one was another job all the way in lower Manhattan. But at least it wasn't in awful Bowery. I wouldn't want Todd to lose his car too.

Killing is frowned upon, and people normally aren't supposed to kill each other for obvious reasons. Taking a person's life is a hard thing to grasp for some people. People have lived their lives as long as you have lived yours. And then suddenly it's done, over. Gone. Imagine yourself at this time just stopping. And then you no longer exist. There will be no more future memories. Everything that could and would have been will not be.

To take a person's life and feel no shame requires either insanity or stupidity. I might be neither insane nor stupid. I might be both. But I felt no remorse In killing a person, no shame in it. As long as it was fair then it didn't change me. I had to use my skills against my enemy in order to outsmart him and eliminate the threat.

I drove by the familiar roads of yesterday, still with caution on my mind. They would come for me or at least try. But when and how?

There was something wrong. There were ambulances, police cars, fire trucks, and news vans crowded outside the jewelry store. Traffic gave me an opportunity to get a more direct and focused look.

The windows were gone, and the entire inside was charred and black. There had been a fire. This was no coincidence. They'd killed Saul for his disobedience, and next they would find me.

These weren't thugs. They were killers. I had started something. I knew it. I was right. Damn, I hated being right sometimes. If they did this, surely they would come to see their work with all this attention here in person. If so, it was too late to leave. I was stuck with no way out. There was no point. I may have already been fucked. It would be just a matter of seconds before some gangster came up to my window and blasted me. They would have surely seen me by now. Suddenly, the traffic had cleared, and I made my escape, but not without some nervousness on my part.

The doctor did his work from a little building just before the Brooklyn Bridge. Noisy real estate probably, but he got customers at least—Though it seemed they didn't leave with satisfying results.

I made sure my handgun was on safe like the professional I am, and I headed in. The office was on the fifth floor. But of course, a maintenance crew had to be doing repairs on the elevator this morning. And the vending machine was broken. Just my luck. And I'd left my silencer at home. God, I hated Tuesdays.

I avoided cameras the best I could. But it wouldn't matter if my existence was practically unknown to the police.

The receptionist was cute. I asked her for her number, and she was happy to let me in to see the doctor instead.

It was worth a shot.

THE DOCTOR. **Good morning. (***Looks down at his papers.***) Jeffrey, is it?**

CARTER. **Yes that's me.**

We shook hands and sat down. And he introduced himself as Dr. Allans.

I had to remain professional. I needed not only to keep up my acting and performance but also to remain vigilant and wary of objects around me that could be used to kill without the use of a firearm.

DR. ALLANS. **I'm gonna start off with asking you a series of starter questions if that's OK.**

CARTER. **Of course. Go ahead.**

Dr. Allans. So, tell me, Jeffrey. What brings you here today?

Time to act.

Carter. Well, Doctor, I'm just unhappy. I mean, first off, my job. It's just the same thing every day. Then time flies by, and I have no free time.

Dr. Allans. I understand. It's common to feel that way with a career that seemingly drags on and on, so much that it seems like two days or even a week could fit into the memory of hours.

Now, Jeffrey, how is your relationship with your parents?

Carter. My parents died when I was young, in a car accident.

This was an act. I wasn't the best at it making up stuff on the fly. Overconfident again.

Dr. Allans. I'm sorry to hear that. It must be tough growing up without someone who could truly love you for who are— someone who knows and understands what you can be capable of?

His response was really weird, even for my taste. I tried hard to act like I was listening and not confused.

I sat there and nodded.

Dr. Allans. Over the past month, have you felt depressed or helpless?

Carter. Every day more and more. It just feels like it's stacking up.

Dr. Allans. It can be a rough world out there not knowing what to do next or where to be or what to eat. It really hurts people sometimes because they really are hurt. and sometimes they just can't be helped without proper medication or advice.

Now, Jeffrey, are you currently on any medications or prescriptions?

Carter. No, not currently.

Dr. Allans. I'm gonna recommend you two medications that you should take before going to bed. And don't worry. They're over-the-counter. You don't need a prescription.

Was this man seriously, after only a couple questions, recommending medicine? For fuck sakes.

DR. ALLANS. You should go and buy some ray dol, and calcemin—

I didn't know what these drugs were or what they would do to me, especially combined before sleep. But I got tired of listening. I was literally just bored. I had a job to do but no way of doing it. Poor planning on my part. I looked around and saw the balcony. Maybe? Yeah sure. Why not?

So I just got up and walked over to the glass doors onto the balcony. The door was locked.

DR. ALLANS. Jeffrey, what are you doing what's wrong? Is everything OK, Jeffrey? Talk

This was really awkward. Nonetheless, the act continued.

CARTER. I want to go outside, Doctor.

DR. ALLANS. Jeffrey, I'm sorry. I cannot open this door for you.

Whether I find this justified or not, I have a job to do, and I must do it.

I looked over to the bookshelf next to me to see a bust of some Greek philosopher whose name I couldn't remember.

It seemed sturdy enough, so I tested it on his skull. Sure enough, it knocked him clean out. I searched his pockets for a key to the door. He was lying. He could open the door after all.

I unlocked it and dragged his heavy ass over to push him off. It would look like suicide, and in my eyes, it would be ironic—a doctor of suicide falling victim to his own methods. Literally. Falling. It seemed brutal and fucked up. But what choice did I have? The job could take a toll on you if you weren't careful.

I quickly ran out to the cute receptionist but not before taking the bust along as evidence not to be left around.

CARTER. Oh my God. It's the doctor. He just ... He ... he ... he just jumped. He just killed himself. Oh my God. Someone call an ambulance.

I needed to start a scene in order to cause a distraction so I could escape. And sure enough, a crowd of shocked coworkers had gathered and were streaming into the office to see what had happened. Amid the panic, I left. I was considerably hungry after the ordeal. But alas, the vending machine was still broken. So, I left through the back door and headed down the block. I climbed into the car, leaving the bust under the seat to throw it in the Hudson later.

In and out, just like that. There was a chance I'd done the whole thing so quickly it might have been reckless. But I needed to distract myself from my other worries.

I called Todd to tell him of my success. As my trusty accountant, he wired money directly into my account from the client.

And as promised, I went to the gas station to fill up the tank and then went into the store to buy a nice twelve-pack of some foreign beer whose name I couldn't pronounce.

I got back in the car, but there was something wrong. It all went bad. I wished I hadn't been so reckless. I hadn't checked the getaway for tails, and I hadn't even checked the back seat. It was too late. There was already a gun to the back of my headrest. Kinda figured this was coming; it was just a matter of time.

The guy with the gun told me to drive, so I did. I didn't need to dig myself a bigger hole than the one I was already in. There were opportunities to get out of this situation. For example, I could slam on the brakes, sending my assailant's body forward, along with the gun, over my shoulder. That way, I could grab the gun and his arm, pull him a little bit farther forward, and shoot him in the head.

First off, we were in traffic. And second, the next guy they sent might not be as friendly. They would just kill me on the spot, and I wouldn't see it coming. I had gotten careless. Maybe I should offer him a beer.

> CARTER. Hey, buddy. You, uh, thirsty back there or what? I got some premium shit up here. Might be good.
>
> GANGSTER. You think you're funny, do you? Think you can fuck with us and walk away? No. You're fucked. And you don't get a lawyer.
>
> CARTER. Really? Cause my cousin—
>
> GANGSTER. I said shut up.

At this point, he rammed himself into the back of my seat as a very poor and embarrassing attempt to shut me up. Why couldn't he just hit me? I was still in traffic, so not in much danger. Maybe he didn't want anyone to see. Or maybe I was to be left unharmed to be dealt with by the boss. Curiosity and overthinking filled my mind.

I followed his directions for around twelve miles until we ended up on some dock works in New Jersey. I hated New Jersey, and if I needed to, I would make any attempt possible not to die here.

I stopped inside some hangar with black Cadillacs and tinted windows. Scare tactics don't work on me. I'd seen them all.

I got out of my own volition, where I found around five other fuck heads pointing their guns at me. I was almost flattered at how dangerous they thought I was. They must've seen my record.

I looked around to see an office at the top of some stairs in the back corner of the warehouse. I knew where I had to go. So they didn't need to push me there.

These guys weren't very careful from what I could tell. At many times, I could have disarmed and killed them. These guys were rookies. They weren't competition. They were followers—jealous even.

To make these pigs think I had standards, I showed some common courtesy and knocked on the office door first.

It was opened slowly, which gave me a decent opportunity to view the surroundings as I was walking in.

Then I saw her. It was the boss. Or at least this was the conclusion I came to at first. She was blond and around thirty, and to be honest, she was not fucking hot.

I sat down in front of the desk on a nice quality rolling desk chair with only three wheels. I couldn't expect much. It looked like this placed had been long since abandoned.

CARTER. **Good morning**

I held out my hand, smiling. But she was in no mood. She even had the audacity to light a cigarette instead.

Boss. **Do you know who we are? Do you have even the slightest clue?**

She was also a bitch.

CARTER. **Jumping right into it, huh? You must be a busy lady. Well, no. I don't know, I'm afraid.**

Boss. **Well, we know who you are. We know exactly who you are.**

I was getting bored. At this point, she pulled a file from the desk and began reading. "Andy McGraw was born February 26, 1996, in Los Angeles and lived there for nineteen years, at which point he enlisted in the United States Air Force as an engineer. He served in that capacity for some time—enough for him to achieve the rank of staff sergeant and enough time to have twelve confirmed kills, most while helping Navy SEALs in the Middle East. And now he goes by Carter."

I was aware of the file she was reading. It was a fake—an altered document, a fabrication. The name was accurate for this stage in my career. The story behind the origin of this document comes later. For now, I was curious how the fuck she got it in the first place.

CARTER. If the theatrics are supposed to scare, me you've got the wrong man, miss.

BOSS. Why would I want to scare you? No, no. We just want you to understand that knowing who you are is an easy task. We have power. We have friends in high places.

And you decide to try and fuck us over and attack two of my men.

It was embarrassing. She was acting like some sort of leader. Maybe I was just sexist, but she didn't seem to fit the part very well. She must be new, or her father really wanted a son instead.

BOSS. We know where you live as well. So there's something to sleep on.

Sleep? They weren't going to kill me. They needed me. Or I'd have been dead already. Something was not going to go in my favor today. I was sure.

BOSS. We also know about that poor innocent doctor you just threw off a building.

She was trying to find a pressure point.

Don't give them one.

CARTER. Well, it was a balcony actually. And rumor is he actually jumped off.

BOSS. Don't give me that shit, Carter. We saw you. And by the way, he was an innocent man. He did nothing wrong. I personally put up that contract to see what you would do—to see if you had any sympathy, any shame.

CARTER. So, I guess I'm here for my payment then?

It was the best and worst part of my day. On one hand, I'd pretty much been kidnapped. But on the other, I could fuck with these clowns.

BOSS. You're heartless. Besides, your guy at the bank already paid you.

OK, now she might know too much. But maybe she was guessing, and my reaction would tell the truth.

CARTER. Bank? You already put it in my account?

BOSS. Carter, we got Saul to tell us where he got you from.

Well, damn. She wasn't bluffing on this one. I was growing bored of this, and I had shit to do anyway.

CARTER. OK. So am I supposed to feel something? Fear? Anxiety? You knowing this information doesn't really make me feel uncomfortable. If you read deeper in my file, you would have seen it says I'm a trained psychiatrist. (This was also fabricated.) I used to pick slow minds like yours for a living. I can control my emotions and use them to make the next move before my adversaries can understand their own. I'm not retarded, miss—

ANASTASIA. Anastasia please. My friends call me Anastasia.

The fuck was going on? Friend? She was mocking me.

CARTER. Right, Anastasia. So tell me—and get right to the fucking point—what do you want from me?

ANASTASIA. OK, Carter. You're an experienced man. I'll give you that. But you're record also says you've been admitted to rehab on two different occasions—once before and once after your enlistment. That tells me you have flaws. So, you can't tell me you're perfect, no matter how much you think you are.

That took me by surprise. The government didn't tell me they'd put that in the file.

ANASTASIA. Tell me, how is your relationship with women?

I was, at this point, confused beyond fucking comprehension. I thought she was likely still looking for pressure points. Even all the other goons in the room raised an eyebrow or two.

CARTER. Huh?

ANASTASIA. I'm just curious. Your record says nothing about marriage.

CARTER. You're not my type. I prefer women without daddy issues.

She slammed her fist on the table.

I found her pressure point.

Damn, I'm good.

ANASTASIA. I'm not here for your fucking jokes, Carter. All right, you want me to get to the point?

CARTER. Well, that is why I'm here after all.

ANASTASIA. You work for me. Or we start war with the Outlaws.

Not entirely what I was expecting. But yeah, fuck.

CARTER. Oh shit.

ANASTASIA. Yeah. That's right, Carter. We own you now. You are our fucking property. Every single thing you do from now on is under supervision. You can't be trusted, but I'll give you credit, Carter. You're good at what you do. So now you're fucking ours.

CARTER. So, what am I, a fucking prisoner for war? Like what the fuck do you think this is?

ANASTASIA. We'll be in touch, Carter. Now get the fuck out of my office.

This could have been worse. But to be honest, I was pretty pissed off. This bitch thought she can just use me as some sort of pawn in her imaginary war against the patriarchy? I needed to call Todd.

CARTER. So you're telling me some of these fuck heads are just gonna be at my apartment. Is this something you just thought of, 'cause it's something I sure as shit haven't heard of before.

ANASTASIA. Get out, Carter.

I was done with this bitch anyway.

She opened her hand toward me to shake my hand. I just smiled and walked away.

CARTER. Oh, and by the way, you should consider redecorating. It's like a psych ward in here.

Was that the best I could come up with?

My two new best friends were, of course, Italians in suits. I'll admit they fit them well. They even looked mildly sophisticated. However, looks could be deceiving.

Al and Marvin were now my roommates and personal bodyguards who would live with me and probably drink all my beer. Bastards. The drive home was quiet and uneventful.

I walked by Sandy on my way to my door.

SANDY. Oh hey, Carter. How was work?

CARTER. Oh, not bad. One of the recruits accidentally pepper sprayed himself. But you know, recruits do recruit things.

SANDY. Ha.

Her almost uncomfortable laugh made the scene awkward. *Change the subject,* I thought.

Time to break these dummies in.

CARTER. Oh, this is Al. He participates in the Special Olympics. I mean, he doesn't look it, but damn he can waddle fast. He's to stay with me as a part of some corporate thing to show our sympathy for the NYPD and Special Olympics collaboration this year.

SANDY. Right.

She was very confused. But I was having a good time. Naturally, these guys weren't allowed to speak. They thought they had some sort of cover to maintain. But they'd warm up to me soon enough.

CARTER. And this is Marvin, his husband.

I moved forward to whisper to Sandy.

CARTER. He's not as cool, and I think he might be gay.

SANDY. Well you three have fun … I guess. So … see you later, Carter.

CARTER. Yeah. See you too.

I was skeptical at first. But now I think I was starting to have fun. I showed Al and Marvin over to my door and had to be a good host.

CARTER. Well, make yourselves at home. It's not much, but its ho—

Marvin and Al got in my face.

MARVIN. Let me fucking tell you something, pal. We're not your friends. We're here to make sure you don't fuck around.

AL. We're here to do a fucking job. And if you ever try something like that again, I'll bust your fucking face in—in front of your fucking girlfriend.

Humorous.

But what exactly was I supposed to not be doing? Maybe Anastasia just wanted to bust my balls and piss me off.

I grabbed a beer and offered the hardworking men some food. But they just called me a faggot and sat on the couch.

Not as humorous.

They just sat there relaxing with their feet up on my fucking coffee table like they were on break.

This was a joke; I knew it. But there had to be something more behind it. Scope out my apartment so they could kill me in my sleep? Or maybe these guys were here to kill me but only while I was vulnerable because they thought I was just that damn good. I had to stop being so selfish.

To be sure, I'd have to do something stupid—something I hated.

I'd have to stay awake the whole night and watch these clowns, understand their intentions. But I still had to contact Todd somehow. But how? I supposed I'd just text him. Safe and calm.

CARTER. You boys like call of duty or something? I mean you can watch TV or something. It's not like you have to be miserable here. Put on like a soccer game or cooking show or whatever it is you Italians like. I mean you guys obviously aren't here to kill me.

Good. Make them think you're sure you're safe and calm. That'll ease 'em up and make them vulnerable if I need to strike.

AL. No thank you.

CARTER. You sure? I'm pretty sure I got *Goodfellas* on Blu-ray around here somewhere.

MARVIN. We're fine.

CARTER. Fine. I'll fucking use the TV then.

I jumped on the couch from behind and settled right in between them. This was my place after all. I shouldn't seem intimidated by these thugs. Just for added aggravation, I turned on the TV and swung my arms around the top of the couch and behind their heads.

They obviously minded this move but they didn't protest. I just had to stay awake for another twelve hours until 6:00 a.m. according to my watch. That's when I'd start my morning routine.

CARTER. So we gonna talk? Or are you guys just gonna sit here all night? I mean sure you guys probably might want to fucking kill me for—

Holy shit. These were the same guys from the jewelry store. This might make things worse for my night.

CARTER. Holy shit. You guys are from the jewelry store.

AL. Would you shut up?

CARTER. All right. Look, guys. I don't want you to have a personal grudge against me for what I did. I'm sorry OK. I was there to do a job. And I gave you the money too. So I hope we can put that behind us and move on as friends.

I was trying to be sincere. After all, it was better for me to have as many friends as possible—the more the better. Originally, I wanted to be just anonymous, but it was kinda too late for that.

They still just sat there quietly.

I handed my beer over to Marvin with a smile on my face. He looked over but turned away. So, I nudged him for a second try. He slowly took the beer and shamefully enjoyed it.

CARTER. There you go. We're friends now.

I got up and handed Al a beer as well. He didn't seem like the kind of person to look out of place. So, naturally, he had no choice. I was warming up to these guys—that was until they searched through my cabinets for weapons and God knows what else.

It was only a matter of time before I had to kill these guys. But I didn't care. I didn't like them anyway. I was just faking my kindness again.

I could do it right now even. I was always aware of weapons in my surroundings and what could be used to harm, maim, or kill.

Maybe I could actually get some sleep. Or maybe I was lying to myself and being lazy.

I left the TV on and took a shower. And sure enough, when I got back, those rotten cocksuckers already had four beers each.

My mood had changed. But at least I was safer and, sadly, sober.

These guys weren't going to kill me. Or at least not yet. So why was I here? How had all this happened? What was going to happen next? So many questions still yet to answer.

I fell asleep on the couch around midnight, only to be jostled awake four hours later. I get cranky when I don't sleep. It really just pissed me off. I almost retaliated right then and there. He was an intruder after all. He had no point in being here. Neither of them did. I knew my rights, but I also knew the dangers.

CARTER. What, in the fuck do you want, Al?

AL. Don't you get fucking snippy with me. We got shit to do. Now get up. We're leaving.

CARTER. Al. You can't just fucking wake me—

No. Don't argue. Just get this shit over with. It was either follow orders or death. No matter how stupid these circumstances may be, I had to play the game.

CARTER. Never mind. Sure, pal. Let's go.

AL. Marvin's in the car. Don't worry about breakfast. We already sacked your fridge. You're out of cold cuts, by the way.

He was trying to piss me off probably after my recent antics. Cocksucker.

We got down to the car, and I noticed something funny. Someone had just dumped what looked like the contents of their entire fridge on the fucking sidewalk, coincidently right under the balcony of my floor. Now controlling myself would be a challenge.

We drove to some fucking bar on the east end of Brooklyn just to get some payment at five in the morning. Then we went to the hospital to check in on some gangster. And after that, we went all the way to Staten Island to go to church at nine in the morning.

Now, I'm not particularly religious. But this morning, I was considerably unmotivated to partake in running around the city to do these menial tasks. Was this a punishment? An orientation? Every time I asked Al or Marvin, they just laughed. This was a joke.

Todd texted me to say he had a job, but I told him I was busy. I'd never done that. Maybe he'd sense my stress and come and kill me. I could only hope.

We saw Anastasia around twelve for lunch after a couple back and forths through the boroughs and even New Jersey at one point for gas because Marvin was retarded and couldn't drive.

This was the only time I'd been able to eat all day. It was time to relax. The deli itself had a nice old-fashioned theme to it, with struggling, single mother waitresses and abusive bosses. I could see it in their eyes. They were overworked and underpaid. I can't save everyone. So I just smiled politely as we were handed menus. My smile faded when Anastasia walked in though.

ANASTASIA. Hey, Carter. How has your day been so far?

AL. He's had a fun time so far.

CARTER. Look, shithead. I can talk for myself.

I was breaking.

CARTER. This is a joke, isn't it? This is some punishment for me doing my job as your rival, isn't it? I mean that's the only option, the only conceivable reason for this bullshit.

ANASTASIA. I just want to see if you can be trusted. That's it. You think you get a shiny fucking suit on your first day. No. You have to earn it.

I was getting impatient.

CARTER. Anastasia, tell me this. What if I get up, walk out of here, and never fucking talk to you ever again? How would that feel? What would you do to me?

ANASTASIA. You're not afraid of us?

CARTER. What? No. I just think this is retarded in my honest opinion—like I won't fuck with you anymore.

ANASTASIA. Wow you must really hate hard work and authority. It's not surprising you ended up here.

Was I really being lazy? *Wow, I'm a scumbag.* No. It just must be my exhaustion and hunger. Yeah that was it.

ANASTASIA. Well, if you do, I won't stop you. But I'll kill your neighbor.

These people were sick. They were fucked, maybe even more than me.

CARTER. Anastasia—

ANASTASIA. You're useful to us. You have potential. And you can see how nice I've been so far. I don't want your skills to go to waste in this cold, dark world.

I sat there disgusted and silent. Did I care about Sandy? I mean, it would be horrible to say I wouldn't care if she died. But we were just neighbors. It wasn't like we were married. Should I care? *Jesus, what is wrong with me?* Maybe I felt a connection with her. Was I really considering this?

Thoughts raced through my head. Here I was, overthinking, overanalyzing, and contradicting myself at every turn. I was at war with myself in my own head.

CARTER. Then use my skills, Anastasia.

I had no choice. I had to bend over for these pigs. Either that, or there would be a gang war.

ANASTASIA. I knew you'd understand, Carter. Are you ready for your first job?

CARTER. Sure, doll.

ANASTASIA. Great. We got this little foreign bastard trying to fuck us over in marketing, and I'm gonna send you and Marvin to go teach him a lesson. Everything is already set up. You two just have to show up. I'll send Marvin the details.

She wanted me to make more enemies. Psycho.

CARTER. Marketing? What do you mean by marketing?

ANASTASIA. It doesn't matter. You don't have to worry. Just do the job and be done with it.

I hope you have good intentions with this. You can't have a bad first day on the job. Well, that's all I had for you. So, I'll just show myself out.

She got up and left. But I started to think the way she's been speaking to me these past two days. It almost seemed flirty, which was weird as shit to say. But she never seemed as authoritative as I would expect a fucking mob boss to be. Weird thoughts and unusual times were upon me.

Then the waitress pulled up to disturb my train of thought, so I turned to my bodyguards.

CARTER. OK, boys. Do we know what we want?

3

It was an exceptionally boring day in my opinion. How far would these guys go in following me? Should I test them?

Yes.

They accompanied me to my apartment again, and I didn't want this to be some sort of habit on their part. I needed some freedom.

I saw Sandy in the lobby.

SANDY. Hey, Carter.

CARTER. Hey, Sandy. How was work?

SANDY. Good. How's the, uh, Special Olympics thing going?

CARTER. The what? Oh yeah, uh turns out Marvin here can't run very well even for a retard. So we didn't get a medal or anything, just some ice cream. And, boy, let me tell you; these two love their ice cream.

SANDY. Oh awesome. Is that true guys?

God, I loved being a fucking scumbag sometimes because Al and Marvin were still the shit end of this fucking joke, and they basically just looked at each other, trying to hold back rage and simply nodded their heads.

Time for an escape plan.

CARTER. Hey, Sandy, are you by any chance doing anything tomorrow for dinner perhaps?

I felt like a Nazi using her like this. I could put her in danger. It was amazing how I could go from protecting her one second to using her as some defense the next.

I could protect her though. I was sure of it.

Confidence was my friend.

SANDY. Um, I mean sure, like OK. I just have to finish up some work at the vet. But OK.

She was nervous. She was excited. She was happy. I felt even worse. But my morals told me to ignore the feelings that weakened me. These were, in fact, dark times.

Maybe this was a good thing. Not being some bitchless loser. What was wrong with me?

CARTER. How does around six sound? I could pick you up here, and we could go to this nice place I know in Queens. It's a little family German place. I hear from people at work that it's really good.

SANDY. That sounds great, Carter. I'll text you when I'm home. We could maybe leave earlier. I'd just have to have Nancy take care of the kids while we're gone.

Nancy was this nice old woman who lived next door. So it all worked out.

CARTER. OK. Sounds good, Sandy.

I went on my way with my smile giving me pride.

SANDY. Uh, g-good night, Carter.

I stopped, turned around, and said good night as well. Was this what freedom would be like? It'd been so long already.

We got up to my apartment, and of course, the goons had nothing to say but more empty threats and looting of my cupboards for any food they could find.

Their anger filled me with happiness—so much, in fact, that I could sleep easy tonight. I was sure of it.

Todd decided to text me right as my eyes were getting heavy. It was amazing to have all my happiness taken away in just seconds. The texts went like this:

TODD. Any update on my car, you fuck?

Cheeky bastard.

CARTER. Mafia's using it. Out of my control, unless you want to talk to them about it.

TODD. You disappearing with my car and avoiding contact is pretty fucking suspicious, I hope you know.

CARTER. Fuck off, Todd. We can have a beer soon all right. You think I want your shit box? I am literally being held hostage in my own apartment. You can start a fucking war if you want over this. But trust me. You'll have your car back, and I'll make it up to you.

TODD. Hurry the fuck up, Carter.

CARTER. Goodnight. Love you too.

Todd was a good friend. He'd understand this better in person. But what could I do? I'd just have to wait for an opportunity. What an odd situation I found myself in. I wanted action. Well, I guess I got it.

I was happy to have the opportunity to sleep this time—to feel well rested and cheerful for the first time in what seemed like months when, in actuality, it was two days.

After a long night's sleep, I woke up energized and optimistic. I went into the living room to see Al and Marvin had brought back breakfast from the deli down the street—maybe because there was physically nothing left in my apartment to eat.

I was confused, but I didn't know why. I was speechless still, assessing my predicament maybe. Still not knowing what was next, I was still waiting for an opportunity to escape.

My bagel was cold.

MARVIN. Eat up, Pal. We got a big day today.

He was smiling when he said it. What had she meant by marketing? Something strange was going to happen. They were happy. They shouldn't be, not in my presence.

CARTER. So, guys, you think you could, by any chance, keep your distance for my date tonight? It would be greatly appreciated.

AL. You know what? If you do a good job today, we just might.

Another smile. Were they going to kill me?

They could sure as shit try. With that thought, I now needed to be on edge—to be ready. Anything could happen, and it just might. I needed to expect it.

AL. You wanna drive this time, Carter?

Why would they want me to do that?

CARTER. No. I'm more of a backseat driver anyway, Al.

AL. If you say so. Hurry up. We gotta leave soon.

I finished up and got dressed. I saw no reason to rush unless I was forced to. They weren't paying too much attention to my morning routine. I grabbed the gun behind the mirror. I didn't trust these bastards' sinister smiles. They couldn't fool me.

We got down to the car with no problem, not even a run-in with Sandy for one of my scummy remarks. I felt safe. But that's how they wanted me to feel. I sat in the back.

We drove for what seemed like hours. Fucking Crown Heights traffic.

CARTER. Just a quick question, guys.

I leaned forward resting my arms on their headrests.

MARVIN. Shoot.

CARTER. Is there a reason we need to go through little Israel to get where we have to go?

They were so surprised by the bizarre remark that their faces shifted instantly.

AL. Do you have like a fucking problems with Jews, Carter?

CARTER. No. I'm just asking why we're taking a weird-ass route here.

MARVIN. That's pretty anti-Semitic to say, Carter. You should be careful what you say nowadays.

I looked back and forth at them, confused. They had to be joking. I, for one, never held back from my opinions. I wasn't trying to be offensive. Everyone in Queens had their own nicknames for certain places.

CARTER. You're fucking me, right? You guys woke gangsters or something?

Weird morning to start.

Eventually, we ended up at the Holland Tunnel. So it was beyond me why we needed to go through Crown Heights in the first place.

Why not ask?

CARTER. Why did we need to go through Crown Heights if we had to be in New Jersey?

AL. What? You got another anti-Semitic remark to say, Carter?

They were joking. I was just on edge. *Don't let them get in your head.*

I don't know why people live in New Jersey to be honest. It's a shithole of a place. In my opinion, I think I'd rather live next to a meth lab in Detroit then some noisy factory in New Jersey. Just my personal opinion. And don't even get me started on the New Jersey Turnpike.

We eventually came down a dirt road and pulled in to some old, abandoned warehouse just off the turnpike.

Yep, this is New Jersey, I thought.

CARTER. What is it with you people and warehouses?

MARVIN. In case we need to kill someone.

Nice one, dickhead.

There was already a van outside next to a car or two. They were waiting for us—or me.

We walked inside, and Al closed the door behind me.

It was a nice empty space with a couple greasers on catwalks watching the main entertainment. Another couple were just standing around the chair.

Jesus Christ.

Some poor bastard with a bag on his head was surrounded by torture tools.

What the fuck have I gotten into?

This was the foreigner meddling in marketing.

I'd seen it all, but this made me sick. But why was I sick? I'll admit I had to see this shit in the military. But this was bad. Maybe I was out of practice. Or maybe I knew this man could be innocent.

They wanted me to feel this way. They wanted me to, watch? Participate? They wanted me to appear vulnerable.

I couldn't be, no matter how awfully this could go. I had to keep my composure—it might just keep me alive—even if it required a terribly sick sense of humor. But who would break this silence?

CARTER. Let me start off by saying this is the worst bachelor party I've ever been to.

Some of them smiled. I knew I had the right crowd.

CARTER. I'm Carter by the way.

MAN ON CATWALK. We don't need introductions. We don't need anyone's names. We just need to work.

They really were going to torture this man. And they didn't trust either me or each other when it came to what would happen when this was done.

I sat on one of the countertops nearby to watch. I knew Al and Marvin were going to watch me carefully. They wanted to see my reactions. They wanted to see my composure.

Al sat next to me.

They started.

One of them took the bag off the head of the man in the chair. He was Asian and covered in tattoos. He seemed terrified, as he should be. They were gonna kill him when they were done.

GANGSTER. What's your name?

Lo and behold, the guy didn't speak any fucking English. But they didn't need him to speak English. That's why the other guy kept heating up a rusty stake with a blowtorch.

I turned to Al.

CARTER. What kind of marketing was this again?

AL. Don't worry about it, Carter. Yaks aren't gonna be a problem around here?

CARTER. Yaks? Yakuza?

He kept silent. I knew his statement was a fucking lie. "Not a problem around here"—he probably never had to deal with these guys or at least never kept them alive. I had to deal with yakuza when I was stationed in Japan. They made me fear. I felt fear—true fear. I had seen them do awful, horrible things. They just might have to kill this bastard, or he'd come back for revenge.

The yakuza kept their organization like a holy tradition past down for generations—because, to them, it was. They were trained killers and wannabe genocidal maniacs. My fear in them was well placed. But my position in this scenario was not.

The screaming—it just kept going and going. I realized these guys must've been experienced in torture because of how long they could keep this guy alive.

I just wanted them to be done—to just kill him already. I had been here for over an hour now. They wanted me to crack. But no. I just put on a smile—no matter how sick I felt. I needed them to feel intimidated. After a while, I didn't feel sick anymore.

Some time had passed. They were exhausted. They only communicated in Italian, even though they knew English. They just didn't want me to know what they were saying. I was sure of it.

Al motioned to me.

They picked up the body, and I was almost forcibly shoved out the back door with the rest of these guys, looking out onto the empty field in the backyard.

They handed me a bolt-action rifle.

Marvin had his pistol out pointed at me behind my back.

They want me to kill this man. I felt less bad than I would have otherwise, knowing this man was in the yakuza. But still, there was something in the back of my head telling me no. *Ignore it.*

MARVIN. You shoot this chink, and we'll set up his bitch."

This man was pushing around an Asian woman. She was squirming. She was terrified. The yakuza screamed and limped over or at least attempted to.

This was chaos.

They put the man on his knees, looking out into the field with a gun to the back of his head.

The torturer whispered in the girl's ear.

TORTURER. Run.

At least she understood him. Maybe him shoving her right after made her understand.

She ran into the field. She was running away.

Al pointed his gun to the back of my head.

AL. Shoot.

I thought I'd considered every possible outcome, but I hadn't seen this coming. I just hadn't seen it. I've trained not to hesitate, but they were pushing it.

I wished I had more of a choice.

I took a deep breath.

Every step she took made it a harder shot for me.

If I let her get away, they were just gonna kill me. I didn't want to be a selfish person; I had been that person all my life. But I could kill these pigs. I just had to do it.

I aimed.

The yakuza man was crying. How was he even still alive? Was it love that kept him alive? Would that be something I'd ever feel? And I mean real love, not being horny and fucking around with the town bicycle. God, I needed to grow up.

I shot.

There was silence as she fell to the ground. They were laughing. He was screaming. I could see it. But I just couldn't hear it. Why couldn't I hear it? Was I getting my sanity back after all these years? Was it PTSD? Was it shame?

They lowered their guns and left the man alive. It was time to leave. Just like that, we were done. Mission accomplished.

But I didn't feel successful.

The sound came back, and all there was—all I could hear—was the man crying. I knew this man couldn't be innocent with his ties, but she was.

This was what they wanted me to see. This was what they wanted me to feel.

I felt it.

I started to tear up.

This wasn't fair. Why me? Why did this have to happen to me? Why hadn't I shot the gangsters instead? Was I that selfish? There was so much guilt I almost couldn't breathe.

The car ride home was quiet.

There was nothing I could say. Was I a horrible person? I mean, I had been forced, but this could have all been avoided if I could have just obeyed the fucking law. I could've just stayed in the service. Maybe I should start thinking about retirement.

We got back to my apartment around five. We had been there the whole day, and I hadn't even realized it. I was just so in thought about it all.

AL. OK, Carter, it looks like this is it.

CARTER. What do you mean?

I grabbed my gun, ready to pull it on them. I was ready.

MARVIN. You're free to go.

I was relieved from slavery, but could be charged with murder.

AL. We told you, you behave, you get your wish. Go on your date. Do whatever. Just don't go too far.

We got out of the car, which let me know I could at least have Todd's fucking car back. I'd forgotten about the date. How would it go now after these thoughts about having killed an innocent women?

MARVIN. We'll be in touch, Carter.

He held out his hand for a handshake.

Although I was sickened by the events that had transpired today, I had to keep up appearances. I shook both and they were on their way.

I got into my apartment and instantly threw up in the toilet. I felt like crying. I was so ashamed of what I had to do. I was a monster. No. I was just a slave. But I was free after some horrific initiation.

I cleaned up and put on something semiformal. I had a date to attend.

I knocked on her door, and she came out dressed a little bit more formally than I was. I felt outclassed.

CARTER. Wow.

SANDY. I feel overdressed. I'm sorry. I can change.

CARTER. No. It's OK. We'll just go somewhere where you'll fit in.

She blushed. Why was I on this date again? I didn't remember because as soon as she opened the door I didn't care anymore. I felt happy.

SANDY. Nancy will take care of the kids. So we'll have nothing to worry about tonight.

I just smiled, and we set off on our little adventure. I drove of course. She had a little Jewish in her after all.

I'm joking. It was because she's a woman.

Also kidding.

SANDY. Why don't we get some Chinese food?

She was joking. But she had no clue. The joke was so badly timed and awfully placed that it made me laugh. I genuinely thought it was funny.

We settled for some fancy restaurant on 32nd Street.

I don't usually like fancy food because it doesn't like my wallet. But it was time to relax. I had nothing to worry about. I was celebrating my freedom, not my crimes. It came back to me. I forced myself to ignore it again and hide it with a smile.

The restaurant was clearly pricey. I could see other people's dishes. I could see the menu. The food had to be good; it just had too. I knew the locals.

The waitresses even spoke more than one language. This was a real taste of sophistication. The outside venue was also quite pleasing with all the homeless around. I may sound sarcastic in this, but I really didn't care. It gave me an opportunity to impress Sandy, who had trouble understanding the waitress and reading the menu.

CARTER. Ich habe die bratwurst und das frau habst salad.

All I did was order, and both Sandy and our waitress were surprised by my secret talent. The waitress smiled, said danke, and walked away. In truth, I didn't know German at all. I'd pulled out my phone a couple minutes earlier for google translate. The waitress knew it, but Sandy didn't.

SANDY. Where did you learn German?

CARTER. I-I picked it up in high school.

I picked it up on Google.

She loved German. She was happy, and so was I. I stayed away from drinking. I didn't want to embarrass myself or look unprofessional. I had to drive anyway.

She looked lovely. Was I in love? I didn't know why, but I had the sense she could be something more. you know? It just might've been time to retire. Or maybe it was because I knew she cared, and I just hadn't had something like that in a while.

I loved the German food the place offered. My stomach didn't, but I could make it home before I had an accident, so I wasn't completely worried. She didn't really want desert, and neither did I—not with my stomach.

I looked over her shoulder at one point and noticed a familiar group staring me down at a bus stop. I had seen them at the warehouse. They weren't gonna ruin my night though.

We got the check and drove home around seven thirty. The night lights were mesmerizing. We talked about work on the way home. I had to lie, and it felt wrong. But it would probably be a last date if I told her I'd killed an innocent woman today.

I parked Todd's car and walked her back upstairs to the apartment.

SANDY. I had a fun night, Carter. Maybe we could do it again sometime.

I looked at her with a genuine smile.

CARTER. Are you busy tomorrow night?

SANDY. Actually, I have to take care of some family problems tomorrow.

Something to do with divorce most likely.

SANDY. I'm available the night after though.

She wasn't as nervous this time. She was warming up to me.

CARTER. Same time?

SANDY. Same time.

She kissed me on the lips and shut the door behind her. Now I felt a flurry of emotions. On the one hand, terrible mistakes had been made today but at least I had a nice date. I didn't even know if I was gonna be busy that night. It was just some heat-of-the-moment thing.

I guess now would be a good time to text Todd and tell him he could have his shit box back now.

It was still in my head. How could I forget? A woman was dead because of me.

Now did I work for these bastards? Things still didn't make sense. Should I go after them?

Or were they expecting that?

Time would tell. Maybe I should pay the old bank a visit—clear all this shit up.

I didn't even feel tired. I just needed to forget what had happened. I needed to move on. It was over. But the action could be redeemed— maybe. I'd think about this. I slept terribly.

4

I woke up around ten and just laid there for a while. It was so relaxing. I could finally be well rested after an unusual and stressful week.

I took my time making breakfast and tea for a little brunch to get my day started.

I had to settle that Outlaw fiasco with Todd. That was something not to look forward to. I might as well get that shit over with, though. And to think, I had been having a good morning—until I just *had* to remember about cleaning all this up.

Shit.

Pants, shirt, cigarettes, and shades. I was geared up and good to go. I just couldn't forget a shit-eating grin. The car was still in the same spot I'd left it in surprisingly. I thought maybe my bad luck was over. I couldn't confirm anything yet. I had, in fact, promised Todd a full tank and a case of beer last time I was in this position—before I was fucking abducted. I didn't remember what beer I'd gotten last time. I think it was some Asian beer or something that didn't taste very good. Maybe I'd get something European this time.

I knew Todd, the sick bastard, only used premium gas in his tank. But he wasn't getting that today. I didn't care what he said. I mean, I didn't know much about cars except the gas prices, and the gas prices were fucked.

I pulled into the bank and parked in the handicap spot just for a minute while I ran in. The teller smiled and said good morning, to which I replied likewise. They were even giving out free lollipops.

CARTER. Do you by any chance know if Todd is in?

TELLER. Yes, but I think he might be with someone.

She may not know this but I really don't care.

CARTER. OK. I'll just knock anyway.

TELLER. Oh no. It's all right. I can tell him you're here for him. What's your name?

I just smiled and went on my way to piss off Todd, while I was being pestered.

I knocked.

TODD. Yes. Who is it?

CARTER. Carter, you busy?

The door opened, and his little customer scurried off. Obviously, my purpose here was more important.

TELLER. I'm so sorry, Todd. I tried to stop him.

TODD. I appreciate it, Shelly. But next time, let this one in specifically. He's one of our larger accounts.

I smiled at the teller and closed the door. It was kinda time for her to leave.

CARTER. Todd, I'm surprised. You're in a good mood today.

TODD. Carter, I do not give the slightest fuck right now OK. I've been up since I in the morning. I have a migraine. There's been a white van parked outside my house all week. You're here. And I'm pretty sure I have a kidney stone.

Maybe not a good mood after all.

CARTER. Sounds rough. You know what I did yesterday?

I shouldn't try and start a competition.

TODD. Yeah, I read your text. It's fucked.

CARTER. So fucked.

TODD. This whole thing is just bad. They haven't come after us, just you.

CARTER. Thanks, Todd. That's very reassuring.

TODD. Look. I'm sorry for what happened. Are you OK?.

CARTER. Just another day.

TODD. You're sick.

That's exactly what I wanted people to think. It creates fear. And in this occupation, that led to less conflict. But sometimes, as I knew, it didn't always turn out that way.

TODD. You want to get a beer or something?

CARTER. You know what, Todd? Yeah. You can come over, say, around nine, and you can even sleep there if you want—or to get away from the van you're so sketched out about. Unfortunately, I can't help you get away from your kidney stone.

TODD. I'm down. Yeah, I'll stop by, but—

I dropped his car keys on the table just to see his smile.

CARTER. I'm taking the day off.

TODD. OK. I can let that happen.

CARTER. Oh your parked in a handicapped spot.

And there went the smile. I closed the door as soon as he threw a book.

I grabbed a lollipop on my way out.

I thought I had the bastard stumped with that one, and then remembered I had to get a cab.

I stared out the window and said nothing for the whole ride. I just told the cabbie where I needed to go. and he drove. I needed my time to reflect, my precious alone time. I felt like crying again, like breaking down and just collapsing in on myself and praying for safety and happiness. Had I been overthinking everything my whole life, acting sane when there was always an opportunity to get help, which I refused?

The way we grow up is just the way we live. Where I came from, we were told to hold ourselves together in instances of severe mental scarring. What had happened to this place, this world? People—so many of them were evil people, cruel people. Was I any different from the cruel and horrid? Could I justify my senseless killings and bad nature? Knowing what I'd done and the innocence I'd destroyed, should I be happy?

The driver stopped in front of my apartment, and I could just see my own reflection in the window staring back, seemingly without emotion. I faked a smile to ignore my self-pity, paid the man, and went on my way.

For me and many others in my wake, these would be bad times. I was sure of it.

5

The elevator was down, so I trotted my sorry ass up the stairs. God was teasing me at this point.

I got to my door and almost thought I lost my keys. I was getting frustrated, but I couldn't let aggravation get the better of me. I needed to remain calm. Today was my day off.

There was someone in my apartment. There was someone here. I could feel them waiting for me. My blanket wasn't on the couch, and my cabinet wasn't fully closed, and I could see it from here. It was the one where I kept an extra gun.

Those goons were here. But if they wanted to kill me, they wouldn't have waited for me in my apartment would they? I couldn't be sure.

What was my game plan though?

They knew I was here now. I could just open and close the door again and fuck with them or turn on the TV and leave. Or I could just go room clearing.

I started slowly moving gun drawn and eyes peeled. First, I went past the couch and then the kitchen. Next, I headed toward the cupboard behind the couch. I kept my steps silent and my breath slow and steady.

Marvin jumped out of the closet next to me. Next thing I knew, he was trying to choke me out with an extension cord. It got me to drop my gun. We fumbled around a bit as I tried to ram him into the walls of the hallway. In the chaos, the gun got kicked and lost. I rammed him into the wall multiple times until he loosened his grip.

I could then twist around and hit him in the face a couple times until my neck got the better of me, and we both collapsed, with me gasping and him regaining himself. He regained himself a little quicker than I did, giving him time to grab a glass on the countertop and chuck it right at me. I could get my arms up just in time, but that wasn't to say it didn't hurt because, goddamn, does glass hurt.

The cord was on the ground, and I was pissed off—like really pissed off. He lunged at me, and I had enough. I stood up, and I just started whipping him with the plug side of the cord. Now, I'm no Indiana Jones, so I managed to whip myself too, which made me think about a different solution. I recoiled in pain.

He ran at me again with a blind punch out of anger. I used his momentum against him and spun him into the wall. I knew that had to fucking hurt; I could tell by the hole. He was still moving though. So I flipped him over and punched him till his eyes fucked off, and he was unconscious.

At first, I thought about killing him but what was more important was finding out what the fuck was going on. From the looks of it, it was just Marvin here. So, I got a chair and tied the bastard up.

I tended to my wounds until he came to. I also grabbed a beer and stood behind him and waited.

His eyes started to open. And by the look on his face, that headache must have been brain killing.

I just stood there waiting for him to be cognizant and at least a little aware of his situation. He looked around.

He was panicking. He was scared. He was breathing way too hard. I walked around so he could see me. The shoe was on the other foot. I was in control, and as an aside, he could understand the pain of the yakuza.

CARTER. Hey, Marvin.

He sat there boiling in his emotions and said nothing.

CARTER. Marvin, I'm just gonna be straight with you. Just tell me what's going, or I'm just gonna kill you. I'm done with you fuck heads all right.

MARVIN. Al's dead.

CARTER. Damn, Marvin. That sucks. What's that do with me?

I tried to sound as sarcastic as possible to express how little I cared.

MARVIN. Don't start that shit with me. You fucking killed him after that shit last night.

CARTER. Marvin, you guys were watching me last night. What the fuck are you talking about?

MARVIN. You're a fucking liar.

CARTER. Who told you Al was dead?

MARVIN. You put his body on my doorstep.

I needed nothing more from him. He was talking nonsense. I wouldn't be able to convince him of anything. So I might as well kill him, and shit would it be satisfying.

MARVIN. You think you can lie. You think you can deceive us. You think you're smart, huh?

I walked away and laughed at his senseless yelling and got a plastic bag.

I watched him suffering and gasping for air. He squirmed and screamed, and I had no remorse. And soon enough he had no breath.

But what was he talking about? What had happened?

I took his phone. I knew his passcode from seeing him constantly scroll through messages in the car—1989, the year he was born I guessed. Not very secure at all.

I called Anastasia.

The long ringing made the scene uneasy, until she picked up.

It was silent for a second, and she was waiting for Marvin to say something. She didn't expect it to be me.

CARTER. Anastasia, he's dead.

She must have been shocked, as she was still silent.

ANASTASIA. If you have time before you die, try begging the yakuza for forgiveness. And if not, I can always tell them.

Fuck.

A set up. I was a goddamn pawn. Shit, maybe all of us were.

CARTER. So, this is loose ends, huh?

ANASTASIA. Think of it as smart and convenient marketing.

CARTER. It was just a jewelry store, you dumb bitch.

Silence.

CARTER. Anastasia?

Dead end here now.

Dead in the end more like it.

It was all quiet with my thoughts until a knock sounded on the door.

I grabbed the gun and aimed it, inching closer and closer. I looked through the eyehole, and for fucks sake, it was Sandy's nanny. Old hag could have gotten herself killed.

I opened the door and inch with the chain lock on, making sure Marvin wasn't in sight.

CARTER. Hey, what's up?

NANCY. I heard yelling. Is everything OK?

CARTER. Yeah just ... uh ... watching football. Don't worry. Everything's fine.

NANCY. Are you sure?

I looked behind me to make sure Marvin hadn't moved before responding.

CARTER. No, yeah. I'm fine. Thanks for checking though.

NANCY. OK ... well, take care.

CARTER. yeah. Bye.

She could tell in my voice there was something off, and admittedly I was a little shaken up now, knowing Anastasia had pinned the murder of the Japanese man on me. Now the yakuza were going to come kill me, and it had something to do with this business. And well, yeah shit. I couldn't really get out of this one, could I?

Now what should I do?

Do I arm up and stand by and wait to die? Or do I leave and run? But if I ran, they'd kill Sandy. She didn't deserve that. For now, maybe I should just get rid of the body. That was what was important right now. I hadn't been expecting company today, so I didn't really have a body bag lying around. I had to use my good duffel bag. He was big too—heavy as shit and only barely fit.

I cleaned up, grabbed my duffel bag, and made my way to the

subway. I made sure to look twice at everybody and every car and take note of everything that didn't add up.

It was a busy time down here, which made me nervous. And me looking at everybody made me look suspicious. I passed the turnstile and hitched a ride to lower Manhattan.

The long ride gave me time to think.

It had been a long week. Sheer chaos surrounded this whole situation, and I didn't like it. I hated it and wanted to just escape. It was kill or be killed, I guess—and all because I wanted to be a badass. I could've gone to college. I could've done so much. But no. Right now, I was dumping a body on the subway with cameras everywhere. No, I'd just dump it in an alley somewhere. Fuck this.

The train stopped and I trudged my sorry ass up two flights of stairs and through a sea of people. I turned into the first alley I came across and dumped the bag next to a dumpster. I was being lazy. I was frustrated and pissed. I kept walking till I got to the boardwalk, taking in the view over the Hudson River. For a while, I just stood there with a cigarette leaning against the railing.

I stared over at New Jersey for a bit, still thinking of escape. But who the fuck would want to escape to New Jersey? I mean shit. Couldn't trade hell for heller. I laughed and tossed the dart in the water, watching as it sizzled and sank.

I stopped and remembered.

Todd was coming over to my apartment, and it'd probably be best that he and I kept our distance for a while. So I'd just call him and tell him to fuck off back to the bank.

He didn't pick up.

I called again.

He didn't pick up.

I called again.

Nothing.

I started walking faster and faster now. This wasn't good.

I retraced my steps back through the alley, even noticed the smell of a bloody mess I'd left behind, so I knew I was going the right way. Down the stairs in Greenwich I went and hopped the turnstile, with the cops ignoring me. They didn't care at this point, and neither did I. I needed to get home and save my friend—my best friend.

I got on the subway, and all I could do was wait. Missed call after missed call. Todd's phone just kept ringing. It's impossible to explain how hard it is to just sit there and wait, knowing there is nothing else you can do, knowing it was all your fault. I was getting impatient. I was getting angry. I was getting paranoid.

The door opened, but I wasn't where I wanted to be.

Fuck it.

I booked it, pushing and shoving anyone in my way.

I was risking everything on Todd, and I wasn't even thinking. This was against everything I'd taught myself on not getting caught, but I didn't care. Why was I doing it? Did I realize how limited my options were?

Sometimes, recklessness is just fucking fun.

I ran into an empty backstreet with a lone car. So, I just pulled my gun on the guy in the car.

CARTER. **Get out of car. Get out of the fucking car.**

He was so shocked he nearly pissed himself, swear to God. If anything, he should have thanked me. It was only a Nissan. But shit was she nimble. I revved her up to her limits, driving like a drunken bastard on his way back to the bar. There may have been traffic but only on the road; the curb was just fine. Wait. Did I just steal a fucking car? What the actual fuck was I thinking?

It was stupid what I was doing. I was risking everything. But the more I neglected my rules, the more satisfying it was and the calmer and more focused I became. Running red lights and sticking to less populated roads to avoid most traffic and most police, I flew over the bridge and through the alley toward my shitstay.

I ditched the car an alley or two away, and I could hear sirens echo behind me. The less I cared, the more fun I had. I ran up the stairs to my floor, drew my gun, flung open my unlocked door, and aimed in.

Todd freaked out to see me aiming directly at him.

TODD. **Put that thing away, Carter. What's wrong with you?**

Never had I been so furious in my life. I'd risked everything over nothing, yet I was more or less relieved.

So, I lowered my gun.

CARTER. Todd, you should really answer your phone.

He checked his phone to see my messages and tried to laugh it off.

TODD. My bad.

What an absolute piece of shit. Now I had to get rid of a stolen car.

TODD. You could've fucking shot me. What's wrong with you?

I walked and talked to the fridge and left the gun on the countertop.

CARTER. Well, you know that bitch in Greenwich I was talking to you about.

TODD. Yeah, I guess.

CARTER. Well, I guess the greasy whore told the yakuza about that incident yesterday. And so one of the thugs came to kill me today. So, I killed him and dumped him in an alley, and now the yakuza are probably gonna come to kill me.

TODD. Woah, woah. Slow the fuck down. What are you talking about?

CARTER. You want a Bud heavy or some Japanese IPA shit?

TODD. Carter!?

CARTER. I'm being hunted now, Todd.

TODD. I'm sorry, Carter. I wish the Outlaws could help. But intervention could start a war.

Very reassuring

CARTER. I know, Todd. I'm just letting you know.

I got a beer out of the fridge for both me and him.

TODD. So, should I be here? Like am I in danger now too or—

CARTER. You can leave if you want, but then you'd miss out on the free beer.

TODD. True.

We stayed silent for a minute, with Todd enjoying his beer and me trying to.

TODD. Carter.

CARTER. Yeah. What's up?

TODD. That van was there again today.

CARTER. You think it's feds?

TODD. Carter, they're closing in. They already had a big bust with the rider side of the gang. It's just a matter of time before

someone talks, and they start coming for the bureaucrats—
that is, if they aren't already on their way.

CARTER. You know, Todd, I don't know anymore. Maybe this is it. Maybe it's the end of the road with what could be either a gang war or justice for the community. Now I know what I've done isn't what someone would consider the good deeds of a valued citizen. But shit, maybe I should get caught. I'm just a fucking killer.

TODD. Don't lose your mind on me now, Carter. We still have our freedom. Let's enjoy it while we have it and not be sorry and beg for forgiveness.

CARTER. We're just running out of options here, Todd. The wolves are closing in.

TODD. I don't want to sound like I'm abandoning you, but it's you. You're running out of options, and if shit hits the fan, the syndicate will abandon you. I know you don't want to hear it, but you already got a pretty fucky rap sheet with the higher-ups, so yeah.

I just sat there and finished my beer. He was right. He was absolutely right. I was my own worst enemy with this. But what now? What next? Pray? I stood up.

CARTER. You know what? I don't want this night to end off on a shitty note. So, why don't I put a movie on, huh? You want to watch something?

TODD. Actually, Carter, I think I'm just gonna go home. I wish you the best of luck, and I will see you again. But with all this shit, I'm not ready, and I'm not prepared.

My smile faded with an empty can in one hand and a remote in the other.

TODD. I'll be seeing you, Carter.

I was a little bit sad. But wait, how did he get in?

CARTER. Wait, Todd.

TODD. What?

CARTER. How did you get in?

TODD. The door was unlocked.

Oh my God.

CARTER. Todd. You might want to leave.

And that was that. Todd left, and I was left on the verge of a complete mental breakdown. The wolves were closing in. I didn't know how many and how good they might be. Would I die? Would I be tortured? The worst thing was having to wait for something like this, something you couldn't avoid—like justice.

Should I leave? Should I ambush them? The door may have been unlocked, but they couldn't already—still?—be here. I'd be dead by now, right? Or had I actually forgotten to lock the door in all the chaos of trying to dump a body?

Panic started to set in. I thought about the bad things before I thought about survival. I needed to calm down. I needed to think. I acted. I got my gun, checked the ammo, and started room clearing.

First room—swing door open, check behind door, scan room, all in matter of seconds. It wasn't harder than it sounds; it was just training.

Don't rise to the occasion. Fall back on your training.

Bedroom done, I moved to the bathroom, the closet, and then the office. All clear. Even the fire escape door was locked at the end of the hallway. I must have been overreacting, overthinking, overevaluating.

I wouldn't be able to sleep tonight, knowing I might be in danger. So, instead of sleeping, I got Marvin's death chair and put it up in clear view of the door. It had some of his blood on it, which I'd failed to notice earlier. But it didn't matter. I'd just get rid of it in the morning. I just sat there, gun in hand, waiting patiently, thinking I should go out in a blaze of glory.

Todd texted me to say he'd made it home safely. It was good to have at least a little bit of relief for now.

It got dark, and my eyes got heavier and heavier. I kept myself up with constant loading and unloading my magazine. I was bored, and fidgeting with the safety kept me entertained. The click was satisfying.

Gunshot.

I woke up.

It echoed through the whole building. The cops would be called any second. It had to have been the ground floor. That poor receptionist.

This was my time. The yelling bounced up the stairs, as did the screams and doors slamming in either escape or pursuit. It all just got closer and closer. This was happening.

I slowly stood up and slid the chair off to the side with my foot and slowly aimed up at the door.

Louder and louder, closer and closer, they came. I could feel them at this point. There must have been at least three or four of them. They got to my floor. It just went silent. It seemed like time stopped. I looked around, and I could even notice the dust flying through the air. But it was all just so slow, so quiet, so empty.

So dead.

And then a single creak sounded outside the door.

My focus snapped back to it. And I was gonna be the smart-ass to shoot first. The door flew open. Before the figures behind could barge through, I put three shots to the door while I moved closer, taking the point man in the shoulder and neck and a secondary man in the chest. When I got to the door, I shut it back with the force of my body. Then the motherfuckers broke through the fire escape door at the other end of the hall.

They took a couple shots at me, but I moved forward, took the couch as cover, and shot once. I hit this second point man in the stomach, causing him to stumble toward me. I sped toward him, grabbed onto his belt, shot twice toward the secondary man behind him—one in the chest and one in head. My human shield was bleeding all over me. Behind me, the front door slammed open again.

I turned myself and my shield to face the last two assailants, and my shield was getting heavy.

I fired three times—one for the newest emerging point man, one to the shield's head, and one for the secondary man firing from the shoulder. He dropped his gun.

My gun jammed. Fuck.

My shield fell, and I moved closer toward the wincing last man, trying to fix my gun as I went. But with all the emotion, I just got frustrated. So I slammed the gun on the guy's head, and he fell to his knees.

I put him in a choke with one hand and pulled his hair with the other, just to bully him.

CARTER. **Not so fucking smart now, are we fuck head, huh?**

He didn't speak English. He spoke Japanese. There was no turning back now. I just snapped his neck.

I surveyed the scene, getting a grasp on what I'd just accomplished, what I'd just survived. I was proud. Nine shots, six dead, and one stoppage—equaling one reason I didn't like Glock anymore.

Nancy stood in the doorway with a rolling pin as a weapon.

We locked eyes. My emotions went dead. Someone who I had mistaken for an angel was standing in my doorway as my killer. She would bring me to justice. But I thought the gunshots had already attracted attention. And I don't know why I didn't expect police. But shit, the killing part was over I guessed. I just stood there with my blood-soaked shirt and a guilty-ass look on my face. I didn't even know how to reply. She looked terrified. So I thought I'd break the unwanted silence.

CARTER, *voice cracking.* Hi.

6

This cold and dark interrogation room would probably be my home for some time. But it was too damn uncomfortable to sleep, and I was exhausted. For some reason, though, I wasn't scared. I mean, I knew I was caught. I knew It was over. But maybe I'd be safe now. I always expected to be scared whenever or if ever this moment came. But maybe I was just too tired to care.

What should my game plan be? What was my defense?

I was alone—just me, myself, and the water the detectives had given me about an hour ago. I supposed there was a reason for all this waiting. They probably had a lot of paperwork to do, given what had just happened. I wasn't gonna do that stupid lawyer shit just yet. I'd at least see what they knew—that is *if* they knew anything—about me. My record was clean. They wouldn't find a damn thing on me. No tickets, no bills, no phone, nothing. I'd be just fine.

My chair and the table were bolted to the ground, the door had no knob, and the camera was pointed at me. But that funny-looking one-way window was very shiny indeed. This was no small-fry interview. They were scared of me. Something that may not help my case was the very bloody clothes I was still wearing. And Marvin's chair was probably on its way to evidence as I sat here. No matter. They just might assume, given the bloody mess of a crime scene back at my place, all the biological evidence was related to the bodies there.

Finally, after ages of discomfort, the door just opened.

INVESTIGATOR. I'm gonna have you read this.

He put a rights advisement in front of me.

INVESTIGATOR. This is your advisement of rights. Read it over and tell me if you understand or not.

Was I going to be stubborn? Nah, fuck it.

CARTER. I understand completely.

I didn't even look down to read the whole thing. I had been a cop before. I knew it all too well.

INVESTIGATOR. Good. That's the hard part out of the way.

I tried to impress him by acting like I knew it all. But I just managed to hate myself for it. Fucking cringe-ass shit.

Annoying already.

CARTER. Hard? Did you expect me to be stubborn? I am willing to cooperate 100 percent. I have nothing to hide, sir.

He laughed at me. The bastard was mocking me. And as his laughter went on, my smile slowly faded until it was a look of despair.

INVESTIGATOR. Carter.

His laugh turned to a smug look.

He put a file on the table.

INVESTIGATOR. You contradict yourself. I mean, you say you're not going to be stubborn. But then you also act like you're innocent, and I'm not buying it.

CARTER. I don't think you can say that, Officer. Are you aware of the concept of innocent until proven guilty?

INVESTIGATOR. That would be true if you didn't kill six men in your house. And you know, you being who you are, it's a very unusual scenario I'm afraid.

CARTER. I'm confused. I don't know what you mean.

COLTON. Well, first let me introduce myself. My name's Special Agent Colton. I work for the FBI.

He put out his hand to shake mine, and I nervously accepted. I was still confused and now even more unnerved. How did the FBI get here so quickly? And why did they want me unless he thought this was gang-related—which it actually kind of was now?

COLTON. Do you want to hear a story?

CARTER. A story about what?

COLTON. A story about deceit, lies, and betrayal, of course.

CARTER. I don't think we have time for that or even if it's related.

COLTON. Well, of course we do. We have all the time in the world. And trust me. It's very relatable.

CARTER. I don't have a choice, do I?

COLTON. Not really. It's more of, uh, you know, a question with no actual answer. It's more of teasing actually—a rhetorical teasing.

CARTER. You're a very unorthodox detective.

COLTON. You're a very unorthodox man.

CARTER. OK, Colton. Tell me the story.

COLTON. I'm happy you changed your mind.

He opened the file and started reading.

COLTON. Well actually, I have two stories for you. But we'll get into it in a minute. Just let me find where I should start.

I grew more and more nervous. After all these years, all these actions, all these bullets, and all this blood the feeling got so high, it fell off and shattered into pieces—until there was nothing left but fear.

COLTON. Tristan Mitchell was born March 18, 2001, in Long Island Jewish Medical Center to a loving, silver-spooned family with no debt and no worries. Tristan Mitchell attended Rosemary Catholic High School later in life for three years until mysteriously not graduating, at which point, he faked a diploma and joined the United States Armed Forces, more particularly, the United States Marine Corps.

Throughout Tristan's three-year military career, he spent most of his time overseas in the Middle East, being accredited with over twelve confirmed kills in Fallujah. Now, no doubt this would take a toll on this man's mind. So, maybe it isn't a surprise that, through investigation by the NCIS, it was found that three of the twelve kills were civilians who, quote, "got in the way," as is said in UCMJ court documents. At any rate, poor Tristan was discharged from the military for being mentally unfit, at which point he was to be escorted to a psychiatric facility in Virginia. He later disappeared, either before or after getting on the plane.

Now, the funny part about the first story is that it doesn't have an end, but it has a beginning. The trouble with your story, Mr. "Carter," is that it has an end, but it has no beginning. Andrew Carter McGraw first turned up somewhere in Missouri when he hitched a ride to—

I snapped and banged my fist on the table.

He stopped and looked up at me, but I just couldn't bear to look back at him.

CARTER. That file ain't fucking true. That shit's fabricated. You can't hold that against me. I was framed.

The story had some truths in the beginning and toward the end. I could admit that. I was framed, and I had to escape. The government promised me those files were destroyed. I took a deep breath.

CARTER. So, now what? You imprison me?

COLTON. I didn't get to mention your ending yet Tristan. The thing about your ending is that it can go a couple different ways.

My fear boiled in to aggravation and anger. It seemed like everything I'd taught myself just went out the window.

CARTER, *mumbling*. Unorthodox as shit.

COLTON. Say that again?

I looked up at him, still trying to come to terms with the situation.

CARTER. You want something from me, don't you?

COLTON. Well, that depends if you're still willing to cooperate, Tristan.

CARTER. Stop calling me that.

COLTON. It's your name, Tristan. You can't keep running from what you did.

CARTER. You read it yourself, Colton. Tristan's MIA, presumed dead. But Andy's alive and well.

COLTON. You know what? Sure, if that's what you want. Sure fine, whatever. But look. Now, the FBI is willing to clear that whole war crime in Fallujah of yours and anything else leading up to this night, including that little number you pulled on that psychiatrist a bit ago—but only if you are still willing to co-operate, Trist- er, I mean Carter.

Todd was right. They had been watching us. They probably had started during the whole jewelry store fiasco.

CARTER. I am willing to cooperate.

Nothing left to lose.

COLTON. OK great.

He sat back in his chair and killed his shit-eating grin.

COLTON. Bring them in. I want you to bring them all in. And I mean every last one of them—from the Outlaws to the Mafia and maybe even the yakuza if you try hard enough.

The FBI will grant you freedom in exchange for being an informant and a whistleblower.

CARTER. I'm not sure if that's entirely humane for me, Colton.

COLTON. Well, I'm not too sure if you care, Carter.

I'll give you my phone number, and you can be on your way. We'll do some paperwork on our end. And then you're free to go. You'll have one week to provide me with some-thing, or we will come back for you. Remember, Andy, we're always watching.

He slid a business card across the table and walked out just like that. I had been granted freedom but with the expense of taking everyone else down with me. They wouldn't let my actions slide. As soon as I brought someone important in they'd put me right next to them. I wasn't stupid, only careless.

I sat there for a second and eventually got the nerve to get up. I walked around in a daze, as if I was pushing through sludge for a min-ute—until I got in front of that window. *Who could be on the other side?* I thought. FBI? CIA? NCIS? I don't know why, but it just made me laugh. And then I spat at the window and awaited my departure.

7

My apartment was still bloodstained, but all the bodies were gone. The police never even bothered to get a mop. So, now I was stuck with it. At least they left Marvin's chair. Then again they did take my gun and scraped my dignity, and here I was this whole time thinking I was a badass.

They didn't take my beer. So, I indulged myself and sat down on the couch. Then I had an idea. So I called Todd, and he actually picked up this time.

CARTER. Todd. We need to talk start heading over.

And then I just hung up and continued drinking. I couldn't talk on the phone. I was too paranoid. So many thoughts were rushing in all at once. I needed to slow down and think before I did things now—be more careful.

I had been stripped of all of my dignity and was now forced to be a slave to the government once again. But this was ridiculous. I was pissed off now, and the drinking didn't help.

I thought about going over and talking to Sandy. But that could just put her in more danger. It was bad enough that Greenwich knew about her. I was just glad the yakuza didn't, and sooner or later, they'd come back here. They couldn't just let me get away.

Sandy would probably even move herself and kids miles away. It was obvious she would know had what happened here. It was literally next door.

So, maybe in that case, I shouldn't be waiting around here for Todd. And maybe I just shouldn't be living here to begin with. You know what? I should actually fucking leave, like right now come to think of it.

The sudden realization of countless waves of enemies changed my mind about relaxing. There was no more leniency, there was only danger.

There wasn't much I should really need, except maybe a change of clothes for at least a week's absence and a suit for my funeral. No gun, no ammo. But Todd should be able to help with that.

I packed up my shit and then left immediately afterward. I called Todd again on my way out but not before passing Sandy in the hall and making it all the more uncomfortable. We just stopped and stood staring at each other for what seemed endless. She saw my full bag and my empty face and slowly backed away, still saying nothing.

I couldn't say anything either—could only watch her go. I had hurt her in the worst way—leaving her with fear and mental scarring that would last forever. Even if I did say something, there would be nothing that could justify her having to see what she'd seen.

It actually made me sad to push her away by showing what I was capable of and what I could do when pushed to my limits. She didn't deserve this. So, I would take my destruction elsewhere and leave her safe.

I continued on, trying not to look back; it would do me no good to regret and distract myself from wanting to live on. The thoughts of retirement came back—of the escape I so desperately wanted. I was in over my head. Focus on this first.

I called Todd again.

CARTER. Hello?

TODD. Yeah I'm on my way. What's so important?

CARTER. It's best not to say shit on the phone. And you probably shouldn't come over. Why don't we get some breakfast? My treat.

TODD. You want me to pick you up?

CARTER. I'll take a cab and text you the location.

TODD. All right. See ya.

CARTER. Yeah, bye.

Feds were probably wiretapping me, so it would be best to talk in a public restaurant at a private table.

Outside, I kept walking for a while. It was at least a block or so until I decided to call a cab. But then I stopped and caught something out of the corner of my eye down the alley.

That Nissan I'd stolen the other day was just piling up dust all the way down there, and it would be a shame to let it go to waste. Surely, the FBI would turn a blind eye if I just kept using it, right? It seemed like they would be OK with it—I mean, so long as I did what they wanted from me. Yeah, it should be fine. Good thing I'd left the keys in there.

I started it up and made my way to a busy enough diner I knew about in Brooklyn.

Today was gonna be a good day. I could feel it—no traffic, free car, and a plan to win. I could see a familiar car with tinted windows, or make that two of them, in my rearview mirror, keeping their distance. They were probably fumbling through records to see if I owned a car they didn't know about. It put a smile on my face.

I found myself outside some cheap coffeehouse and thought it was good enough. I didn't feel like driving all the way across town to the diner, which was overpriced anyway. I texted Todd to show up. Finding a parking spot was somewhat difficult. But then I remembered I'd taken this ride off some old guy. Sure enough, right under the visor was a handicapped mirror pass. So, parking just got a whole lot easier. I walked inside with pride and got myself a table and waited.

Sooner or later, a waitress came by to bug me.

WAITRESS. **Good morning, sir? What can I get you?**

CARTER. **I don't want coffee. So do you guys have tea?**

WAITRESS. **Y-yeah we do what would you like?**

CARTER. **Well surprise me, I guess I don't really care.**

WAITRESS. **Yes, sir. Will that be all?**

CARTER. **Yeah that's it. Thank you.**

WAITRESS. **I will be right back.**

CARTER. **Uh-huh.**

I should've been more respectful. I knew that. But it wasn't on my mind. Some people say, "Oh, it's not hard to just be nice to someone." I could be dead any minute. Nice was not a priority.

The tea came by more quickly than expected. However, it tasted like ass. It was some iced shit, and I hated tea with just a bunch of fucking ice cubes in it. It was forty-five degrees out. Why the fuck would I want a— Never mind, whatever. I just ordered to be nice anyway.

Todd took his sweet time as usual, showing up almost an hour and a half after the text.

I waved him over, and he sat down.

CARTER. What the fuck took you so long? There's like no traffic today.

TODD. And when there's no traffic, that means everyone is parked instead. So I was looking for a spot for a bit.

CARTER. That's funny, I just parked in a handicap spot.

TODD. Not surprising coming from you. I thought you said you were gonna catch a cab. Where did you get a car?

CARTER. It doesn't matter. I called you because I wanted to talk to you, in person. In case you didn't know, after you left, a couple guys showed up a few hours later, and I maybe killed six or seven. I don't really remember. But the important part is I'm OK. I just can't stay there anymore. So, I was thinking about a safe house, but a safe house with a location we're willing to give to the feds.

TODD. What the fuck are you talking about? are you autistic?!

CARTER. Some fucking hit men or some shit came by and tried to kill me.

Todd's face sank; he looked petrified. He couldn't even believe what I was saying.

TODD. Is this some stupid little joke you came up with?

CARTER. No. The feds have literally been tailing me all morning too.

TODD. And you brought them here? To me?

In all fairness, I didn't think that one through. So much for my focus.

TODD. What the fuck is wrong with you?

CARTER. Todd, I need you to listen to me. You have to trust me.

He was skeptical, and he was scared. He couldn't escape now. He was stuck in this with me at this point—some dirty trick that just conveniently happened my way.

Todd took a deep breath.

TODD. What do you need?

CARTER. Look, we can give up a single safe house that's empty, and I can deal with this.

He shook his head.

TODD. So, the feds are watching you right now. And you thought it would be a good idea to meet up. Are you actually retarded?

He stood up and was about to leave until I grabbed his arm and pulled his ass back down.

CARTER. Todd, listen to me. They're not after you, OK. They want me. They want me to fucking take out the gangs, and I am not here to snitch you out or put you in danger. You got nothing to freak out about. I have a fucking plan, Todd.

TODD. Oh really? What's that?

CARTER. I want a partner and a gun.

TODD. I'm not trying to be your partner, Carter.

CARTER. I didn't say you, Todd. I want you to give me someone we can turn over and give away to the feds and maybe, you know, frame the feds for having someone die while in their custody. We'll anonymously report it to the news and get them off everyone's ass except mine. I'll be gone by then. And I suggest you leave, too, and then we would be in the clear.

He stopped panicking and looked me straight on.

TODD. Carter.

CARTER. So, you'll help me, right?

TODD. You are fucking insane.

I shook my head.

CARTER. Todd, are you going to help me or not? We can both get away from this. But we'll have to leave everything behind.

TODD. Carter, that is beyond fucked.

CARTER. Todd we have limited options here. Either we snitch out everybody and go to prison and get shanked, or we run and hide.

TODD. You realize this is all your fault, right, Carter? You brought these people down on us, and you want me to leave everything behind.

CARTER. Todd, look I know, all right. I know it's all my fault. I fucked up, and there's nothing I can do to change that. If I fucked it up, then I should be the one to fix it. I just need a helping hand.

TODD. Carter.

CARTER. Todd,

CARTER. If you won't do it for me, do it for Miranda.

Miranda was Todd's ex-wife, who died in a car accident a few years back. Maybe it wasn't a good idea to step on her grave like that. But he had to let go at some point. His face went angry and scolding, and his tone went deep.

TODD. Don't mention that name.

CARTER. Todd if I don't accept what they offer, they will imprison me. And then they will come for you.

The noise in the background from the other guests seemed to fade in, making me realize it had faded out at some point. I had been so absorbed in the conversation I'd forgotten we were in public.

Todd's face showed he was sorrowful and fearful. But who wasn't in a time like this?

He grabbed a napkin and a pen and wrote something down.

TODD. Carter.

He looked up at me.

TODD. You owe me more than a beer this time.

He handed the napkin off to me and stood up.

TODD. I can see about getting you a partner later. But for now, don't do anything else too stupid, buddy.

I nodded as he walked off.

The napkin contained just an address scrawled in a red-inked pen— the location of the safe house.

The waitress walked back over.

WAITRESS. Can I get you anything else, sir?

I stood up and folded up the napkin and put it away.

CARTER. No. I'm good. I'll take the bill and be on my way.

WAITRESS. Actually, your friends already paid for it.

CARTER. My who?

She pointed over to a table with a couple guys in suits, and we locked eyes. They just waved and smiled.

They were obviously feds; their suits were too cheap to be anything else. They couldn't have heard the conversation between me and Todd. They were too far away, and the place wasn't bugged. So, they must've just snuck in through the crowd while I wasn't looking, which meant I needed to be more aware. They weren't here for trouble, just wanted to remind me they were keeping an eye on me.

So, I smiled at them and left the coffeehouse. I felt around in my pocket for the keys and looked up to see that my car was missing. The feds had it towed. The bastards were toying with me. No matter. In my position, I just might be able to get a free taxi ride. So I tried my luck and went back inside and over to the feds.

I sat down and interrupted their conversation about something unimportant.

CARTER. Hey, boys. How we doing?

They didn't really know what to say.

CARTER. I was wondering, since we're really just helping each other out here, you think it might be possible for you retards to bring me over to this address.?

I took out the napkin and slid it over to the more professional-looking of the two.

They looked at each other and then turned to me.

FED. Do we look like a taxi service, Mr. Mitchell?

CARTER. No. You guys look like a couple of queers if I'm being honest.

I left the scumbags with disappointment and got a cab.

8

The safe house was some apartment in Queens. And honestly, I always had a thing for Queens. It seemed like the nicer part of the city, but my dumb ass ended up in Fremont. The cab dropped me off, and I thanked the cabbie for the ride.

As you can imagine, the feds were curious. Imagine being given a napkin by the guy you're tailing and told to drive to the address written down and having no clue what it was about. As law enforcement agents, you'd want to investigate the location, so of course they followed me.

Now these were one of those three-level apartments with a million copies just one after another, a remnant of mass immigration long ago—identical buildings in long rows with unique residents. Everything about the building was old. The door was frayed, the paint had died off, and the key was in the usual safe house spot—inside the flower pot under its soil.

I walked in and looked around and noticed locations that would definitely house firearms and other goodies. But the feds weren't up for searching an entire building. Nor did they really think I was that much of a threat. So, they just stayed outside in the car on the other end of the street. I imagine they were just told to watch me and not told what I'd done.

I went over to the stash spot behind the picture of a windmill above the couch. The hole behind would be able to store a multitude of cash or guns or ammo, just about anything really. But there was nothing. I moved the table and checked the spot under the rug. Still nothing.

I understood now,

Todd had given me this place because there was nothing here, because nothing of value would be lost except the location. He really had thought I was going to do something stupid. No matter. No problem, right?

Maybe I was just being picky and ungrateful. Maybe at least a fucking new location would be good enough for now.

I looked around, and there wasn't even a TV in the living room. There was a wall mount for it, and there were wires. So, someone just must've taken it and left. Assholes.

I went into the kitchen and looked around for some food. It wasn't exactly barren, but everything had long since expired and was no use. The kitchen sink couldn't even produce hot water, so there was a problem with that too. Just my luck.

I went into the basement to check out the plumbing and see how fucked she really was. I know nothing about boilers or heating, but that didn't mean I shouldn't at least investigate.

The basement had beds and couches—which I personally knew was a violation of NYC housing laws because landlords are dickheads, and politicians like money. So, all seemed pretty normal down here.

The boiler had lights coming off its control panel. I gave up, knowing little to nothing about whatever I thought I was going to accomplish.

I looked around and saw nothing of any interest except a cellar door, which could provide a back door escape if need be. But when I tried the thing, it was far too rusted to swing open. Instead, I would just have to pick it up and move it if I wanted to leave. So, I just left it alone.

The only reason I know all these stash spots is because, at least a month or two ago, I had to escort someone to one of these safe houses, and I had to go through every stash spot they told me and assess the contents. They never had me check the "last lifeline spot."—the "if all else fails," the secret spot.

The boiler spot.

They wanted it secret because it would be a last resort if all other spots failed or were compromised.

It was time to truly test my luck.

I got up to the boiler and felt around it. It was freezing cold. It must've been down for a reason—so someone could store something and never turn it back on. But everything else in the house was gone so maybe whatever had been stored there was gone too.

I felt around to the back of the boiler and against the wall where the pipes were going into. There was just enough room to get my hand in there. I grabbed a hold of something. It felt like it was some sort of box. I pulled it out. Sure enough, it was.

I opened it. Lo and behold, there lay a single sig and a single mag. I took it out and put it on the table. Within the box was a little compartment under some fabric. It seemed unnecessary. But still, it had one of those tracker chips you can buy at a gas station and connect to your phone. I took that as well.

It was better than nothing, but still I found it disappointing.

I now had shelter and self-protection. Nothing to fear except negligent discharge. I went upstairs and secured my gun in my belt line. As soon as I got to the living room, I had a knock at the door. I went over and looked out the window in the living room adjacent from the front and saw a fed and my bag—the same bag that I had left in the Nissan with all my clothes and essentials.

I went and opened the door to hear nothing but sarcasm.

Fed. I think you left this at the café.

I grabbed the bag from him.

Carter. Fuck off.

And I slammed the door in his face.

At least they were nice enough to return what belonged to me. But at any rate, they were still dicks about it. I put my bag on the coffee table and emptied it, trying to find out if it was bugged or not. But I couldn't find anything. The apartment itself was probably bugged or soon would be. So, I would need to limit any business at my new residence starting now.

To be fair, right at this moment, all I wanted was some food. I was fucking hungry. So, instead of staying in and being lazy, I decided to go out instead and live a little dangerously. The thing with Queens is there are actually a surprising amount of restaurants just small walks in between each other. So I got a hoodie and kept my gun and went out for a stroll.

I got only a few feet out my door before the feds' car started, and they were on my tail. This would actually prove to be pretty annoying. How did they expect me to find out information that would be incriminating to the Mafia if they were on my ass the whole time. What a fucking joke. They could at least try to be inconspicuous.

I walked a bit until I got to the corner. I'm no jaywalker under normal circumstances, but these were particularly unusual circumstances indeed. So, I stopped and used it as an excuse to look around and see if there was anyone else following me.

And there was.

There was this guy trying not to look suspicious right behind, and of course, trying not to look suspicious only makes you look more so. I noticed him smoking across the street when I left the apartment but only just noticed he'd been walking behind me the whole time And all it took was a look over my shoulder.

The feds drove off and left as soon as I saw this guy. Was this a hit? Was he going to kill me? He was closing in, but the traffic light was faster. As soon as it said walk, I just turned left and walked away. He was still pursuing my trail, though, so I ran off into the alley and hid in a corner just at its entrance. I heard his footsteps get faster and faster, and as soon as he ran in, I jumped out behind him with my gun out.

He flinched.

CARTER. Hi.

PARTNER. The fuck is wrong with you, Carter? I'm your partner, you fucking retard.

I was a little embarrassed, so I holstered.

CARTER. Oh shit. My bad. Sorry about that, buddy.

PARTNER. Fuck. When they said you were on edge, I didn't think you were fucking paranoid.

CARTER. Stop freaking out. It's not like I just shot you.

PARTNER. No. It's like you almost just shot me.

He must be new or something Todd didn't react this way. But then again, Todd knew me. He was used to near misses.

My new partner calmed down after a couple deep breaths and held out his hand.

ASHTON. I'm Ashton by the way.

I laughed.

CARTER. Where did you get a gay name like that?

He did not laugh.

ASHTON. It was my grandfather's. He lost his life in World War II. You got a problem with that?

CARTER. Relax. I'm just joking.

Annoying little shit already

CARTER. Are you hungry?

He nodded. And we started walking back on track.

CARTER. What are you into? Pizza? Steak? Salads?

ASHTON. I hear they got good pizza in New York, so we could go for that.

CARTER. Oh, not a local I take it.

ASHTON. No. I'm actually from Arizona, but you know how it goes. I get too careless and people come hunting me down and I have to escape.

All too familiar.

CARTER. I know the feeling.

We found a little pizza joint along the strip that seemed to match what we were looking for, so we hopped in and got a table.

The waiter wasn't annoying this time around and was polite and patient.

WAITER. What can I get you gentlemen?

CARTER. I think I'll have a gin for now.

WAITER. Sir, we don't sell alcohol.

CARTER. I'll just have a coke then.

ASHTON. I'll just have a ginger ale.

WAITER. OK. I'll be right back with your drinks.

I looked at him, puzzled.

CARTER. A ginger ale?

ASHTON. Yeah.

Instead of finding him annoying, I straight-up disliked him.

CARTER. OK, whatever. Did anybody tell you anything about a plan? No. Scratch that. Why do you think you're here?

He looked around to make sure no one was listening in and leaned in closer.

ASHTON. We're here to get Greenwich and yakuza to fuck off.

CARTER. Atta boy.

I realized I would have to sacrifice this kid in order to escape. So, at that second, my smiled faded. But I snapped back into conversation.

CARTER. All right, here's the plan, Ashton. Now, Greenwich and yakuza got a little gun-running thing going on, and they're competitors. Now, they used me in order to kill loose ends and distract the yakuza, but that didn't really work. So, God knows what they'll do next. But we are going to intercept their shipments and give them to the Outlaws.

He sat there for a second thinking about it.

ASHTON. Do you think it'll work?

CARTER. Well yes, Ashton. And the only reason we haven't done this before is because we wanted to prevent war. But if they see us two shit rats doing it, then they'll wage war on us, not the Outlaws.

ASHTON. You're insane.

CARTER. More or less just pissed off.

I was going to hit them where it stung and wouldn't stop.

ASHTON. Well how are you gonna know where the shipments are?

Fuck I didn't think about that. Then I realized I'd have to do something I didn't want to do.

CARTER. I'll call the bitch at the top.

He looked very confused.

ASHTON. What are you talking about?

The less he knew, the better.

CARTER. Let's just say I got someone on the inside.

I sat back in my chair and felt like shit until the waiter came back, and then I felt like shit some more.

WAITER. Sir, we are unfortunately out of coke.

I just stared him down for a second,

CARTER. I'll have a ginger ale.

9

I knew I couldn't just call Anastasia, especially not on my phone. it would obviously bitch the plan. Marvin's phone was still in use, as he was MIA. Therefore, no one knew he was dead. Maybe. I scrolled through his contacts and couldn't really find much intriguing. Then I just kept looking—through his notes, his call history, and his pictures. And the retard let it slip.

I realize the importance of not being careless. That was what had kept me living so long.

He had taken pictures of a crate. It was just a crate on a pier, but it was enough. Now, why would someone take a picture of a crate at 3:30 in the morning? And then I looked in his call history to see if a call matched he time the picture was taken. One did, and the call was to Anastasia. I wouldn't need a call transcript to know what they were saying. All I need was to put the pieces together—something that could have been solved as a matter of common sense.

Each picture taken has a location, and so does call history. So I just looked at the address, and that was it. That was where they made they're living—out of a bullet.

But I still had no idea when the next meet would be. For that, I was fucked. But it was still a start.

I wrote down the address and put it in my pocket. Then Ashton walked into the living room, so I turned to him.

ASHTON. You want the couch or the bed?

CARTER. There's plenty of more beds downstairs. It doesn't really matter.

ASHTON. Oh.

CARTER. Look,. Ashton I got a location from my mole, but I don't have a time. So, we're just gonna have to stake the place out. But it could be days. So, we might have to set up a camera.

ASHTON. Fine by me, as long as I get my bonus for this.

CARTER. Bonus?

ASHTON. Yeah. Bureaucrats said they were gonna pay me extra if I got this for them.

CARTER. No one mentioned a bonus for me.

ASHTON. Well, they tell me you're not doing it for the money are you?

CARTER. Mostly I'm just trying to send a message and survive. But I've been digging a deeper and deeper hole day by day, I've come to notice.

He went on his way. still looking around for something to do. He was bored. Finally, he sat down on the couch next to me staring at the empty wall where that TV should be.

ASHTON. Well, you want a beer or something?

CARTER. There's nothing in the fridge.

ASHTON. We could always just go out and get some.

I hadn't slept in two days trying to figure all this shit out. I appreciated the effort, but he didn't understand. And of course, I wouldn't expect him to.

CARTER. I think I'm just gonna go to bed, Ashton. We got a long week ahead of us.

ASHTON. Do you think this shit will work?

CARTER. We don't have another choice, another opportunity. So, we have to take what we have and do what we can.

He went up and off, still not understanding. But I didn't care. I was sleeping in this time. And if my luck served me right, Ashton might have a car.

Sleeping on a couch that is at least forty years old is actually pretty miserable. Plus, this one was not a decent length, so I had to have my feet up on the armrest and my head leaning off the side. It could always be worse. I could have not fallen asleep at all and just lay there with my gun digging into my side.

Just looking up at the ceiling fan slowly spinning on its highest setting seemed to prove this was an unforgiving and unsettling time and place for everybody who had been and would be affected by my actions. This was just a desolate, crumbling apartment long forgotten by time and innovation. Even the kitchen had a calendar with a young and promising OJ Simpson on it, and the light switches were those push buttons from long ago.

The place was frozen in time. Poor thing.

I woke up on the floor the next morning with an unbearably painful neck and an imprint of the rug on my forehead. Sleeping in such piss-poor conditions would make a normal man just groggy, but I had it worse. I just didn't wanna be there to begin with.

I checked my phone and saw that I'd slept for over twelve hours. Unbelievable to me, but I still felt like shit. I never thanked Todd for the partner, but I texted him real quick and got up to see what Ashton was up to. For a minute or two, I couldn't find him so I tried calling for him.

CARTER. **Retard!**

No answer.

His loss. He'd miss out on breakfast.

I checked the cupboard to find a single can of spam that had expired last year. I started to contemplate eating it and then thought about eating out. But then again, I was miserable and deeply frustrated and still too groggy to leave. Then the back door opened.

It wasn't a conscious action to have my gun already aimed at Ashton's chest. I just reacted without even knowing it. Maybe I was on edge. I snapped back and apologized the moment I realized it was him. He of course nearly pissed himself again, his hands up for protection.

ASHTON. **Are you going to do that every single time I show up?**

CARTER. **Only until you realize not to fucking sneak up on me like that.**

I noticed he had grocery bags, which he'd dropped when I'd pointed my gun in his direction. And my grogginess seemed to kill itself off.

CARTER. Oh, you got breakfast.

ASHTON. Yeah. Nothing here is edible. So I decided to get some food while you were asleep.

CARTER. What did you get?

ASHTON. Bagels!

My grogginess seemed to be reincarnated at that point.

CARTER. You're not Jewish, are you?

He looked confused and didn't get the joke.

ASHTON. No

I have nothing against bagels, but I just wasn't in the mood for them.

CARTER. Yeah, sure. I can eat a bagel.

He set up the table with two paper plates and cream cheese. Fucking primitive way of living. Not much of a choice except eat or starve. So we started eating.

CARTER. You have a gun, right?

ASHTON. Yeah. I keep it on me all the time.

CARTER. What kind?

ASHTON. Glock.

Fucking amateur. But then again I only switched as soon as I didn't have a choice of the brand I would get next. But since the other night, I really would prefer something that wasn't made by Glock.

CARTER. Oh, they're nice. I've always wanted one of those.

I put on my shit-eating grin and dashed on some sarcasm because fuck it; why not?

And then he pulled it and set it on the table to try and brag about it, but I wasn't really impressed. Then I pulled out my new sig and set it next to his as an attempt to solemnly tell him to fuck off and keep eating.

ASHTON. Hey, look. Mine's bigger than yours!

I was not pleased.

CARTER. Don't be gay, bro.

He frowned and took his gun back, but I noticed something before he put her away. His gun still had a serial number. Odd, but it was probably nothing. So, I shook it off and put mine away too. And sooner or later, we both finished up.

ASHTON. We might as well check out the spot beforehand and set up if we need to, right?

I looked at my watch to see that, if there actually was a deal, we would be quite a few hours early in relation to the photo. So, we'd probably be fine and not get caught.

CARTER. Sure. Why not?

Do you have a car, by the way?

ASHTON. Yeah. She's parked about a block away. You have no idea how hard it is to find a parking spot in this place.

We set out with our guns and hoodies and went for the walk to the car, noticing all faces along the way. This time, no car decided to follow me. So, they either smartened up and fucked off, or they kept their distance.

Ashton's car wasn't some shitty sedan. So, I was fairly impressed to the fact that it was a newish Volvo S60 without a single dent or scratch to be seen. I was pleased and jealous.

CARTER. You must take good care of your car.

ASHTON. Yeah. I try my best. I just got it a month ago. So, I barely have a bump in the odometer.

You wanna drive?

I looked up from drooling over the car and was almost starstruck. And of course I had to accept.

CARTER. I could definitely take her for a spin. Sure.

It was a good car without a single problem, and it even had a backup camera. I'd never even been in a car with a backup camera. It seemed so fancy to me. But after all it was just a Volvo. And as soon as I ran into a curb, the whole car would be paralyzed. Stupid Volvo electronics. The thing with Volvos is they're built by Germans, but the electronics are made by Italians. So, seeing a fair language barrier, they can't really make a functioning car half the time. But they still make do with what they have.

We drove along for a bit, trying to not get aggravated by the excess traffic into Manhattan. But there was nothing we could do about it. So, we mustered on while Ashton gave directions.

The closer and closer we got, the more and more familiar it seemed. And then I realized something. This was the same warehouse they'd brought me to what seemed like ages ago. This was that place. Holy shit. I knew of it. And sure enough, I was right. But I drove past, trying not to look suspicious.

ASHTON. It was right back there. You passed it.

CARTER. What? You want me to stop right in front and get out and try and look as obvious as I can? You're very new to this. I can tell.

Ashton sat back and said nothing. He knew I was right and didn't see a point in arguing.

CARTER. We'll just find somewhere to park and then, you know, scope the place out.

He didn't know it was familiar to me. So I didn't need to mention it to him. As usual in lower Manhattan, it took a stupid amount of time to find a parking spot. But eventually, we got around to it and hopped out around three blocks away.

I expected at least an ambush walking up. But then again, they might not even think I was still alive. Or, if anything, they likely thought I was still in custody. They'd think that they'd be safe.

I started inching around alleys and corridors, seeing if someone was on guard. And lo and behold, an empty pier. No boats.

CARTER. Ashton, come on up here.

I got my eyes set on a ladder leading to the top of one of the seaside hangars. Rusty-ass ladder. Probably would need a tetanus shot after this. We finally got to the top and went down, lying on the roof to minimize the chance we'd be seen.

ASHTON, *whispering.* You'd expect the sort to put locks on those ladders.

CARTER. Why are you whispering?

He shrugged it off.

CARTER. The thing with New York City is we have something called politicians who'll let a homeless man jerk off outside a school and not have him arrested. So, why would they put lock on a ladder?

ASHTON. Actually?

CARTER. Not really. I pretty much made it up.

We kept crawling forward until we could get our heads over the edge and get a look at the pier and at that all-too-familiar hangar with a dumb bitch and her crew.

We stayed around for a couple minutes, and then we saw a glimmer of hope. A totally inconspicuous, lone Italian in a suit walked out of the hangar.

CARTER. There it is, Ashton.

ASHTON. What? Do you know him?

CARTER. Not personally. but there wouldn't be a lot of reason for a well-dressed European to be strolling around a commonly used gun-running pier—unless something was going down soon.

I knew what I had to do. I would have to stay here and wait till the sun went down. Being so patient would suck. But I knew my goals were far more important than my deteriorated mental health.

CARTER. Ashton.

ASHTON. Yeah. What's up?

CARTER. Something is gonna go down tonight. So, I'm gonna have to wait here until they come.

ASHTON. You're really determined about this thing, huh?

I looked at him.

CARTER. You betcha, pal.

ASHTON. Well then, what am I gonna do?

CARTER. Well you'll get the snacks, of course.

He wasn't pleased with that. He probably felt useless from the way I'd been talking to him. But he had to understand this was my thing. This was my problem and my plan, and if he talked back, it wouldn't actually matter, because I was gonna have the poor kid killed anyway But I tried not to think about that part. Still, Todd knew he needed to send someone useless because Todd knew he'd be dead in the end. Why would he send this kid? There didn't seem much wrong with him besides the fact he was new.

May God have mercy on us.

Ashton sighed—obviously not pleased.

ASHTON. Well, what do you want to eat, Carter?

I'd go easy on him this time.

CARTER. Here. Take my debit card. Just get whatever you want for
both of us. And maybe get some binoculars too.

Now he was pleased.

ASHTON. Oh shit. All right. Thanks.

He crawled off. But I had one last thing to say before he left.

CARTER. Don't buy too much shit, Ashton, only the essentials. I'm
not trying to go broke all right.

He nodded and went down the ladder.

Now I'd have to play the waiting game.

Todd still hadn't texted me back, and it had been almost an hour
since Ashton had left. That guy was still just standing there, just waiting. He was waiting for a meet. He had probably come early to check
for security. But, damn, he must've been blind not to see me. And it
was odd the guy had to stand there so long. Maybe I'd increased their
security measures with all my stunts and their lack of knowledge when
it came to my unknown location or even whether I was alive, for that
matter.

I saw Ashton pass by in his car. It was getting late. I double-checked
my watch. Two and a half hours. At least I got a little warning before he
came sneaking up on me. But the little shit didn't have to go out and buy
a buffet. I would definitely be checking my purchasing history when I
got back to the bank—if I ever got back there.

It was another couple minutes till he parked and made his way over
and up the ladder.

ASHTON, *whispering.* Carter.

His head popped up over the ladder.

I rolled my eyes.

CARTER. Thanks for making yourself known this time, Ashton. I
greatly appreciate it.

He crawled over with a backpack and returned my debit card.

CARTER. You get the car washed?

ASHTON. What?

CARTER. You took a bit of time. What did you do?

ASHTON. Traffic. And to be honest, I did get lost for a mile or two. Whatever.

ASHTON. How can you see shit? It's dark as fuck.

CARTER. I barely can. but they'll need light at some point.

Ashton handed me a bag of chips that had been severely crushed, but I smiled at him with hidden anger.

ASHTON. Anything happen while I was gone?

CARTER. The man has had six cigarettes and two phone calls from what I've seen so far.

I desperately wanted a cigarette now too. But it would be risky, given the likelihood of it drawing the attention on over.

ASHTON. All right. I can keep you awake if you need me to.

CARTER. No need. I'll be fine, but I can do the same for you.

ASHTON. Don't worry. I can keep myself up.

CARTER. Suit yourself.

After another couple hours of waiting, four more cigarettes, and another phone call and after Ashton fell asleep, the traffic in the area died down when everyone got off late shift. And then there was a van pulling in.

God, was I prideful. My ego was nearly about to burst thinking I was a goddamn genius and all.

I shook Ashton to wake his useless ass up.

CARTER. Retard, wake up.

He jostled up, confused and exhausted.

CARTER. Look down there.

ASHTON. Oh shit. All right, let's go.

He was getting up, but I pulled his stupid ass back down to my level.

CARTER. What are you doing, dumbass?

ASHTON. I'm gonna go down there and steal those guns or some shit. I don't know.

My hands were still firm and tight on him, clenching harder with aggravation.

CARTER. You don't know what you are gonna do because you were just gonna go down there and get yourself shot?

ASHTON. Well, isn't that what you do—not plan ahead.

I released my grip.

CARTER. No. We are gonna see where the weapons go and follow that, like memorize the license plate so we can catch them somewhere else and not compromise the integrity of the opportunity of this fucking place. That way, they won't know we caught them here and not somewh—

ASHTON. OK, OK. I'm sorry. I'll just follow your lead.

CARTER. Yeah good. Just do that. But be ready to memorize a license plate and remember what the transport looks like.

He nodded, still anxious to get himself shot I was sure.

We were patient. Or at least I was, with me trying to make sure Ashton was still awake. It was shifty to see. But thank God for the lights above license plates and the carelessness of the cocky.

At this point, there were two vans. One had just pulled out from the hanger, and the other had come off the street. Throughout the whole ordeal, the only person to come out of either van was the same person who'd been standing there the whole time. They must've trusted him to do all the work because that's what he did, but they all wanted their own privacy.

The guy would open the back of each van and basically switch the crates. He'd put a crate from one van into the other and vice versa. I had no clue if this was an attempt to confuse pursuers or what. But there was only one way to find out.

As soon as the van's doors closed, we would go for the van that had been there the whole time.

CARTER. OK. Let's go.

I started crawling back until I felt it safe to get up and run to the ladder, and Ashton was right on my tail.

We got down and started walking to the car.

ASHTON. Why are we walking away? What are we doing?

CARTER. We're going to the car, Ashton.

ASHTON. Shouldn't we at least speed up?

CARTER. Probably not. It would look a little fucky, would it not

ASHTON. You certainly do things differently.

CARTER. Yeah. Fuck off. Where'd you park the car?

ASHTON. It's, uh ...

I stopped and looked at him.

ASHTON. I think it's around that corner?

CARTER. You think? What the fuck do you mean?

ASHTON. I mean, it's probably over around that corner.

I shook my head and sped up my pace. I was about to kill him right here, right now. What a fucking moron. Halfway there, we passed an alley with the car sitting right there. I was speechless.

We got in to the car. And for some reason Ashton thought he was driving, as he walked over to the driver's-side door. After that scare, he was never gonna drive or park again.

CARTER. What are you doing?

ASHTON. Driving.

CARTER. No. I'm driving. Go around. I know the license plate. I know the van. I know the plan. Just trust me on this. Not trying to shit on your piss parade, but I'm driving.

We got in and didn't even turn on the car. We just waited for them to pass,

ASHTON. What if they don't come this way?

CARTER. The pier's a one-way. They have to come this way.

One more time he asks what I'm doing and why I'm doing it, I swear to God, I'll kill him early.

After a good solid five or so minutes, I started to get nervous, thinking I had missed my shot. And then that beautiful bounty rolled on by. But I still sat there, expecting Ashton to ask why.

CARTER. Aren't you curious why we're still sitting here?

ASHTON. I assume to give some distance.

I smiled and turned the car on. At least he was learning.

CARTER. Atta boy.

I gave chase at least three cars behind, and the night caused a visibility problem. But after one of the cars in between us turned off, I just got a little closer and kept on the tail.

ASHTON. Do you think there're guns in there or a fucking deuce?

CARTER. A fucking what?

ASHTON. A deuce, like a fake switch or something.

CARTER. Oh. I mean, shit, it could be. But there's a fifty-fifty. And if we're wrong, we just try tomorrow night and have the same chance until we get the guns. So, yeah.

ASHTON. Fair enough, Carter.

We just kept following and following, and the time just dragged on and on. And after a long enough time, the sun started to rise. We had been up all night, and this guy had been driving in circles from the pier to upper Manhattan to Queens and then to Staten Island and back to the pier.

The looping had gone on for hours, just repeat after repeat. I didn't even want the cargo at this point. I just wanted to shoot this guy off the road and go home.

This motherfucker was really testing my nerves and my very heavy eyes. And how the hell were we already in Queens again? I was so tired time seemed to meld together like it had never happened.

Ashton had fallen asleep a long time prior, and I started to have trouble focusing and not getting distracted. After just enough patience and just enough unnecessary bullshit and all my focus maintained on being inconspicuous, it all paid off when he pulled into an alley.

It was amazing the retards the mafia hired nowadays. I mean I had been around three to four cars behind for the last six or so hours, and he hadn't noticed me for a single fucking second—unless this was about to be an ambush. I shook Ashton.

CARTER. Ashton, get up.

He just about came to life but still had some heavy bags under his eyes.

ASHTON. W-What is it—

CARTER. Get your gun out and put on your mask. We're about to shoot up the Mafia.

This part I hadn't planned all the way through. I would have to kill these two or hold them at gunpoint. In either event, I would have to make a quick getaway. But I smiled, knowing it was better not to wear a mask. Let them remember my face. Let them come out of hiding and come for me. And then I'd kill them all.

Ashton handed me my mask.

CARTER. You know what? I don't need it. But you can still keep yours if you want.

He was surprised.

ASHTON. Copy.

And then Ashton took off his mask, and a smile spread across both our faces.

ASHTON. Let's have these bastards remember our faces.

Bright man. I might just miss him. Or then again, I could just use a kid from Greenwich as a replacement. I was so sure of this kid being bait I didn't even think of who actually deserved it.

We parked in the alley blocking the exit and ran in guns out. We sure as shit caught them with their pants down too. Fuckheads didn't know what was coming.

CARTER. Get on the ground. Get on the ground.

GANGSTER. Motherfuc—

One did not comply. Instead, he reached for his gun. I would have to shoot the kid. He looked young too. But then Ashton shot first. I just stopped and looked at him. To be honest, I was surprised. The guy might be thickheaded, but he was good sighted.

The other gangster went to the ground almost pissing himself, begging us not to shoot. We would have to be quick if we wanted this. Someone would have heard that shot. Ashton kept his aim on the passenger, and I opened the back to see the crate.

I gave the crate a couple good attempts at prying it up with my fingers, but it was little use.

CARTER. How do I get this crate open?

My gun was also now pointed at the passenger. But he was too thin skinned to die for something like this.

PASSENGER. There's a crowbar. It's in the front.

I ran over to the driver's side and stepped over the body. I got the crowbar from under the seat and ran back over.

We were running out of time, and we both knew it.

ASHTON. Hurry up, Carter. We've overstayed our welcome.

CARTER. It's all right. The feds love me.

Bad joke, bad timing.

All the crate needed was one little pry with the crowbar, and she was open. And oh my God, were there a lot of guns. I even dropped the crowbar on the ground in shock and just stood there and stared.

ASHTON. What is it, Carter?

I looked over at him, still wide-eyed and speechless.

CARTER. We're not gonna be able to take these guns, Ashton.

There had to have been at least twenty or so rifles just piled on top of each other, and my God, that poor suspension. Instead of packing peanuts, there were just bullets. It was beautiful. But I knew what I had to do. First, I took a picture of what I'd just captured and saved it for later. Now I had to torch the car.

CARTER. We have to burn this shit away, Ashton.

ASHTON. OK. Well do it quick. We gotta get out of here.

His aim was still pinned on the cowering passenger. So, I ran over and got any papers I could find from the front seat, rolled them up, and stook the roll in the fuel tank. In all honesty, I had no idea if this would work or not. If I wasn't mistaken, newer models had little pieces of metal in the fuel tank to stop you from siphoning, which would also stop you from blowing up a fucking car. However, this van wasn't too new. So, I was mostly confident. Then again, the tank would be pretty low given how long the man had been driving around. Fuck it. I just took out my lighter and lit the edge.

CARTER. Ashton.

ASHTON. What?

CARTER. Run.

He stopped focusing on the passenger, and everyone started running. Ashton and I ran to the car to make a getaway, and the passenger just ran off to find some cover.

Even if this shit didn't work, it would sure piss off Anastasia. And that was all that really mattered. Or maybe it would be better if the police found the burning loot and started an investigation.

ASHTON. Come on. Let's go. Let's go.

Ashton was rushing me as I was starting the car, and I was getting annoyed—almost to the point where I wanted to just sit there and do nothing. What a pussy.

CARTER. Would you shut up and fuck off? We're leaving OK. Shit.

I started the car and reversed at top speed into a blind turnout on the street. It was nothing short of luck, us not getting hit; I had to be more careful. I could see Ashton was more worried about the car at this point And then I simply drove off and followed the flow of traffic.

ASHTON. What are you doing? Speed up.

CARTER. You know, if you were a cop, and you were responding to a shots fired call, would you, by any chance, want to pursue the car speeding away from the crime scene? Or would y—

Our conversation was interrupted by the sound of a deafening explosion just where I thought it would be. And holy shit was I happy. Fireworks in my honor.

Naturally, we ducked our heads and braced as soon as we heard the bang. But it certainly cleared the stress in the car, and I just started laughing. Ashton joined in, and we soon passed by the blaring sirens of the responding cops, who probably now were requesting assistance.

The ride home was short and fulfilling. We had gotten the bastards. But now they would come. I was ready. But then again, there was always tomorrow night. We'd just go for the other van. Another long night and horrible—aka no available—parking right outside the apartment. I was starting to miss that handicap mirror tag, but after a while, we found a spot.

I took out the cheap tracking chip I'd gotten from behind the boiler earlier. I turned it on and just threw it in the back seat. I didn't want to lose the car again. Ashton didn't notice. Otherwise, he would've taken it out, thinking it was an honest mistake.

We didn't talk on the walk back. We were just so tired all we wanted was to lie down, and I was gonna have a peaceful nap. I knew I'd be safe because the feds were back outside. Once we were inside, Ashton went into the bedroom, and I went for the couch.

Todd still hadn't texted me, and I was getting annoyed. He always did this shit. I sent him the picture of the guns and fell asleep.

10

I woke up in better shape than I had been the previous morning. My neck didn't hurt. My body wasn't sore. And best off, I didn't wake up on the floor this time. I was well rested and ready to take on the day ahead. I assumed I was the one to get up first, considering the bedroom door where Ashton had gone was still closed, and breakfast wasn't set up yet. So, I decided to do it on my own. There were still leftover bagels from the previous day, and I was in a better mood to enjoy them.

I looked at my phone and saw Todd had finally responded after the last couple days of silence.

TODD. Jesus.

It was all he said—all he thought he needed to say after what I'd shown him. It made him realize exactly what we were getting into and what we were up against. I shouldn't really say "we" because this was all on me. I'd started this, and I was gonna be the one to end it. Todd had no part in this. But the feds would still treat him as an accessory. Greenwich would most definitely be still scrambling after what happened last night. The police and feds would be right on top of it as well. Colton would be expecting something tangible as well, after hearing about what had happened. I'd missed my chance to get a body last time around because of Ashton's itchy trigger finger. However, he might just have saved my life. I'd be sure to get a body tonight.

I was still curious about how the deal went. Either one of those vans did in fact have guns on them and the other was a decoy and I was just lucky or what? I wanted to know what was in that other van. Whether or not I would have another chance tonight was unknown, but there was only one way to find out. Good thing my sleep schedule was now fucked; I was going back tonight.

I had begun to consider before going to sleep last night whether I really wanted to just run away like a coward or die fighting or live killing. I didn't have many options and even fewer that kept innocent people alive. How did all this happen? It just seemed so unreal, so fake. I had to run away again, and I didn't want to. It was unfair for this to keep happening—for me to be punished for these things. In all fairness, this time around, I wasn't so innocent. But it was the corrupt in the corps who'd made me this way. Or was I just trying to justify myself because time was running out?

Ashton came through the bedroom door as I was making my bagel, and it looked like he hadn't slept as well as I had.

CARTER. You want a bagel, Ashton?

ASHTON. Yeah. I can do with one. But we should get some coffee later as well.

CARTER. I just want tea. Thank you though.

ASHTON. What a night, huh.

CARTER. We got them pretty good.

ASHTON. What's your game plan now?

CARTER. Now we do it again.

ASHTON. How about we tell the Outlaws and get our money and go on vacation or something?

Ashton tried to talk me out of carrying out my plans—and just as I started to like him. Pussy.

ASHTON. I mean, you think the mob's just gonna let it happen two nights in a row? I mean, you'd figure not so. What's the point in going if it's most likely going to be a waste of time?

CARTER. You disappoint me, Ashton. I thought you were smartening up.

He looked at his phone to check a text he'd just received and instantly changed his mind. Odd. Little fucker really needed to make more sense.

ASHTON. You know what? Maybe you're right. If we don't check, who knows what kind of damage we could do this time around?

And then he walked off to the bathroom.

Something was wrong with him. He was acting strange, and he was not doing a good job of hiding it. Was he on the mob's side? And was this another one of the mob's excuses to start a war with the yakuza by pinning it on—

What the fuck am I talking about? The kid's just tired. I need to fuck off and calm down. It was just such a stressful time that I didn't know what was and wasn't a sane thought anymore. Constantly looking over my shoulder was bad enough. Now, I was starting to get paranoid.

Eating my food would keep my mind off certain dark paths for enough time. But then my phone started to ring.

My God, it was Anastasia.

I hesitated for a second, wondering what it could mean for such a fragile relationship. I ignored it. She'd probably put two and two together. Good for her. Now, if she wanted to send more gangsters after me, I wouldn't be alone, and I wouldn't be running away. Ashton came back out of the bathroom.

CARTER. Ashton.

ASHTON. What's up?

CARTER. Get your gun. We're leaving.

Shame he didn't get to eat his breakfast. But we needed to prepare for a definite shit show later tonight. Anastasia would throw a curveball maybe. It felt stupid to go back after what had happened last night. But besides that, it was a dead end. It was like Marvin had tried to clear up his phone of all incriminating information, forgetting just a couple photos. He'd even deleted all his contacts. Maybe he knew they were closing in on him. We headed for the car parked up the road.

ASHTON. You really fucking can't make up your mind on anything, can you, Carter?

CARTER. What do you mean?

ASHTON. I mean, you set your sights on a plan with your little intricate steps. Then the next minute, you throw it all away with a new idea like it was nothing.

CARTER. Well, Ashton, you gotta adapt and overcome new problems and shit. But who knows? Stick with me long enough, and I just might be able to teach you a thing or two.

ASHTON. You know what, Carter, I'd like that.

This time around, I let Ashton drive while I gave out the directions. First stop was the bank. I had to drag Todd even farther down into a panic, and he was not going to be happy at all to hear anything I had to say.

ASHTON. Where are we going again?

CARTER. The bank. You know where the bank is, right?

ASHTON. Yeah. We going to talk to Todd or some shit?

CARTER. Yep. We're gonna beg him for weapons.

I felt bad for Todd; it was like I was ruining his life with every choice I made. There was nothing I could do to soothe his pain but hurt him more and more until I could get him to escape all of this. If I could make up for every evil thing I'd done in my life, I would at least put it into saving Todd. Todd had it bad with losing his wife, and now he was losing his mind because of what I was doing. I couldn't let it happen to him. I couldn't let him go to jail. And most importantly, I couldn't let him get killed because of me.

The traffic on our way was light, and I knew Ashton was starving. But we'd get some food later. And coffee had to still be on his mind. But I was selfish, and all I wanted was my tea. I forced myself to think nonsense instead of focusing on Todd's mental well-being, no matter how important that was. We had to sacrifice a bit of ourselves in order to save our future.

We pulled up at the bank before I knew it. I had to talk to Todd alone. I didn't want to have to bring Ashton in on a more personal situation. He was hungry anyway.

CARTER. OK, Ashton. I'm gonna talk to Todd alone. I want you to get some food and coffee—whatever you want. And I'll call you when I'm done if you're not here when I get out.

ASHTON. You don't want me to come with you?

CARTER. It's nothing personal, Ashton. It's just he's going through a lot right now, and—

ASHTON. OK. Say no more. I'll buy you a tea, too. I can't promise it'll be warm when I get back though.

CARTER. Sounds good. I'll see you later.

ASHTON. Yeah. See ya.

I got out, and Ashton drove off for his breakfast. I took a deep breath before entering, but I got myself together and walked in anyway.

RECEPTIONIST. Good morning, Carter. How can I help you today?

It was good to see she remembered me but I just ignored her and walked off to Todd's office. She was definitely used to that one. I missed coming here. I missed having a normal routine that I could get used to and being excited about new opportunities and challenges. How clueless I had been joining up.

I just barged in like I used to, and Todd's office was empty. He just wasn't there. His books and papers were there. But Todd was nowhere to be seen. I was surprised and went back to the bank teller for help.

CARTER. Hey, where's Todd?

She looked up at me from her computer.

BANK TELLER. What do you mean where's Todd?

CARTER. I mean where is he? What do you mean, what do I mean? It's important.

Everyone in the bank was now looking at me. I was starting to make a scene. Why did I have to lose my temper?

BANK TELLER. I mean he hasn't been in in like four days. I thought you'd know where he is.

Fuck.

BANK TELLER. You could always try his house.

Good enough. I settled for it.

CARTER. OK. Thank you. I'll start there.

I started to walk out after a giant waste of time in a useless place filled with useless people but not without hearing her quick remark.

BANK TELLER. Carter.

I looked back around.

BANK TELLER. As of noon, Outlaw will cut all ties with you. So whatever you want from Todd, you'd better make it quick, or you'll get him killed for sure.

Annoying bitch.

In a full bank with all these eyes staring. Could it be that all these people were killers and mercenaries? She was taunting me, and she loved doing it too. But she was right to give me at least a little warning. Would I really be disowned? Unbelievable. Why hadn't Todd told me? What was next?

I rushed out, calling Ashton. It was ten o'clock, and Todd wasn't too close of a drive. I needed to act fast and ditch Ashton as well; if the teller knew, then he would soon enough. Ashton wouldn't be allowed to do a damn thing after twelve. He may be new. But he wasn't stupid. I was still an official member.

He texted me saying he was on his way, but he wouldn't answer the call. So, I called Todd instead.

I waited patiently for him to pick up.

And waited and waited and, finally, my patience was rewarded.

TODD. Hello?

I was calling on Marvin's phone. He didn't recognize the number. So, this time, he just so happened to not be busy.

CARTER., *voice raised.* They're disowning me, and you didn't tell me?

TODD. Carter, is that you?

CARTER. Don't start shit right now, Todd. I wanna know what's going on.

TODD. I haven't been told anything. No one told me shit. Where did you hear this anyway?

CARTER. Your fucking teller told me in front of a full audience, Todd. They want me gone.

TODD. Calm down, calm down. I'll fucking call up the higher-ups, see what's going on. But let me say, I haven't been told shit about this, Carter, all right.

CARTER. I'm coming over, Todd.

TODD. What?

CARTER. You heard me. I'm on my way with Ashton.

TODD. Wait slow down. Sto—

I hung up. I wasn't in the mood for shit like that today. And I needed to move fast. Thank God Ashton got here quickly enough. So, I made enough of a scene to let him know I was in deep shit.

ASHTON. **Where am I even supposed to go, Carter? You're not telling me anything.**

CARTER. **Just go to Astoria. We're going to Todd's house.**

ASHTON. **Where is that, Carter? I don't know.**

I was too nervous to be a back seat driver right now. So, I just wrote down the directions and gave it to him. I couldn't have this right now. My heart was beating almost out of my chest. It started to hurt.

ASHTON. **Carter, what's going on? I'm clueless here.**

CARTER. **Just be quiet, all right. Just don't say anything.**

I needed my mind to deescalate rash decisions. I needed to slow down and remain calm. I just looked out the window for the rest of the time and hoped for happiness and peace in my life. That was it, just peace. I had forgotten what it felt like already.

Ashton kept driving, but he seemed to be circling in all kinds of different directions. He took empty side roads, passed through dead alleys, and drove along barren shore paths. After a while I started to notice this bizarre act. Was he lost or was he killing time until he could dump me? Did he already know? We kept going for a little longer. At this point, it was around 10:45 or somewhere around there. I can't remember.

ASHTON. **Carter.**

CARTER. **What.**

ASHTON. **We're almost out of gas?**

CARTER. **What the fuck do you mean we're almost out of gas? How the fuck did that happen?**

It's fair to say I reacted with disdain to Ashton's plain-faced statement.

CARTER. **You didn't think to get gas before you picked me up?**

ASHTON. **No.**

There was no emotion in the way he said it—no sadness, no anger, no regret, just nothing. I was going to either ditch him or kill him.

ASHTON. **We're going to a have to ditch the car.**

I stopped reacting to him. He wanted me to react. Something wasn't right here. Something was wrong. Something was very wrong.

He pulled over on a barren road just off a rocky beach. We were in the Far Rockaways or somewhere more reclusive—so distinct from the busy subway train right overhead.

ASHTON. That's it. No more gas.

I was through with it.

CARTER. Ashton, if you're not gonna help, then I'll fucking walk there, you retard.

I got out and went on my way, Leaving him to fend for himself. I would have to first walk up the road for God knows how long. Then I'd have to hitch a ride or flag down a taxi. *Remain calm.*

I walked by an alley to my right. But why was that same blacked-out car there? The same car that had been following me in Queens?

It was a setup.

ASHTON. Tristan!

No fucking way. I turned around to face him. He had his gun out and aimed directly at me.

I stood there in shock. I had been tricked this entire fucking time, and I'd ignored all the signs. The car turned on and pulled out of the alley behind me to block the road. I started putting the pieces together.

ASHTON. Don't reach for your gun, Carter. It's not there.

I was still shocked, so I felt around. And damn, he was right.

ASHTON. I slipped it off you while you were freaking out in the car. You're so clueless when you're panicking.

I finally got the sense to speak.

CARTER. So you're an informant too? Or are you just undercover?

ASHTON. Undercover. Carter, come on.

CARTER. Well why, Ashton?

ASHTON. Carter, this is my first and only warning. Do what you were told and do nothing else, Carter.

And just like that, he got in the car and left. I was left abandoned and enraged. I was going to be barred from the Outlaws in an hour, and now I was lost and disarmed. What did I even do wrong? I had been gathering actual evidence last night. I had been doing what I was told. What the fuck? It just didn't make any sense.

I should probably take my anger out on Colton. I gave him a well-deserved call.

The response was almost instant. And I thought he was a busy man too.

COLTON. Yes, Carter.

CARTER. Is Ashton a friend of yours, Colton?

COLTON. Carter, we had to keep an eye on you. And we didn't know how else to do it. I hope you understand.

CARTER. Well, he just pulled a gun on me.

He hung up on me.

CARTER. Hello?

I felt like slamming my phone on the ground, but I settled for kicking trash cans and throwing them in the street.

Why all of a sudden would this go down—especially all in one day, all in one hour? More pieces settled down next to each other. The serialized gun. Could they have been feds selling weapons to the Mafia? It didn't seem that rare of a conclusion. Everybody knew they did that kind of shit. And all they could do was deny. It seemed like only too good a reason. I knew too much. So, now they were leaving me for the sharks. But why would they tell me to be an informant and think I wouldn't go for an arms deal. Day by day, I just dig deeper and deeper.

I kept walking along for a while, just kicking rocks and pushing over trash cans. Then I remembered about the tracker in the bag. And they say superstition doesn't get you anywhere. I opened my phone to see if I could figure out where Ashton was going.

They were on the way to Astoria.

They were headed for Todd. Not good.

I started running down the road, looking for any signs of life. I spotted a lone car just driving along the road. I couldn't force this one out. I didn't have a gun. Maybe begging would work. I ran over to the front of the car and over to the window.

CARTER. Take me to Astoria.

I felt pathetic. It was just some stoner kid with no heads or tails about anything.

STONER. The fuck you on, guy?

So I just ripped him out of the car.

The car, of course, smelled like pot. But it didn't really matter.

I put the pedal to the floor as hard as I could before the pothead even realized what had just happened.

It was all happening so fast. Todd was my best friend. I didn't want anything bad to happen to him.

I tried calling him, but he refused to answer. I tried texting him, but I ended up on the sidewalk a couple of times.

I managed to get a word or two out through dangerous driving. The text said, "Run away."

It was all I could muster with so many whirring emotions going back and forth and not knowing what to do or how to act. Why hadn't Ashton just shot me? Why hadn't he done anything last night? Why had Colton just hung up after I mentioned him pulling his gun. Were those guys in that restaurant actually listening the whole time and knew what my plan was?

The traffic was nothing but miserable. I was losing my mind. I started running more and more red lights. There was one red light just before Jamaica I just couldn't go for though. There was a cop two cars over, and I knew damn well that wouldn't have gone in my favor. So, it pained me to be patient, but it had to be done.

The light seemed to take forever. But eventually, it turned green, and I went on my way. Then the cops' light turned on. But they weren't going for me; they just ran right on through at a hefty pace. My tracker wouldn't load at this time. So, I kept going, speeding up behind the cop. But then I noticed he was going the same way as me—all the way to the end.

The squad car parked right outside of Todd's apartment.

I stomped on the brakes right behind him, almost crashing into them. But they were already out of the car and walking toward the already kicked in front door.

I ignored their yelling and made a run for it. I didn't want to think. I just wanted to see. I wanted to know it wasn't happening—that everything was OK. But then the whiplash kicked in when one of them grabbed me, taking me away from the door.

I just started crying. I just didn't want to be here anymore. I didn't want any of it to be true. I didn't know anything but sadness, and I just broke right then and there. I just broke. Now, I wasn't defending anything. I had lost my brother, and now I was empty inside. They wanted to send me a message. Or had they just gone after the wrong person? He could be fine, though. I mean it wasn't like he was a stranger to combat.

They didn't let me in—even after the paramedics arrived. By this time, they had sat me down on the curb and wouldn't let me see what was happening. They didn't think of me as a suspect. It was just protocol for friends and family not to be allowed to disturb the crime scene. I didn't say much to any question they asked. I just blankly looked away down the road, still in shock. I forgot how to act. I forgot how to do anything but deny the situation.

The EMT's wheeled out the body on a stretcher in their bag, and I was fixed on it. I was starting to tear up again, and I had to look away. I had to forget what was happening. But how could you?

OFFICER. **Sir.**

I didn't look up, but I held my head up to show I was somewhat listening.

OFFICER. **You said you had just come from work and saw the police vehicle, but you failed to mention where you work.**

I thought about it for a second. I couldn't say I worked at the police academy. So, I settled for something else.

I looked up at him.

CARTER. **I'm a federal agent, Officer.**

He wasn't buying it, and I wouldn't either if I saw a special agent driving around in a shit box like that. But I had a little something up my sleeve.

OFFICER. **Do you have a badge or any way you can prove that?**

CARTER. **I can give you my boss's number. He could back up my story.**

He was still unamused. But if Ashton really wanted me dead, done, and buried or even arrested, he'd have done it earlier. They were still using me. So, it was time to use them.

OFFICER. **I guess we can start with that.**

He took out a pen and his notebook, and I relayed information as he wrote it down.

OFFICER. Thank you. But you don't have your badge on you.

CARTER. No. I just rushed from work when something popped up on our scanners.

I'd have to bullshit my way out of this one. The cop then walked off to make the call. Meanwhile, the other officer started to annoy me as well.

OFFICER. Is that your car over there?

The cop pointed to the heap of shit that would soon turn up stolen if the little bastard hadn't called yet.

CARTER. Company car. Tight budget this time around.

OFFICER. Uh, right.

An awkward silence ensued as the officer talked with Ashton on the phone. I was getting nervous.

OFFICER. Good pay?

CARTER. What?

OFFICER. They pay you good over there?

CARTER. Uh, yeah sure.

Did this guy actually believe me? Was I that good of a bullshitter or was he just retarded?

Then the other cop hung up and rejoined the group.

OFFICER. You're free to go, sir.

It was just a phone call. What had he done? Threaten his life? Alas, I was right. They did need me for something. It was quite a risky choice, but it had all worked out. I at least expected a fed to show up in person. But no. I was free to go, just like that.

OFFICER. It is with a solemn heart we tell you we're sorry about what happened here—sorry for your loss, Mr. Mitchell?

He held out his hand, and I accepted. The name they'd given went to show the feds still had jokes on their side.

CARTER. Thank you, Detective. I hope I can get some money together for a funeral arrangement sometime this week.

DETECTIVE. Yeah, you'll have to set that up with the coroner's office. I can give you their number.

He gave me the coroner's card, and I took it.

DETECTIVE. We'll just wait for the officers to be done inside, and then we'll be on our way.

No interrogating, no more questions. What exactly had Ashton told him? They didn't even bother about the very suspicious-looking car I'd shown up in.

After another hour or two, the boys got together and left. They definitely didn't find any of the guns Todd kept lying around. I went inside, but I just stood there without even touching the door handle. It took a lot of strength to try and walk in. I just took a deep breath and closed my eyes and went in.

There was no blood. But it looked like there had been a struggle. It smelled of alcohol pads, so this time, they'd at least taken the decent measure of cleaning up.

I picked up some of the furniture and put it right side up, just to make it a little neater. They'd even left the cracked picture frame of Todd's wife on the ground where it had fallen or been knocked. I picked it up and put it back up.

I sank into the couch, knowing this was all my fault. I had killed Todd, and I felt utterly awful. I was horrible. Even if he was alive, he wouldn't forgive me. He had known the risks, but I'd skated past them in my head. He'd tried to warn me, and I hadn't listened. I started tearing up again.

I told myself something. Every single one of them has to die. The Outlaws disowned us, the FBI disowned us, Greenwich hunted us, and so did yakuza. I now had nothing that would keep me from dying— nothing left to protect, only me. It was time to suit up.

The first step was to kill Ashton.

11

Todd kept a stash at his house, which would always come in handy if things got hairy. I would take pride in using his guns for vengeance. Todd had around three rifles in the basement, along with two shotguns and three pistols. The garage had around the same, except one of the rifles didn't cycle properly for some reason. No matter. The kitchen cabinets had a couple extra more—not to mention the stockpile of ammo in the couch. I had a setup now, with a rifle, three pistols, and a shotgun. I went into the garage, strangely surprised to see Todd's car after all this time. Serendipity.

I loaded up the car. Then I felt something—a little footstep creaking in the next room over. Someone was here. Then there were more footsteps. I inched myself over to the doorway with a rifle in hand and a pistol in my waistband. This would definitely take away some of my anger.

I swung out from the garage, sweeping the living room with my sights. In them, I saw five Italians soon to be dressed in blood.

I took the farthest one on the right, while sweeping, using two shots for one in the head and one in the wall behind. It was a little sloppy I know. But the second one to the right of the previous took one to the chest and one to the heart.

I started taking shots, and I jumped behind the couch for cover. I had to move for something better that might be bulletproof. But they had to take cover too.

I ran forward over the couch suppressing fire at the target that was farthest away, taking cover outside. But that wall wasn't bulletproof, so he only took a shot in the side and started limping away. I kept moving forward, passing a guy on my left who was using a wall as cover. He grabbed my rifle and put his pistol to my side. I slammed his hand up against a wall with my side, disarming him. Then I pulled my pistol for two in the stomach.

The last guy threw his gun out from a wall and walked out, surrendering. I used my rifle to put one in the head. No mercy.

The injured bastard kept limping off into the woods, so I shot—one in the back and one in the head. They wanted war, then that was exactly what they'd receive.

It was time to leave after the encounter with the men, obviously Greenwich. Everyone would know what had happened here, and they would learn to fear me more. I heard very distant sirens, so I got the car started and opened the garage door and went on my way. What still escapes me is why the pothead didn't call in the stolen car. Guess he didn't want that possession charge. Lucky me.

It was time to kill Ashton, the coldhearted bastard. I remembered that tracker in the car—the one I'd placed just for parking, convenience at its finest. Currently, my tracker said he was hanging out in Brooklyn.

Suddenly, I remembered about sandy. It would endanger her life for me to check on her. But—

I shook it out of my head, but they really could have gone for her too. The risk was too great. How could I protect her if I couldn't protect Todd? Oh, poor Todd. I tried to ignore it. I could at least pass by, just to make sure, you know. Like some sort of creep. No. I was just making sure she was safe.

I slowly passed by my old apartment.

Then I saw her up on the steps smoking a cigarette. She didn't see me, but I knew she was safe. That was all I needed to know.

I kept on down the road and looked at my phone again. Ashton was going home. I pursued. He was headed in the direction of Bushwick. He was going nice and slow through traffic. He felt no danger. But he shouldn't have been so careless.

I pulled into an alley nearby to wait for there to be less of a distance between us. So patient I was to kill this man. I felt determined and motivated to strike this killer down. It was sad to see corruption every now and then. I knew most people in law enforcement and federal positions were decent enough people. But scumbags like Ashton and his pals gave the good ones a bad rap.

I only had to wait for a couple more minutes until I could pull out and be on his tail. I took a couple turns until he was finally in sight in that once beautiful Volvo. *No mercy*, I thought.

Two cars in between me and him, and he didn't know Todd's car and presumed me dead.

He pulled into his driveway. I drove past to park just up the road. I looked in my mirror to wait until he went inside. I turned off the car and brought a pistol. I headed up to his house. But what would be a good point of entry? Window? Back door? Let's just calmly try the front door.

I went up his driveway with a smile and a heart of anger. Pulling out my gun, I went up to the front door. I thought again about being calm and just decided to kick the door in. So, I did. The door flew open, splinters hitting the walls and pointed right at him. He was right through the doorway into the living room—surprised for sure.

CARTER. Ashton.

He didn't move for a gun. He would know I'd be too quick.

CARTER. Let's have a chat.

ASHTON. My wife will be home any minute, Carter. Please.

CARTER. I said let's have a chat.

He sat down on his couch, and I pulled up a chair in front of him but not too close. I needed my reactionary gap just in case. It was time to find out some information.

CARTER. You killed Todd.

ASHTON. You got him killed yourself, Carter.

CARTER. Don't try and guilt me. It won't work.

ASHTON. After you sent that photo, I had no choice.

CARTER. The feds were selling the guns, right? That's why they were serialized, right?

He said nothing.

I raised my voice.

CARTER. Right?

ASHTON. Yeah.

Now it makes sense.

CARTER. But why would Colton tell me to go be an informant if he didn't want me to find the guns?

ASHTON. We just wanted you out of the way.

CARTER. And so why didn't you shoot me back in the Rockaways?

ASHTON. Because—

He took a deep breath. Now he was my informant.

ASHTON. Because Greenwich wanted to kill you. So, we let you go knowing you were too risky.

CARTER. You in with the Outlaws too?

ASHTON. No.

CARTER. You bullshiting me, Ashton?

ASHTON. No. We were trying to get to the Outlaws through you. But they ditched you.

CARTER. How do you know that?

ASHTON. You think you're the only one we have on the inside?

CARTER. You sent Greenwich after that phone call, huh?

ASHTON. You just gave us your location. So we did, yeah.

All because of a goddamn jewelry store.

ASHTON. We're trying to have them kill each other off, Carter. We're the good guys.

CARTER. Ashton shut up.

We just sat there for a moment in silence while I wrapped my head around it all.

CARTER. What about Sandy?

ASHTON. Who the fuck is Sandy?

I smiled. She was safe from all this. But the yakuza still needed to be taken care of, and I hadn't heard from them in a while. Time to wrap this shit up.

CARTER. How long you been married?

ASHTON. Five years, Carter.

CARTER. That's almost as long as I knew Todd.

ASHTON. Carter, please. We thought you both knew about the feds in the van.

CARTER. You know what really gave you away.

ASHTON. What's that?

CARTER. Your gun was serialized.

His face sunk.

ASHTON. Shit

I did what I had to and put one in his skull. He thought he could get so far away from all this and murder. I avenged a comrade and took justice on a killer. He was no better than me, but I was the smart one. A little light bulb appeared in the back of my head, and I had to try it out to be sure. I rummaged through the closet in the living room and found a decently large bag. In fact, it was large enough to hold a body.

A perfect fit.

It was time for my plan to come to fruition. I grabbed his car keys and didn't bother cleaning up the blood. The wife could do that when she gets home. *No mercy. Seek revenge on those who have wronged you and put them under.*

I dragged the bag outside and down the steps. Couldn't carry the bastard. He was just too heavy. But I could manage to get him in the trunk. I didn't care about being seen. I was gonna call them later anyway. His car had a full tank. But I don't know if you could really call that ironic or more or less annoying.

I cut off some guy on my way out and headed for the pier. It was around seven, so I had plenty of time and plenty of darkness.

The roads were a little busy, but I was in no rush. So, it didn't really matter all too much, except for getting a little impatient. But I managed to get closer and closer minute by minute.

I heard no noise in the trunk, which was always a good sign. If they hadn't already, the cops would be scrambling over the new scene at Todd's house and his missing car. But now I had a new car—though, on second thought, they might find Todd's car and see Ashton's scene. I was rambling. But fuck. I left all my weapons in there. Still, I should be back soon.

I got to the docks, but I just passed by it, like normal. They had increased their protection, with totally inconspicuous sentries standing around looking like criminals. I pulled up a little bit away. I hadn't thought about having to carry the bag. So, I was a little stumped. First, I'd need to clear a path.

I got out and moved toward my goal with my hoodie up. Avoiding being seen by all the guards and eye contact was difficult. But around this time, it was rush hour. So, they couldn't possibly notice everybody who walked by. I got to the other side of the hangar and hid in an alley to watch for a bit. There was a back door to the hangar, but it would definitely be guarded on the other side, even if it was unlocked. I saw a guy go up and just knock, and they let him in. That easy, huh?

I waited a minute or two to prepare myself for a sneaky bastard action. Good thing poor Todd had silencers stocked up. I screwed a silencer on and took a deep breath. It was time to go.

I moved out from the alley and went up to the door and knocked. I looked around while waiting, making sure no one was watching. The door opened. Big mistake.

One in front and one on the left side of the door, but the door opened inward to the right, so that would make three people. *Be quick,* I thought. The man in front wasn't looking, but the one on the left was. I stuck the gun in his stomach and shot once. Then I slammed my body up against the door to block the other guy. Next, I took two shots at the man in front starting to turn around—one in the chest, one in the neck. The door I was using as a shield was very thin, so I thought, *Why not?* I put two through the door at waist height.

Three were dead, and no one else was in view. But the others sure as shit would come back. The hangar door was closed; I was safe for now. There were already bloodstains on the ground, so I didn't think to worry about that, just the bodies. I painstakingly carried the bodies over to a laundry basket in the corner that was being used as a trash heap. One by one, I picked them up and carried them over. I had to be quick too. But I swear I tweaked my back or something.

I decided to pick them up instead of dragging them to avoid leaving streaks on the ground. The van was here. I opened the back and saw the crate. Perfect. I left and headed back the way I had come to get the car. I walked a little faster than I had last time because of the limited time I was working with.

I got back to the car in no time. But I really wasn't gonna drag Ashton's body through the streets, was I?

I put the car in reverse and just backed up down the street, looking like a maniac with cars honking and people swearing at me. I reversed into the alley, but I drew the attention of one of the guards, who came over to see what was going on. So, I got out.

GUARD. What the fuck is going on?

CARTER. I got some guns in the trunk for you. Sorry about the delay.

GUARD. The fuck are you talking about?

I walked over to the trunk, and the guy followed to see what I had. I opened the trunk and showed him the body bag.

GUARD. What the fuck?

I pulled out my gun and put one in the back of his head, blood and brain matter splattering on the inside of the trunk. The fucking mouth on him though. What a sailor.

I took the bag out and left the guard's body behind the trunk. I picked up Ashton with all my strength and carried him over to the door and through to the van. No one investigated the area, so I was still in the clear. My back was hurting, so I dropped him right behind the van. I took the crowbar that had so conveniently been left nearby, and I opened the crate with swift ease.

It was full of money—and not just a couple thousand ones. These were hundreds, and there weren't just thousands; there had to have been millions. I stood there for a second in awe. But I got myself together and emptied the crate on the floor until there was nothing but pocket change left. I opened the bag and recoiled. He was starting to smell. I lifted Ashton up, put him in the crate, and sealed it back up.

I started piling the money into the blood-soaked bag. Blood money. It almost made me laugh. But I managed to do it. And just like that, the old switcheroo was done. Now, I needed to wait for the feds to show up. I hauled the now much lighter bag over to the trunk and closed it up. I sat in the driver's seat, feeling so relaxed it was hard not to fall asleep.

The radio didn't have anything good on, and I couldn't watch *M.A.S.H.* on my phone without reception. So, I got bored fairly quickly. I settled for playing with the seat adjustments. It was so cool—with all the electronics and little knobs. I was like a little kid. The AC even worked without hesitation. I went through the owner's manual about three times, seeing that Ashton had gotten a fairly priced package— neither the cheap nor the expensive one, going instead right down the middle.

The feds showed up and pulled through. I checked the time. It was around eleven. I forgot how quickly time passed. I made sure to see the license plate before they were out of sight. I instantly called the cops.

DISPATCH. 9-1-1. What is your emergency?

CARTER. There's been a kidnapping over at the pier. They have guns and vans.

DISPATCH. What is your location?

I gave them the address and the license plate numbers of both vans.

DISPATCH. OK. Stay on the line.

CARTER. Oh my God. He has a gu—

I hung up, proud and satisfied with what I'd just accomplished, although I couldn't stick around for the fireworks. I had to leave before the cops showed up.

I started up the car and made my way back to Ashton's to dump it. But I needed to be careful. The feds wouldn't save me this time around. It was a much quicker and softer drive on the way back, with little to no traffic in some places.

I made my way over the bridge to Brooklyn with a song in my head and a pep in the gas pedal. Some people didn't give Billy Joel enough credit.

I slowly made my way through Brooklyn and dumped the car in a spot a block or two away. But I wasn't going to forget the bag. I also took my bag of clothes I'd left in Ashton's car.

I walked down the road and over to the block where he lived. There were at least three or four cops cars outside and a grieving wife sheltered in a detective's shoulder. I wasn't gonna stare too long. So, I unlocked Todd's car and threw the bag in and went on my way.

Where was I gonna go, though? I was exhausted, and there was no home for me. The feds would soon enough have an APB out on me. So, where to now? Oh, that's right. I literally had a giant stash of money in the bag. I'd just get a hotel somewhere. But I couldn't be close by. New Jersey sounded good right about now. But goddamn, I'd never thought I'd say that.

I made my way over with very heavy eyes, taking it easy, figuring I'd arrive sooner or later. The Holland Tunnel actually looked very satisfying at night. But I couldn't fall asleep to it. I had to keep driving. I drove another couple miles inland and settled for a Marriott. I pulled into the parking lot, thinking I might have to dump the car sooner or later. My clothes were soaked in blood. So, I took off my hoodie and said it was good enough. I took the bag and made my way to the lobby. I waited patiently in line until it was my turn.

CLERK. Hello, sir. How may I help you?

CARTER. Yeah, I would like a room for around, let's say, three nights.

CLERK. OK. Will you be paying by debit or credit?

CARTER. Uh, actually cash, if that's OK.

CLERK. OK. If I could see an ID or passport.

I had a couple different IDs just for this occasion. I was never that clueless. I took one out and handed it over.

Tom Stevenson

Good enough. I didn't care.

CLERK. OK. That will be $312.

I only had hundreds, so I opened the bag and pulled out four. Some of them had blood on them, but I handed them to her anyway.

CLERK. Umm.

CARTER. Oh. I'm sorry. Had a nosebleed earlier.

She slowly handed over the key card, and I trudged off with my bag, ready to have a good night's sleep.

12

I never felt so well rested. I slept like a baby. It was wonderful. Thomas Stevenson was ready to take on the day as a new man. But first, Carter had to finish what he'd started. I took a shower and changed out of my clothes. I was now on top. I thought I was the one ahead of the game. Now that I knew their plan, I could be ten steps ahead of them.

I was starving. So, I went downstairs to get some complimentary breakfast. First off, I headed for the complimentary bar. I slept in till around eleven, and by the time I got downstairs after getting ready, it was already twelve. So, having a drink or two at this time was perfectly acceptable.

BARTENDER. What can I get you?

CARTER. Gin and tonic on ice.

BARTENDER. Yes, sir.

I wasn't really down there for mediocre liquor. I was only interested in the news above the bar.

CARTER. Hey, can I have the remote? I just want to watch the news.

The bartender handed over the remote alongside a gin and tonic. I turned on the TV and immediately flipped to NY1 for the ever-so-trustworthy local news. And there it was, and it was beautiful—my finest work so far.

NEWS REPORTER. Last night, an anonymous phone call led police to an illegal arms deal between two federal agents and two suspects with known affiliations with the Mafia.

It worked. Colton would not be happy with this one. Nor would Anastasia. But that was exactly what I wanted. This would make the Outlaws ignore my existence even more. I didn't blame them, though. They were not the bad guys. They just didn't want to get themselves killed.

> NEWS REPORTER. The body of Special Agent Richard Ashton Mathis was found alongside the bodies of ...

And here I thought he'd lied about his name. But no. The police had already been investigating the special agent's disappearance, and then they'd found him in an arms deal. That would definitely confuse the whole situation for them. But the feds would catch on real quickly—at least the shady ones would.

About now, the higher-ups would want to look into some internal corruption within the bureau. They'd really picked on the wrong guy. But what was the score here? What would be next? I guessed now I'd just wait for another opportunity to show itself.

I thanked the bartender for the pick-me-up and went on my way. I was rich now, maybe. I might as well hit the town to buy a better suit. Go raid Times Square and—who knows? A new pair of shoes couldn't be all that bad.

I went upstairs and got dressed for a different occasion. I put on the cheap suit I'd gotten in Missouri all too long ago and thought, Why not? Be talk of the town. Some new hotshot whoring for attention. That'd definitely draw out the Mafia. But then again, how deep did the corruption go through the feds? How much firepower could they throw at me? It was also true though, that big spenders didn't put off too much of a scent, especially if they lay in cash like Scrooge McDuck.

I went downstairs, feeling like the most interesting man in the room. I got to my car and got it started up. It was time to set the mood. I blared the radio and made my way back to Manhattan. I always hated the traffic before getting onto Holland Tunnel. The New Jersey side seemed so much worse. It was like everybody was leaving the hell they called home and making way for New York because, after all, who'd wanna stay in New Jersey unless you were doing a drug deal, dumping a body, or hiding from the law?

I got through it all after an unnecessary long amount of time waiting. I drove down the street, praying for a decent spot and settled for parking down near the Battery. Lucky spot.

I left the car, making sure to at least hide the extra guns a little bit, so I wouldn't have to find more, and walked up toward Times Square. It was my first day off in a while, and I was going to spend my heart out. I made sure to have my money and wallet in my front pocket, because God knows you couldn't trust you wouldn't encounter a pickpocket around this time of day.

First stop was watches. I needed a new watch because I'd already had the current one for about a month, which was way too long in this case. I could've just bought a Rolex, but that would've been too douchey. And it would just end up being stolen anyway. I also wanted a watch that could take a hit or two without breaking entirely. Plus, I wanted Swiss, because why wouldn't I buy Swiss? I got a Tissot T-Race that had all the features I wanted—durable, Swiss, and fashionable.

My suit was cheap and uncomfortable, so I went another block or two down to the most expensive tailor I could find. I wanted a black suit. Of course, I didn't need some fancy, colored, simple people's suit. I was no simple person. I went in and got sized up for my trousers, shirt, and jacket. I even got to walk out the same day with it. They were really quick; they barely had to size a suit to my fit. Guess I just had a pretty regular body type. Noted.

I stepped over a couple crackheads on my way to get some tea at some bougie-looking cafe. Might have been a Starbucks. I can't remember. But it was very nice and well made—definitely what I needed. I even managed to buy a new pack of darts on the way, and they didn't even want my ID. But then I just felt old.

It was a little bit of a hike, but I also made my way to Bowery to see the old CBGB and relive some memories I'd never thought I'd see again. The club even had a live anniversary show coming up soon. But I probably wouldn't make it.

I left Bowery fearing for my life from a couple more crackheads. I stopped at the 9/11 memorial to pay my respects. It was really impressive to see, and even though I personally hadn't been affected by it, the memorial was always quite a site to see.

I made my way back to the car with various other prideful purchases that I knew I didn't need but didn't hurt to buy. I got over to the car with no problem. I put my stuff in the car and closed the door. I was so close to getting in too. Then a man just appeared out of nowhere behind me. Scared the shit out of me.

MAN. Carter.

I just turned around and looked at him with my hand on my back, ready to unholster at any second. I didn't say anything.

MAN. There's no need for that, Carter.

He was Asian, and he was wearing a suit. And that could only mean one fucking thing.

MAN. Mr. Soko would like to have a word with you.

He motioned to a blacked-out Escalade on the other side of the street.

MAN. We only want to talk, Mr. Carter.

I spoke up, skeptical about the friendly gesture.

CARTER. What does he want to talk about?

He kept motioning to the Escalade.

MAN. You have my word. We only want a chat, Carter. No violence.

This could be one of the stupidest traps I'd ever fallen for. Or it could be an actual peace treaty. I had the opportunity to clear my name with the yakuza. I should take it before I missed the chance.

CARTER. OK.

I took my hand off my back and started walking over to the Escalade with the courier. I was still extremely unnerved by what was going on, and I didn't trust them for a second. But if they wanted to kill me, they would've sent this guy to shoot me in the back of the head.

The door opened for me, and I was expecting to be treated like royalty. I got in and got myself comfortable.

The man sat next to me, and he closed the door. I was in the middle seat in between the courier and another man. But it wasn't like there wasn't enough room. There was plenty, and I was very comfortable to say the least.

We started driving off.

The man in the passenger seat shifted around to face me.

PASSENGER SEAT. I hope you understand we have to confiscate your weapons before you meet Mr. Soko.

It made sense. In that case, these fellas were actually pretty polite. I slowly reached behind my back and pulled out my handgun. I even cleared the weapon and put the safety on to make the scene even less tense. I handed over the clip, the gun, and the bullet from the chamber.

PASSENGER SEAT. Thank you, sir.

And then he just turned back around and put it all in the glove box. If this Mr. Soko was such an important person, why didn't they just put a bag over my head to keep me from knowing the location? Did they want me to trust them that much? Did they really think I was dangerous? I was flattered. But then again, I should really stop inflating my ego all the time. It couldn't be good for my mental health.

The car was full and quiet, which did make the situation a little awkward. But I was comfortable, so I didn't really care all too much. We drove in circles a couple times and took unusual routes, which was probably to lose a tail if we had one.

We drove up and down Manhattan at least three times, which definitely took time. But eventually we made our way to the Bronx, where I saw signs of the trip coming to an end. Only we then drove back over to Manhattan, at which point we almost instantly turned around and returned to the Bronx.

We drove through the Bronx for another thirty minutes until stopping. We had finally arrived. The house we pulled up to had guards all over it and the house itself must've cost a pretty penny. That was clear just from its location alone, not to mention its immense scale

We didn't pull in the drive. We just parked on the curb because the driveway was already filled with identical Escalades. I wasn't worried. I was only curious.

I got out and accidentally stepped in front of the man from the passenger seat while I was still looking in awe. He then apologized and gestured for me to carry on. What an interesting culture. I'd killed their friends, and they were treating me like a king. Weird.

I walked up to the front door with my pickup entourage following me closely. I attempted to knock on the door, but the doorman on the inside had other ideas. The door opened, and I just walked on in, looking around, still confused by the sudden respect, although I was not going to complain. I just might've earned it, you know.

I couldn't help noticing all the eyes watching me, though, as if I was important. I wasn't used to it. I was directed to a closed door protected by two Asian guards with rifles sponged across their chest.

COURIER. **Please knock and address yourself in order to enter Mr. Sokos's office.**

The big man, huh. Either I would be killed or forgiven for what I'd done. Then again I could be held captive or exiled and banished. I slowly walked up to the door, still skeptical about it all. I looked back at that same courier, and he nodded, signaling my acceptance.

I knocked twice but didn't really know the proper way I would need to address myself. They couldn't have been too used to outsiders on their own turf, and I didn't know the customs.

CARTER. **Uh, it's Carter.**

I could feel them eyeballing me after that one.

The door was opened by another interior man, and I was let in. It sure was an office and a fancy one at that. Overflowing bookshelves were filled to the ceiling; intricate paintings hung on the walls; and, of course, there was a handmade, hand-carved wooden desk—and Mr. Soko, himself seated behind it.

He was a balding, middle-aged Asian businessman, as all mob bosses tend to be, the Asian part exchangeable depending on the mob. He looked up from signing his probably illegitimate paperwork to greet me.

MR. SOKO. **Good afternoon. I've heard a lot about you.**

He had a slight accent, but I was very surprised to see such politeness out of a mob boss who worked for an organization responsible for sex trafficking, drug sales, murder and many other underworld operations. The daring man was even brave enough to have a smile. No shame. As awful as these people may be, I nonetheless had no choice but to show the same respect I was being afforded.

He put his hand out to shake mine, and I pretended to be graciously accepting.

MR. SOKO. Please have a seat.

I took a seat in front of the desk. All the guards left the room and closed the door behind them, and it was just the two of us.

CARTER. So what's going on?

MR. SOKO. We are aware that you were forced to kill some of our members.

And I want to apologize for our reaction without proper investigation.

Things were looking up for me. I was now ahead of the game, ahead of the curve, ahead of it all.

CARTER. I'm sorry I killed six of your men.

MR. SOKO. You merely defended yourself.

We would also like to thank you for your attacks against the true killers.

He undoubtedly was talking about Greenwich. But he wanted something, didn't he?

MR. SOKO. And the enemy of my enemy is my friend.

He had said it with a mischievous grin.

CARTER. And all good battles are won without fighting.

MR. SOKO. You are a scholar.

But ...

Fuck.

MR. SOKO. We are in the middle of a war that cannot be won with words. You are a small fish in a big pond where you do not belong.

CARTER. I'm not quite sure I understand.

What was this old man going on about?

MR. SOKO. You are strong and useful, but you must choose a side. You can either escape, in which case, we will not pursue you, or you can punish those who have hurt us.

It was an ultimatum that I hadn't seen coming. My plan wasn't to escape. But was I really going to arm up with these monsters? Was I any different though? And did I really think I had somehow been forgiven for what I'd done? Few choices remained. But at least I had a choice this time around.

CARTER. What would accepting entail for me?

MR. SOKO. Return to the Outlaws and be absorbed by the yakuza.

Jesus Christ, the man was insane. Achieve total power and eliminate the competition. This man couldn't handle it all, and I couldn't let him. But what could I do? What choice did I have? Although Mr. Soko seemed important, he couldn't be anything more than another pawn in the chain of criminal bureaucracy.

CARTER. And if the Outlaws refuse?

MR. SOKO. They are business men. They'd be foolish to refuse.

They wouldn't possibly let me just leave and escape. This was an illusion of choice. I would be a very valuable pawn. But right now they were just asking nicely. It was their way or being thrown off the highway, so to speak. They were threatening me, but they didn't want it to be obvious. So, I told them to stop messing around. We didn't have to lie to each other. I didn't need to play any more games.

CARTER. Let's cut the shit, Mr. Soko. I don't mean to be blunt. But let's be honest. You're not gonna let me escape. You're not gonna let me leave. And you know I won't either way. But you want something more out of this.

His smile faded, and it was almost as if his expression turned into anger. But he wouldn't take it out on me. He wasn't making the rules. There was always someone higher up telling people what to do, how to act, and what to say.

MR. SOKO. If you don't want a choice, then I will give you an order. Go to the Outlaws, and together, in good time, we will control many assets that could prove useful profits.

Finally, we were being straightforward and honest. It was all I needed and wanted.

CARTER. Well, when you put it that way, Mr. Soko, I have no choice but to accept.

I stood up and set forth on my leave and disappointment. Once you're in the game, you just can't escape. You can't leave. There is no winning or losing, only death or justice. My plan did, in fact, work. But

I guess I just forgot to plan ahead again. I had been so excited and exhilarated by the first couple steps that I'd forgotten to have a getaway plan.

CARTER. I appreciate your hospitality. And, well, yeah. Goodbye, Mr. Soko. It was a pleasure to meet you.

I held out my hand, but he just sat back in his chair and refused. Stubborn old man couldn't accept being caught. So, I just turned around and walked away. I got up to the door, and it opened for me, thanks to the guard on the other side. That little gimmick was starting to get creepy.

COURIER. Are you ready to leave now?

CARTER. Yeah. I think I'd like to go back to my car now.

We strolled back out through the doors and down the driveway and climbed back into the car. Just like that, I was in another deep hole. Now, the thing was I would fix these problems, but then another one would come back, only it would be worse and more complex than the one before it. I had no way of knowing what would happen next. But right now, I needed to plan this out and sure as shit plan an ending this time.

An escape would be nice. But where would I go? Canada? Mexico? Jail? The FBI hadn't arrested me yet, and I couldn't be that hard to find. So, maybe they weren't using all their manpower. I mean, after all, Colton wasn't exactly the most law-abiding of agents. Maybe that could explain the lack of reinforcements. He just might not want the higher-ups to know what he was doing.

So, maybe I could deal with them tonight—just snitch them out to the news, and I'd be safe. But then I'd have more problems to deal with and then, again, a lack of escape. Maybe I should deal just with Greenwich and the yakuza first.

The Outlaws weren't on my hit list. But I definitely wanted to clear something up with the old chain of command, starting with my only just recently former boss, Drew.

13

I was very surprised the Outlaws had settled with me just being left to fend for myself. I knew an incredible amount of information about the Outlaws' dealings—so much it was a wonder they were letting me live. I mean, I knew account information and asset locations. I was a witness to a multitude of serious crimes. And of course, I knew where some key locations were; I'm talking important and prominent figures in the gang, most notably their house and headquarters address.

I got back to the hotel with no worry or superstition of tails. There, I dropped off my newly purchased products and got dressed into a more normal attire. It was a shame. I really wanted to wear the suit. But I didn't really need to stick out too much.

To cut to the chase, the Outlaws headquarters were in Jersey City. That point always confused me. I mean, I knew the Mafia and yakuza had connections in Jersey City, seeing as how close it was. But I thought the Outlaws were smarter than that. If there was any prison I would be thrown into, I wouldn't care, so long as I didn't have to live in Jersey City. I just felt uncomfortable living near it. All jokes aside, it's not per say a terrible place to live. But it's not on my list of likable places.

I had a cigarette to calm my nerves and went on my treacherous way to hell on the border of home. The New Jersey Turnpike had factories stretched along the shore, which always made for a sore sight—or maybe a foreshadowing—before you got further into the state. I only disliked the northern part of New Jersey. The southern aspect was actually a lot nicer, with more to do and see. But for some reason, I couldn't think of anything at the moment.

Traffic on the turnpike was awful around Easter; it was packed and slow—almost unbearable. Nevertheless, hour by hour, I made what should've been just a twenty-minute drive into three hours of crawling forward and stopping every few hundred feet. I drove around for another hour or so to find a parking spot close by and managed to somehow find one outside Liberty State Park. It was a lucky find, but the cops around here would find any excuse to ruin a perfectly normal day. It's no hate toward the police in general; it's just the ones in New Jersey were dickheads.

And to think Tom Stevenson was born here. Poor guy.

As soon as I got out of the car, I got a whiff of that unique smell—a mixture of sewage and homelessness. If I kept shit talking about New Jersey, I'd just make myself miserable. Maybe I should calm down with all that. I had to make my way further in the downtown area. From what I remembered, my old pal Drew was in the basement of some obviously out-of-place coffee shop in a prime real estate area. I didn't know why they didn't just move. The location itself was suspicious. But then again, hide in plain sight, I guess.

I walked for a long while, getting lost many times along the way. I managed to find a hot dog stand, where I stopped to get a Coke and lunch, just to keep myself less starving and much less aggravated, even bring a little joy to my mood. I found a coffee shop near city hall, but it had been closed down by health inspectors according to the door. Directly across the street was the place I was looking for. *Must have been some ugly competition*, I thought.

They no doubt didn't want to see me. But I could just say all I wanted was some coffee. I jaywalked across the street, smiling at all the cars honking and flipping me off. The traffic was pretty light. So, I only managed to annoy a couple people.

I got up to the door and walked in. The place wasn't too crowded; it was afternoon anyway. There were cameras inside and outside, and if they weren't already, they would all be trained on me very soon. They were at least paying attention. I got in line and looked up at the menu to see what I wanted to order. But I was skeptical. Did I actually want a coffee this late in the day? Or should I just get a bagel or something? I mean, I already ate a hot dog. So, I was a little full. But I could do with a snack maybe.

I could just wait and tell the barista to get Drew. But God knows he wouldn't leave his bunker for anybody. The man was a paranoid freak when it came down to it. With me showing up like this, who knew how nervous he might be. The person in front of me stepped away, and it was my turn. But still, I wasn't so sure what I wanted.

BARISTA. Can I help you, sir?

Whatever. I'd just get some water or something.

CARTER. Yeah, uh, can I just get water … in a cup. I don't want a bottle.

That was the thing with these businesses. You'd ask for water, and they'd give you a bottle so you'd have to pay for it. But if you got it in a cup, then it was free. Cheap bastards.

BARISTA. Of course, sir. Would there be anything else I could get you?

I wasn't here to be a very patient person, so I'd just spit it out.

CARTER. Is your manager in by any chance?

She looked confused, as a well-trained Outlaw should be. Throw off the scent, they tell them. If you don't know them, you can't trust them. Act stupid. I wasn't buying it.

BARISTA. Um, sure. Are you a friend of hers or something?

CARTER. Of course. A longtime friend. I've known him since the service. Just wanted to come down and surprise him.

It was a lie. I only had met Drew on a number of occasions, and he didn't like the way I worked. My excessive force made him even more paranoid. It was only a matter of time before he gave me up to the Mafia.

BARISTA. Oh, uh, yeah. I'll just be right back.

I waited at the counter while a couple people formed a line behind me, waiting to order. But they didn't have to wait long.

Out of the kitchen, the barista returned with a woman in her thirties. This was not Drew, not even close. This was probably just a cover, but it wouldn't fool me.

MANAGER. How can I help you, sir?

CARTER. Yeah, are you the manager here?

MANAGER. Yes, sir. I am. Is there a problem?

The barista just stood there looking nervous, probably just here only to pay off college. But the manager just had a smile on her face. I hated customer service.

CARTER. I was actually looking for Drew. Is he no longer the manager here?

MANAGER. Uh, I've been the manager here for the last five years since we opened. I've been the only manager here. Maybe you're confused with another store close by, sir.

Annoying. But at this point I wasn't up for an acting game anymore.

CARTER. Listen to me, all right. Go downstairs or whatever and tell Drew that Carter is here, all right? I've had a fucking stupid-ass week, and I'm not up for any more bullshit, all right.

I got myself more and more aggravated and eventually started a scene.

CARTER. I've been shot at, kidnapped, threatened. I'm responsible for Todd's death and now the yakuza are out to kill Outlaws unless I talk to Drew and tell him to stop pussyfooting around and fix his shit.

The manager's smile faded, and the employees and customers looked at me in shock. There were no more smiles, no more conversation, and no more happy afternoons.

MANAGER. Sir, I'm now asking you to leave. And if you do not, I will have no choice but to call the police.

This might be the wrong coffee shop. I'd thought I was so sure. But was I right the first time? Was the closed-down place across the street a cover, and it was still operational. Uh-oh.

I didn't really know how I could fix this. I could just walk out and act like nothing happened—just another crackhead in Jersey right. It was still very silent. Everyone was waiting for my response. And frankly, I didn't really have any.

Carter. Can I have my water please?

While all eyes were on me in the silent room, the manager turned around and angrily grabbed a cup and poured some water. She came back to me and held it out. So, I took what I had asked for and surveyed the room.

Carter. What's the matter? Never seen a crackhead before?

It wasn't my best joke. Nevertheless, it was time for me to leave with my water, and so I did. They probably wouldn't call the police if I did what they asked. But maybe I should calm down every now and then—either that or just ignore it like I was already used to.

I jaywalked back across the street, with the same outcome as before. This time, I looked closer at the closed coffee shop. I could, of course, just ask the rival store what had happened here. But I didn't think I really wanted to walk back in there. This place also had cameras. The thing was there was a little blinking light right on the lens. These cameras were on. I tested to see how attentive they were. Sure enough, as I walked around, the cameras followed me.

I looked up at the camera and waved. They would definitely be surprised to see me still alive. But of course, I still needed to get inside. I knocked a couple times and looked back up at the camera, which was still watching me. So I just yelled at it.

Carter. Open the goddamn door, Drew. I'm not in the mood.

I put my face up against the glass door and peered in at the dark, empty shop. Finally, three armed bikers came out of the basement with shotguns and came over to the door. It was annoying how these people overreacted. They unlocked the door and opened it.

Carter. Finally, some good customer service.

They pulled me in and shut the door behind me, locking it back up again. They were on edge, and any wrong move could set them off. I would need to be careful with how I presented myself now.

Carter. I mean no harm. I just want to speak with him.

My hands were up, but I was armed. I wouldn't be able to get to my gun if they lit me up. But they wouldn't dare compromise the location—unless I just had.

One of them walked toward me. He still had me locked in his sights.

BIKER. Turn around.

I turned around.

BIKER. Start walking.

I started walking.

I walked over to the basement door they had just come from. This had to be the shittiest gang in the city. I mean, Jesus Christ. They had an internal power struggle in leadership that had torn the gang into bikers and bureaucrats, and God knows, it hadn't gone well. No experience in business, just crime. Just brutes and desk jockeys, the gang had fallen apart and was on a steep decline. And I had been there for all of it.

I arrived at the basement door.

BIKER. Downstairs.

I stubbornly followed these orders, doing everything they asked. According to city code, you weren't really allowed to have a weapons armory in your business basement. But the Outlaws just had to ruin that, didn't they. I slowly got to the bottom of the staircase with my hands still up, just waiting for someone to do something stupid.

Drew's office was right in the back left corner of the basement. But I had to get stripped of all weapons first.

One of the bikers threw me up against the wall and patted me down and got my gun and withheld it.

They were so lucky they were Outlaw. I would've killed them without a second thought otherwise. They knew they had the upper hand, though, so they wanted to stretch their power to see how far they could go. Brutes.

They finished their search and directed me toward the office. All I wanted was just a friendly little chat. We got up to the office door, and they opened it and pushed me in. Lo and behold, the man himself was leaning up against his desk with his arms crossed and wearing a definite look of disgust. The room had three extra guards ready to draw. This was not a good situation.

DREW. You got a lot of balls showing up here, Carter.

CARTER. Drew, buddy, I didn't have a choice.

DREW. We are neutral, and you're bringing conflict right to our doorstep.

CARTER. Drew, that's the problem with you. You never understood. All you wanted to do was play gangster and expect that everybody else would just let you invade their turf. Drew, shit doesn't work like that.

I got comfortable and sat down.

DREW. Are you trying to justify your actions?

CARTER. All I did was follow orders and defend myself, and you gave me up.

DREW. All right. Everybody get out except him.

He pointed right at me. And at first everybody looked confused. But the toy soldiers wound themselves up and set off out the room, looking down on me as they passed and closing the door behind them.

DREW. Why did you think it was a good idea to show up here, Carter?

CARTER. You're not gonna like the reason, pal.

DREW. Carter, I could never understand your fucking lack of emotion. Like what is genuinely wrong with you? You think everything is a game.

CARTER. All right. The yakuza came to me and asked for a truce.

DREW. OK. That doesn't mean you get your position back.

CARTER. Their main man in Brooklyn says, if the Outlaws don't help them take out the Greenwich cocksuckers, then the yakuza will come down here and deal with the Outlaws.

He just stared on and then shook his head. He wasn't happy. But it wasn't like it was my fault. Maybe, though, I was just selfish. He turned around and sat down at his desk with his head in his hands.

DREW. Carter, what the fuck have you done?
        You've ended us.

CARTER. I can help you, Drew. And in return, they'll let us go, and we'll have freedom again.

DREW. It's not that simple, Carter. It was never that simple. We can't just go to war with the fucking yakuza and win.

He got up from his seat and started pacing around. He was panicking.

CARTER. You can always try and run away, Drew.

What if I just tried to get into his head—use his paranoia against him.

DREW. Carter, what would I get out of this, huh? I'd only be in more danger?

You'll never understand what leadership is like.

He didn't know anything about me.

CARTER. Drew.

They killed Todd.

He looked up, straight into my eyes and stopped pacing. He was both our friend. We both knew, respected, and loved that man.

DREW. Carter.

Get the fuck out of here. Leave the city and never come back.

I started backing up toward the door.

CARTER. Then I'll be as dead as you.

I left him with that thought and looked for the guards to return my pistol. I found him at the top of the stairs.

CARTER. Can I have my gun back?

He just looked at me menacingly. He didn't want to give it back. If they wanted to play like that, I could play their fucking game.

CARTER. OK, bud. Don't lock the door. I'll be right back.

I was getting my rifle.

I left the coffee shop and headed back toward the car, which was parked so far away. I wasn't getting lost this time. I just had to retrace my steps and move on. I managed to find my way back to the car without the same trouble I'd had before. And with the luck I had, I only encountered a single homeless man scoping out my car.

CARTER. Hey, fuck off.

HOMELESS MAN. Look, man. You got any change or just some food. I'm starving.

I had the opportunity to give this homeless man hundreds of dollars. Or I could use him to my advantage. But how could I? Why would a homeless man be lurking around my car anyway. Me of all people. It didn't add up, especially given my circumstances. I got a little nervous, and then I overreacted.

HOMELESS MAN. Please. Just anything will do. I'll take anything.

I unlocked my car, reached in, and grabbed an extra handgun. I pointed it right at him. Broad daylight—how could I be so stupid? At least I didn't get a parking ticket. Needless to say, he was very surprised.

CARTER. **Who are you? Fed? Greenwich? Outlaw? Who are you?**

He held his hands up in fear, not knowing what was going on, not knowing what he had done wrong.

HOMELESS MAN. **I-I-I don't know. What are you talking about?**

CARTER. **Walk away.**

He just wobbled off as fast as he could and did not look back. What was I thinking? Why would I do that? Why did I have to be so on edge? It may have been a park, but I didn't see anybody close by or in the parking lot. I could be safe, but there was no way of knowing until it came back to bite me. I was about to close the door. Then I realized. Was I just going to go in guns blazing and threaten those bikers into submission? How would that work? It would just be another stupid idea. I still wasn't thinking properly.

I would buy him off.

The money was blood money anyway, and I wasn't going to retire yet. It was for Todd. I owed it to him to avenge him. The money meant nothing compared to that. I emptied most of the money bag into the back seat and covered it up with the blanket that was also covering a rifle and extra ammo. The bag must've had around $250,000 in it. But it was still just pocket change.

I got my bag and decided against the rifle and set off back the way I came. I tried not to get lost this time, and sure enough, I didn't. I was just angry. And God knows, I shouldn't be; more anger would just lead to more bad decisions.

I came around the corner and noticed the bikers were just hanging outside. Surely, though, they wouldn't let me in this time. I walked across the street and into an alley close by in order to get to the back door instead. I strolled over to see a lone biker guarding the rear entrance. I kept walking until he noticed me.

BIKER. **Hey, what the fuck you want?**

CARTER. **I want my gun back.**

I kept walking, and he pulled out my gun.

BIKER. Come take it, bitch.

CARTER. Are you really gonna shoot me in the middle of the day?

I kept walking toward him, and he started backing up. He wasn't allowed to shoot me. I knew it, but he should have at least looked where he was walking. He slipped up and got his foot twisted in a garbage bag. He looked down to see what had happened, and I made my move.

I ran toward him. He looked up, noticing my movement. But I had already thrown my bag in the air, and it was coming straight toward him. He was blinded long enough for me to run up and disarm him. I bent his wrist as far back as I could until he shrieked. I got my gun back and thought it would be better If I used it as a hammer. I just started slamming the grip again and again on his face until he kept quiet.

I expected his noise to alert the two guards at the front. So, I went to the corner and waited. They both came around close together at the same time.

I kicked the second man's knee and made him lose his balance as the other one turned around to greet me. But I already had my grip on his face with another hammer technique and then slammed my grip again on the top of the second man's skull. He went limp. The first man fell to the ground, and I grabbed the back of his collar and slammed my grip down again, knocking him out.

I didn't care about the damage I had just done to the three bikers. My grip may have been a little bloody, but that was just wear and tear. Must hurt getting two hundred fifty grand thrown at you. But oh well. Not my problem. Just my luck, the back door was locked. What would even be the point in guarding it? Like what the fuck?

I went back through the alley and back up to that glass door. I didn't forget to look up and smile at the camera before I kicked in the glass door. I kicked right under the doorknob, and it swung open. But the amount of force I applied broke the glass and shattered it into pieces.

I roamed in and headed to the basement door. I didn't need to kick this one because I knew it wouldn't be locked. I went downstairs and passed a bunch of bureaucrats staring me down. Some of them were even trying to get out of my way in fear. I might be acting too violent down here. But like I said, the point wasn't threatening into submission; it was negotiating and working together. Still, force might be required unfortunately.

I went back over to Drew's office and tried to open the door, but it was locked. There could be guards in there, too. So the next step really shouldn't be to kick it in. I knocked and tried to convince him.

CARTER. Drew, open the door. I have something to offer.

No response. So, I knocked again.

CARTER. Drew, I know you're in there. I just want to give you something.

DREW. Carter, you come in here, and I will fucking shoot you. Go away.

Drew couldn't even aim. He was not going to shoot me. And if he was, then he'd aim for my head and hit the wall behind him. He was just that bad.

CARTER. Drew, I have been nothing but fair. I'm coming in.

DREW. Carter, I will shoot you.

CARTER. Unlock the door, or I'm just gonna kick it down. I really don't care right now.

DREW. I'm warning you, Carter.

I gave a nice, good kick to the door while all the spectators stood, looking on in shock. They had no idea how to act. The door swung open, and I went in.

Drew wasn't kidding. It was like I could actually see the bullet whizzing past me. I couldn't have been fast enough to get out of the way, though. I was just too unlucky. The bullet went past and grazed my left shoulder. I recoiled in shock but was still aware enough to draw my gun and point it.

CARTER. What the fuck is wrong with you?

DREW. I told you I was gonna do it, Carter.

CARTER. You didn't have to fucking shoot me.

I looked at my shoulder, but it was nothing—a graze sure. Unlucky or not, though, it was only a graze. What a fucking scumbag.

DREW. Why'd you come back? To kill me?

I threw the bag on the table and put my gun away to tend to my shoulder. That really stung, but it was fine. I was just even more pissed off now.

DREW. What is this?

CARTER. It's two hundred and something grand.

He opened the bag to call my bluff but then he looked up, his face pale.

DREW. Carter ... where the fuck did you get this?

CARTER. Spoils of war, that's all. They killed Todd, and I took their money.

DREW. So, now you're trying to pay me into switching sides.

CARTER. Drew, it was never about switching sides; it's about fighting for the same cause. You may not like the yakuza, but I hate them even more. And in the end, we have no fucking choice, Drew.

He sat back down with his hands in his head, still thinking about the whole damned situation. At this point, some guards came in to investigate the gunshots and were almost about to shoot me again.

BIKER. What the fuck's going on in here?

DREW. It's all right. Everything's fine. I have it handled.

BIKER. Are you sure?

DREW. Yeah. Just leave us.

I interjected, knowing my problem was a little bit worse.

CARTER. I mean I could do with a bandage at least or something. I have just been shot at.

These dickheads had the audacity to look me dead in the eye and just walk out of the room like nothing had happened.

CARTER. Drew!

DREW. What?

CARTER. Did you hear what I said?

DREW. We'll help you later. Whatever. I'm still just trying to wrap my head around this.

CARTER. Todd is dead, and I'm not gonna let it be for nothing. He is dead because of me, so sparing a little money to influence a gang is no problem. I don't care. I'm trying to forgive myself and avenge him, and you should too.

DREW. Carter.

What have you done?

I took a second to think about everything that had happened over all of this—all the bloodshed and lies and deception. What could I even say to Drew to explain just exactly what I'd done, what exactly I'd caused and what, above all else, I was going to do next.

CARTER. I'm just trying to figure out how to do the right thing.

He sat there, still and lost. I could almost hear all those thoughts racing through his head now. *What's next?* he would think. Paranoia is a tricky thing to avoid, especially when people wanted to kill you.

DREW. Doing what you ask, I would have to take all my resources and forbid the orders of the dons and get ourselves on a hit list in the process. It's not even realistic. It's just stupid, Carter.

CARTER. Drew, I've made it so we're fucked either way. So, in reality, you don't have a fucking choice.

It was like he almost wanted to cry. But God knows, it would do nothing. His voice was even starting to dry up, like he'd been screaming about life for years until he finally gave up and did what needed to be done.

DREW. OK, Carter ... I'll do it ... but only because I have no choice. I want that to be known.

He went silent. I tried to think of a response. It's like Todd wasn't even on his mind. How could he forget a longtime friend like Todd?

CARTER. What about Todd? Are you doing it for him too?

DREW. Would Todd want me to do it for him?

CARTER. Todd always avoided conflict. Would he do this if it were your death instead?

You're goddamn right he would.

DREW. Then we'll do it for Todd.

First aid kit's the next room over, by the way.

CARTER. Fuck off.

14

I sat on some countertops in a kitchen in the next room, trying to fix myself up the best I could. I'm no medical expert. But with my limited knowledge, I was confident and pissed off. Drew walked in to reassure me and fill me with more regret, even though he tried to motivate me.

DREW. I'm still not sure exactly how I'm supposed to help, Carter.

CARTER. Drew, the only goal I have is to kill Anastasia, the Greenwich boss.

DREW. And then me and all my men are ostracized from the Outlaws.

CARTER. Every victory requires sacrifices. But if you were ever winning, you'd understand that.

DREW. I don't like this, Carter.

I dressed my wound, got up, and decided to leave.

CARTER. Now you know how I feel.

He knew we'd be in touch. The mystery was just whether he would actually go through with all this. I shouldn't even think I just gave up all that money for this. But it was for Todd. And even I had to make sacrifices every once in a while—even if I really didn't want to. I still had so much to accomplish, so many things to do. I wasn't done with all this chaos, and I really wanted to be. I had done the most dangerous things I could even think of. But still I just wasn't done. How long would this have to continue? How many more sacrifices would I have to make?

And how many more people would have to die? It was something I shouldn't think about. I just had to man up and press on into the great unknown—into the great mistakes.

I walked down the block and headed for my car. I looked around as a usual precautionary measure to see if I was safe and if I was being followed or tailed. Sometimes, it was good to be paranoid. But in Drew's case he was paranoid all the time and left no room for thought or taking action. I wouldn't consider myself a leader; I was more of a critic. I knew how to lead, and I knew what leaders did wrong, but I couldn't really apply myself. Or was I doing it this whole time? I didn't know. I walked for another couple minutes until I found my car in the parking lot.

There were police.

I hid behind another car in the parking lot and looked on as two cops were investigating my car. The plate would definitely come up as a stolen vehicle from a crime scene. But who would have called it in? It must've been that homeless guy. Or were the police just passing through the parking lot. That seemed unlikely, but I wasn't really be able to tell. Their guns were drawn, and their lights were on. I'd have to find another way home now. Shit.

I had no money on me. I'd just given a bulk of it to Drew, and the rest of my money was in the car. It was time to hit the ATM.

I sneaked out of the parking lot and went down a different road, trying not to be seen too many times in the same location. I found an ATM a couple blocks from the scene, and no one was around. There were cameras in ATMs. Did I really want to show my face? Was there another way to get money right now? I could always just go back to Drew and say, "Hey, can I have some of that money back?"

I'd look like a complete retard if I did that, not to mention possibly compromising Drew if I hadn't already. I decided to take the chance. It wasn't like they didn't know I was here anyway. I put myself in the ATM's view and put in one of my cards. I stood there patiently while it loaded. I couldn't remember the last time I'd actually checked my bank account to see how much I was actually worth.

Card declined.

No. There was no way. I almost didn't know how to act. I still had faith and put in another card.

Same result.

I almost wanted to just start punching the screen. I didn't need to make a scene. It would take a certain amount of strength to actually break the glass but even more to just walk away. I was nothing—or at least I felt like it. I had no money, and the feds had frozen my bank accounts. Why didn't I have a backup plan for this? Why didn't I prepare for this? I had nothing. I was completely and totally fucked. Just when all hope was lost and I was thinking of quitting, it just had to get worse. I needed to move on. How could I expect to take on a gun-smuggling ring, including the Mafia and the FBI without getting fucked over? I needed to calm down.

I wished I was just dreaming. I wished it would all just end. I didn't need to freak out like this. So what? I had no money. *Grow the fuck up*, I told myself. *Todd was killed, and I'm just gonna give up? The fuck I am.* I was belittling myself as a means of empowerment. Did it work? A little, but there were still moves to make.

I don't recommend hitchhiking. It's really not a safe choice. But then again I wasn't going to fucking walk; that was for sure. And no matter how much I didn't want to, I put up my thumb and walked down the road like some bum or dirty hippie. I wasn't proud, and I certainly wasn't happy.

Cars and trucks and all sorts of scumbags passed by me, heckling me and honking. I would honestly do the same thing. So, I couldn't really be too upset. But then again, my day just had to get worse, didn't it?

A van slowed down next to me, and I thought it was just here to actually help. But no. The door slid open, and men were there to grab me. Italian men. Greenwich. I thought it would be hard to identify someone of a certain a race just by their appearance, but the big noses gave it away. And I wasn't being hunted by Jews, at least I didn't think so. Nevertheless, they jumped me and pulled me in.

I squirmed and kicked the best I could, but then they put a bag over my head—which pissed me off. Also, I couldn't really see all too well, obviously. I got a few good knocks in on the people in front of me, but the men behind were an entirely different problem. I felt a paralyzing pinch in my back. I was no expert, but I thought I'd just been tased. My body went limp, and my lungs emptied. I was out of breath and out of ideas. I tried to recover, but I wasn't really too much of a match against all the other hooligans.

I think they expected the Taser to just knock me unconscious. I don't know how it goes for other people, but in my experience, that had never happened. So, what do these retards do? They tased me again, trying to make me unconscious. All the electricity went to my emotions, though, and I was enraged.

CARTER. **What the fuck is wrong with you? Are you retarded? Fuck off.**

I took off the bag and started swinging again. Yet again, I was unmatched. I turned around to face the scumbag with the taser, and he just had to do it again. This time, it actually worked. I don't remember much after that except waking up with a headache. Here I thought I was some sort of genius. But no. I actually got tased until I was pissed off and unconscious.

I woke up blind and tied to a chair. I knew this because, yet again, I couldn't see. and you can usually feel it when you're tied to a chair. I don't really want to beat around the bush here, but I just want you to understand I wasn't too thrilled about the whole outcome of the Taser. I tried squirming around a bit, but it didn't really do anything. I was basically just still, all my efforts hardly moving me. The chair was bolted down too. Or at least I think it was. But at this point, seeing jack shit, I didn't know anything for sure.

There was movement behind me. So I stopped everything to try and listen. They were just watching me struggle. They didn't want to help; they just wanted to enjoy my suffering. Was this actually the end? I told myself to ignore that thought immediately and just be patient. So I was. I stopped squirming and just sat there, waiting for my time to come.

There was a point where I was just bored. But that came and went after I sneezed in the bag and therefore all over my face. It wasn't my fault I couldn't be accommodated with at least a decent bag over my head. Minutes turned into hours, but who was really counting? I didn't know the time, and I wasn't going to count the seconds. Still, I just had to wait.

After waiting very patiently for a very long time, I almost fell asleep—until the bag was violently ripped off my head. From the looks of him, the guy was an Italian. But who really cared? I had dealt with enough of these goons anyway. All they had going for them was their ego and their pride. I mean, sure, I might have some of the same values. But I was the one tied down to a chair. My location threw me off quite a bit though. I looked around in bewilderment. Hallways to the left and right disappeared into corners and turns. Pipes and wires stretched along the wall into the distance. Was I in the lower levels of some factory or chemical plant? Must be in New Jersey then. That's where all of them were anyway.

The chair was, in fact, nailed down to the hardened cement floor, which, for normal reasons, would just be stupid. But of course I was no normal reason.

MOBSTER. **Carter, right?**

Honestly, I was going to respect these people. I wasn't going to beg for my life. So, yeah, he knew who I was, and he wouldn't forget. But if I was going to die, I was going to die with a shit-eating grin.

CARTER. **Yep.**

He didn't take my smile personally; he only assumed he'd be having a whole lot more fun. Torture.

MOBSTER. **Do you know why you're here, Carter? You know what? Yeah. You know what you did. So, I'm just gonna come out and ask you.**

Who are you working for?

I was gobsmacked. I mean, these guys thought I was so good I had to be working for someone or had some sort of training or just hated them. It was the funniest thing I'd heard all day. It really was just hilarious—so much so I even started laughing right in his face. I couldn't help it. These guys actually knew nothing—completely nothing. Clueless brutes.

The man, now embodying anger, slapped me, trying to gain power over the situation. I had worked quietly and subtly to loosen the restraints on my feet, and I was in luck because the bolts on the leg of the chair had pretty much rusted away. *I can get out of this,* I coached myself. *Plan ahead. Kill later.*

MOBSTER. Something still funny, Carter?

I admit I wasn't smiling anymore. But I tried to explain the best I could.

CARTER. Yeah ... only a little bit.

MOBSTER. I'm being polite with you and just want a polite response. So, answer the question. It's not hard.

CARTER. Buddy ... look, I've been kidnapped. I'm tied to a chair. I'm probably yet again in New Jersey. And yeah, I'm just not in one of those moods, you know.

MOBSTER. How do you know we're in New Jersey?

Huh, that was actually funny. With my such cynical mindset, even stereotyping didn't go out the window with common sense.

CARTER. That certain smell of shit in the air.

MOBSTER. Well, actually, it's a sewage treatment plant. But good guess.

Still, New Jersey, so I was very much pleased nevertheless. I knew my location or at least had narrowed it down. But unless I could send a distress signal, it just didn't matter. My hope was instantly shattered. Feet restraints even looser, and still no one was looking at my feet.

CARTER. Joke's on you. Now I know where we are.

MOBSTER. Why would it matter if you're a dead man anyway?

Even less hope; that was amazing.

MOBSTER. So, don't bullshit me, Carter. Who are you working for?

CARTER. You wanna know the truth?

MOBSTER. It could help you out a lot, yes?

CARTER. No one.

He didn't believe me. He laughed and just ignored what I said. I was just that much of a badass, but I couldn't keep letting it get to my head.

CARTER. You think I'm kidding, don't you.

MOBSTER. Explain it to me if you are such a lonesome hard charger. Where'd you get all the guns, weapons, and knowledge of how to be such a pain in the ass?

CARTER. Well, I recommend that everybody should have a military background. It can prove very useful when defending yourself.

MOBSTER. Well, if that really is the answer ...

That was all they wanted. And now they were going to just tie up some loose ends.

An explosion rang out through the hallways. Iron dust fell from every pipe above, covering us with a layer of the reddish flakes. The shock wave wasn't as bad as the noise. It almost just made my ears bleed. The explosion had come from above. But what the fuck was really going on in my life anymore? I just didn't get it—too damn lucky, I guess.

Everyone regained their composure, which even made me remember there were two people behind me as well. The things you forget when whatever the fuck is happening happens.

MOBSTER. Friends of yours Carter?

CARTER. Probably not. You people killed all my friends.

He pulled out his gun, but I had other plans. I gave him a good kick with my free leg, still struggling against the last screwed-in leg and lunged up at him. I slammed his body against the wall and scared the shit out of him in the process. He dropped his gun, and the two behind were hot on my tail. I whipped myself around using the legs of the chair as a weapon, hitting the gunman again and facing the other two.

The other two hesitated, still not knowing exactly what to do. I was in my fighter stance, ready for someone to make a move whilst still aware of the man behind me with,, almost certainly, a broken rib. He started to move around a little bit, so I just kicked him in the head and turned back to once again face the last two retards.

Gunshots broke out, the noise echoing around the cave-like room and the sounds of motion from aboveground making it clear whoever was firing was moving through corresponding hallways. They were getting closer and closer, and it seemed an unexpected rescue was in my view.

Another sound echoed, however.

AGENT. Federal agents. Drop your weapon.

They weren't here to rescue me. They were here to cover up what was going on. When I heard the agent call out, I froze. I wouldn't have been able to react to the men lunging at me if I hadn't been undoing my hand straps the whole time. One lunged at me, and all I had to do was swing with my right hand and fling a chair at him with my left hand.

I remembered the gun and reached down to grab it. Scooping it up, I took aim at the last man standing. He really didn't know what to do. So, after a couple seconds of cluelessness, he just started to panic and ran away.

I knew I had to take the same idea as him. Did either of us really know how to get out of here, though? My best bet was to just run in the opposite direction. I needed to get out. Feds were closing in, and they weren't playing nice anymore. What exactly were they doing here, though? What was their plan? What were they going to do? Kill everybody? Did they even know I was here? Or was this just more bad timing? I was already lost in the disgusting tunnels and ended up having to decide to go left, right, or straight at numerous crossways.

The gunshots and screaming were getting closer. I could hear the federal agents on my tail, closing in. I, on the other hand, still had no idea how to leave. I passed by some metal doors claiming to lead to pumps and generators, but they were locked.

The noises of my pursuers were closing in, and they had to have been coming from either end of the hallway now. My only hope was through the metal doors. I tried opening them again. And just as before, they, of course, still didn't open. I put some more force into it and then ended up kicking one of the doors. Three good kicks, and it was open—with the downside of nearly shattering my foot. The door was still open, though.

In the room was a giant water pump of sorts, along with buttons and lights all over the wall, indicating gauge measurements and other technical shit. But there was also a sewer grate on the ground. Shit. I closed the door behind me and tried to block it off with filing cabinets. For a moment, I just stood over the grate, hating myself. I didn't want to be here, and my head still hurt. My only chance of survival, it seemed, would entail wading through a river of shit. The agents were moving closer, and they'd probably heard the noises I'd made ramming through the door. Or who knows? Even if they hadn't heard anything, they'd start room clearing sooner or later.

I moved the sewer grate and looked down and held my breath. After today, I never wanted to be in New Jersey ever again. I climbed down the ladder a bit but looked back up to restore the sewer grate back to its original position. I jumped off the ladder onto a sidewalk to the streets of shit. The smell was even worse down here. I could barely breathe, so I put my forearm up to try and mitigate the damage to my sense of smell. But I, rather, simply held up the collar of my shirt over my nose—still breathing in shit.

Making my way through the sewers, I stuck to the wall and tried not to get my shoes wet. However, I was not so fortunate. It seemed like I had been walking for miles, just trying to find an exit of sorts—ideally, one that wouldn't lead me into a worse situation. I had come to many turns and connections with smaller "pathways" shooting off into different directions. But I settled with going straight along what seemed the main route. After all, that was east according to my compass, and my best bet was to make it to the coast. Gotta love those little phone apps.

Almost an entire hour had passed since the last turn, and I finally saw light at the end of the tunnel. I finally saw some hope. As I moved closer, the light got brighter and brighter. And at long last, I had made it to the coast. I stepped out and looked at the skyline of lower Manhattan. I reeked of shit, and I needed a beer and a nap.

I started to think about what had happened back there. But no matter how I looked at it, it didn't really add up to any good reason. Was the FBI looking for me? Was it simply that they'd tried to take a hit against Greenwich because I'd made tensions rise over the gun running. Either way, If I hadn't been around these last days, they wouldn't have shown up. I was sure of that. But had they just been executing the mobsters without cause? Or was it all self-defense? Were they trying to burn those loose ends? There were too many questions. But whatever the answers may be, I figured Drew should probably know what had gone down. So, I got myself together and texted him.

CARTER. We need to meet up.

I got up on the road and headed back into Jersey City to look for a bar or something—anywhere that would work well for a chat. I noticed a public park close by. The place seemed good enough. There were plenty of kids; if the cops showed up, they wouldn't shoot into a group of kids. It was an evil thought, but I wouldn't be pulling the trigger in that instance.

I went into the park and sat down at a bench. A decent amount of people would walk by from left to right and vice versa, and it was clear they definitely noticed the smell. They gave me shoddy looks and covered their noses. I just sat there and smiled. It wasn't like it was my fault I smelled like ass. It was just New Jersey in general, I supposed.

I waited around, checking my watch every now and then. And eventually, right in front of me, Drew peered out from behind a tree. It really was comical how paranoid he was. He looked like a retard, and all I could do was act like I didn't notice. I mean, I may have reeked, but even I was skeptical about being seen with him right now. He deemed the scene safe and started walking over, looking over his shoulder every couple of steps. There were other people too. But they were better at hiding. I had seen a guard at least a hundred feet away in multiple different directions. They weren't here to take me out. I knew that.

CARTER. Drew, do you have to look so suspicious all the time?

DREW. You are in no position to judge me, C—

He covered his nose as he noticed the smell.

DREW. What the fuck is that smell?

CARTER. I'm sorry. I'm just trying to fit in.

DREW. You know, that's real funny. But you should really give New Jersey some slack. It's not that bad. It really isn't.
    You didn't text me to talk shit. So, what's so important?

CARTER. I was just kidnapped.

DREW. I can't really act surprised. I'm sorry. I'm just not.

Fair enough.

CARTER. Tensions have risen. FBI just hit Greenwich, and everybody is getting impatient.

DREW. And you want me to do something in regard to that?

CARTER. I just want to know that, after thinking it over, I've realized you're able to help.

He stood there for a second and scratched his face a couple times. It was a tough question. But right now, I didn't want his fear to cloud my judgment. I wanted his anger to fuel his men to avenge a fallen friend.

DREW. Yes, Carter.

I'm willing to fix this.

But only because they killed Todd. Don't think I'm doing this for you.

I smiled. It was all I needed to hear.

CARTER. OK.

You know this is going to be a war, right?

DREW. I'm aware.

He was sterner with his responses now. I could hear the confidence in his voice. It was a certain boost in morale for me, to say the least.

CARTER. Well here's what we have to do. We need to start killing them off, with no mercy and no feeling. They hit us, and I don't care how the big Outlaws feel. If they are not with us, then they are against us.

We are going to show these bastards that the Outlaws won't sit around any longer like pussyfooted lightweights. We will fight back this time.

Do you know how long I've been doing this? You know what? Here's better question. What would you say is our goal as Outlaws? What is our purpose?

I was going off on a tangent and I wasn't going to stop for any weakling.

DREW. We are here to (or at least originally the bureaucracy side was formed in order to) give back to the community—you know, to help those who suffer due to the corruption in the real world.

CARTER. That's right. And you know what, Drew? That corruption has been winning because we refuse to do our job, and we refuse to stick to our morals. We've been doing it this whole time. And right now, at this very moment, it has to change, or this would have all been for nothing.

I was steaming with emotion. I had let it out and had even rose to my feet as I was speaking. I was happy. I could fight back with a force more powerful than just me alone. It was exactly what Todd would have wanted. And by God, I would not rest easy until my conscience was clear and my gun was empty. With all the anger I started to get light-headed, so I sat back down to catch my breath. Maybe cigarettes were not the best option for stress relief anymore.

DREW. Carter.

I looked up, hoping for a somewhat decent response from the oh-so-paranoid boss. *Please just help me, Drew.* It was all I need. It just might be my last option. And after that I didn't know what I was going to do. I didn't even know where I was gonna sleep tonight. Had my time at the hotel run out? Or better yet, I shouldn't go back there anyway. It was time to get rid of all the attention that had been focused on me.

DREW. I'd better start working on my aim then.

Atta fucking boy.

15

First things first. I would need Todd's car back. So, I talked to Drew a little bit more after the park rendezvous, and he told me to get into contact with an inside man in port authority to sneak the car off the impound lot. Drew also gave me a partner—a real one this time—William.

William had been working for the Outlaws for quite some time and had no record of insubordination or deception—no scratches and surely no mistakes. I was exceptionally nervous at first, considering Ashton. But Drew had nothing to do with that, and all I had to do was keep an eye on this new partner. I didn't trust him yet, for good reasons. But there was nothing to worry about. I knew that. Still, though William and I had met under a lot better circumstances, I planned to keep an eye out. Drew said it was only for one job, so it couldn't be that bad.

The port authority mole was in position and waiting for our mark. All I had to do was wait for William to pick me up at the safe house in Crown Heights. He showed up at midnight and gave a couple honks to get me outside. I was pretty groggy, but I eventually made my way outside and to the car and got in.

WILLIAM. Carter, right?

CARTER. Yep.

WILLIAM. I'm William.

CARTER. Cool.

I didn't want to make him feel bad. But I just wasn't up for much conversation. Not only was I tired, I was still pissed off at Drew for putting me in Crown Heights. He did that shit on purpose. I just didn't like Crown Heights. I was like the only one here who didn't speak Hebrew. At least he didn't put me in New Jersey.

WILLIAM. I've heard a lot about you..

CARTER. Are they just rumors or have you heard facts?

I knew damn well I had to be a celebrity at this point, having caused so much chaos over the last two weeks and then suddenly joining back up and sending the gang into war. I was famous among these goons for my instability and bloodlust.

WILLIAM. Well maybe you could prove some things, and then they just might not be rumors anymore.

CARTER. You know, William. I don't really like paparazzi.

WILLIAM. I was only curious.

Sure, I'd quell the curiosity. But I must say, I wasn't used to all this attention from fans. Never thought I really had fans.

CARTER. OK, fine. Ask me something then.

WILLIAM. Uh ... well, I fucking heard you're asking for a war against Greenwich.

Drew really was a little fucking gossip girl, I swear. I'd literally told him a couple days ago, and already people were talking about it. To be fair, that was kinda what I wanted anyway. How could I expect these Outlaws to start war without knowing who they were starting war with. So maybe it was just a good thing that people were talking about it—unless I started another power struggle and broke apart the gang again.

CARTER. Basically, it's not war. It's more about forcing peace.

I thought it was a funny joke.

WILLIAM. That makes no fucking sense. Was that supposed to be a joke?

Dickhead.

The drive to New Jersey wasn't busy, as most people were trying to leave instead of visiting. So, I didn't have to get so impatient this time around—more or less. Mostly, it was just a little bit more tiring. We saw a couple port authority cops driving by, probably responding to a gang-related crime—more specifically, shootings between Greenwich and Outlaws. I was just happy my plan was going well. The crime rate had increased quite a bit, and it was all because of me.

We ended up on the other side of the tunnel and soon found ourselves close to the impound lot, where we parked just outside. It was a little bit past midnight, maybe even closer to one in the morning. The lights to the impound lot were on, mostly because it was dark, which was genuine sarcasm. But nonetheless, the lights in the lot turned off and then turned right back on again.

That was the signal.

CARTER. All right, that's it. Thanks for the ride.

WILLIAM. Anytime.

I don't think so, William. I'm sorry.

I got out and walked over to the gate to the lot. I checked to make sure it was locked. Even though I was still a little tired, I had enough energy to climb the fence, and so I did. I got my pants caught on the way down. But it wasn't too much to worry about. I looked around for a bit and passed by all the shit boxes and victim cars of women drivers and regular fender benders.

There she was. Todd's car was squeezed in between a Suzuki and a mangled Mazda. The mole had told me the key should just be in the front right wheel well, and after feeling around for a bit, I grabbed onto it and pulled it out.

I looked around to make sure it wasn't some sort of ambush and unlocked the car. I opened the door and looked around to see if all my items were in there. The guns were there, which just goes to show the hard work of the police department. But the money wasn't. The money was gone. How the fuck would that be a thing? Someone had obviously gone through the car and grabbed the cash but left the guns. So, there was a little bit of corruption going around. But still, why hadn't they just grabbed the guns? It was time to do some digging.

I closed the car door, and with my angered mood, I decided to just walk into the police department and ask around. The mole said he wouldn't be too busy as regards to manning. But nevertheless, I'd still have to be careful. I didn't have his phone number, but even if I did, I'd still prefer talking face-to-face.

I walked over to the side entrance in the lot and checked to see if it was locked. It wasn't. These had to be the laziest cops ever, I swear to God. What an unusual time so far. I snuck in and listened for computers or movement. I knew at least what the guy looked like for the most part, but his was a pretty common appearance. On the other hand, I could just question the next guy I saw. I guess I was just planning as I went at this point and not sticking to the original plan.

I snuck into an office with a cop at his desk. His back was away from the door. I pulled out my gun and moved in. I, of course, didn't forget to close the door before I walked up though. The closing of the door attracted his attention, but my gun was already aimed in his direction. He was scared shitless and didn't know what to do. He just sat there, staring at me, frozen. The man wasn't even armed. He couldn't do a damn thing.

Cop. W-What do you want? Don't hurt me.

I ran up and aggressively grabbed his head and pushed it toward the desk. I wasn't trying to hurt him. I was only trying to intimidate, and damn did it work.

Carter. Who searched the Nissan in the impound lot?

Cop. The what?

My gun was to the back of his head at this point, and he was almost face down at his desk with the amount of force I was pushing into his skull.

I repeated myself.

Carter. The Nissan outside. Who searched it?

Cop. I don't— W-Which Nissan? What are you talking about?

Carter. The white Nissan that just came in a couple days ago.

Cop. I don't know. I-I can look it up on the computer.

I stood patiently and looked around to make sure I was still safe while I was waiting.

Cop. I-I still don't know what car you mean. We have like nine fucking Nissans out there.

Carter. Search like the fucking license plate or some shit.

COP. Well, what is the license plate then?

CARTER. It starts with like an "X" or something. That's good enough. Try that.

I stood there and kept an eye on the door. The station was still quiet, and the other cops must've not shown up yet—probably still responding to that Outlaw shooting a bit ago. So, while I was still fine, I was in a sketchy situation.

COP. There's still nothing here. We don't have that car.

Feds must be behind this one. And damn were they good at it. Me taking the car now would definitely piss them off—unless they wanted me to. It could be the car was bugged and chipped.

CARTER. Did feds show up with the car?

COP. I-I don't know. FBI agents come in here all the time. What do you mean?

CARTER. Did feds show up acting fucking fishy? That's all I want to know.

COP. Well, I mean, we had some guys come in being dickheads in the lot. But that's it.

CARTER. What do you mean? Explain.

COP. They wouldn't even let us search some of the vehicles out there. Said it was their jurisdiction.

I had all I needed, and now it was time to leave. I sure as shit didn't want attention at this very second. So, I should probably just take the car and leave—and maybe pull under a bridge to search for bugs.

CARTER. You know, you're a pretty useless cop.

He was about to respond, but then I slammed my grip into the back of his head. It knocked him out the first time too. It just goes to show that perfect practice makes perfect.

I still had some Tylenol on me. So, I threw a couple pills on his desk as a way of a tip. But now, like I said, it was time to get out.

I left the room and the building the same way I'd walked in, leaving almost no trace that I had even been there in the first place and made my way back to the lot. I ran over to a control panel on the side of the gate and flipped it on. The gate opened, and I got back to the car and got my ass out of there before anything happened.

William was still waiting, parked just outside. I rolled up to him to explain the situation.

WILLIAM. Is that the car?

CARTER. Yeah, William, this is the car.

WILLIAM. So, let's go switch the license plates.

CARTER. Yeah. But just follow me. We need to search it for bugs first.

He didn't look happy. But I just drove off with him right on my tail. I was a little nervous with my driving. I had just threatened a cop inside a police station, after all, but whatever. It was just another normal day anyway. I drove through the Holland Tunnel again, and just as before, we passed the same cops I had seen on the way there. This time, they were responding to the scene I'd just made at the port authority. And they weren't paying attention to my car when they blasted by, so it looked like I was in the clear.

I got to the New York side and settled for the Battery parking garage but wasn't too happy with the parking fee. William and I parked up on the roof and got to work.

As William switched the license plates, I searched in the car for anything out of the ordinary. It seemed to match up at first. But then I dug a little deeper and found out they had taken my cigarettes too. Cheap bastards. And you'd think I deserved a little bit better than that.

Eventually, William had finished and joined me in the search.

WILLIAM. How the fuck are there guns in here?

CARTER. Lazy cops.

I wasn't in too much of a talking mood. So, I gave him that response and just left him quiet. William wasn't really good at searching. He was kinda half-assing it all over the place. But after a while, we finished up and concluded there were no bugs, no chips, and no trackers. Some of my shit was gone. But at any rate, the car was clear, and the plates were switched.

WILLIAM. So, that's it then.

CARTER. Yeah. You're good to go home if you want. I don't need you anymore. Thanks for the help though.

We said goodbye, and I left first. I drove myself all the way back to

Crown Heights and put the car in the safe house garage. The feds would find out by the morning that it was gone, but it didn't matter. I was still winning, and they weren't using all their resources to catch me. I went inside and immediately passed out on the couch.

16

I woke up in a decent mood. I was well rested and ready to take on the day. I even put on a pot of coffee, which was definitely a different thing for me. But I felt like I needed to enjoy myself. I took a shower and then made myself some breakfast while I waited for the coffee to cool down a little bit.

I stepped back into the living room and put my food and coffee down on the table in front of the couch. I put my feet up and turned on the TV to see some news.

NEWS REPORTER. **Another gang-related shooting occurred downtown in the Bronx last night.**

More of my doing, just like the news from last night. Made me smile.

NEWS REPORTER. **Port authority police are on the lookout for a man who walked into a police station and held an officer at gunpoint, making demands.**

Then they showed the security footage. I may have fucked up here. They had my face, and they had their warrant. I wasn't nervous. Why would I be? If the select few corrupt feds couldn't get me, how could the police?

I started to wonder if Sandy was watching. Did she still think of me? How had I lost her? How had I fucked up so badly that I'd pushed her away?

I knew I should be scared. My face was on NY1. Why didn't I care? I felt more strongly that what I was doing was working than I did that I was in any danger. They could throw whatever they had at me. If they took me down, I'd take them right down with me—down into the gray and out to oblivion. They wouldn't get away that easily.

I didn't really want to sit around and wait for all this to happen without my direction. I didn't want to be some laid-back leader who gave out an order of war and didn't join in the fight. This was my fight. Why should I have to sit around while everybody else was having fun? We were closing in on Greenwich. And who said yakuza would keep up their end of the deal?

I needed a plan B. What if yakuza bent us over and fucked us? I couldn't let it happen. There had to be a contingency plan. I got out my phone and called Drew to see if he was available. It took a while for Drew to pick up. But eventually he picked up. He only seemed to be in the best of moods to talk to me, and I wasn't joking this time around. Profits were up, and we were doing our job for the first time, and we were doing it the right way. We were vigilantes with shady pasts and an uncertain future. The sketchy thing about what we were doing was that the higher-ups of the Outlaws were not aware of our new game plan. If they were, we would never be heard from again. Unless someone snitched, though, we'd be fine for now.

DREW. Carter, what's up?

CARTER. I wanna know if you're available for a little meeting. I just wanted to talk to you about something.

DREW. Is it something I should be worried about?

CARTER. Not really. It's more just about planning ahead.

DREW. Yeah, all right. Sure. I'm available for brunch if you're OK with that.

CARTER. I'm down. You just need to get someone to pick me up.

DREW. Yeah. I'm pretty sure a guy is already close by.

We said our goodbyes, and I waited for my pickup. The convenient thing about my new position was that all these new people I met every day on the payroll were all expendable, each and every one of them. Maybe it was sick and cynical to think of them in that way. But more or less, I didn't care. The inconvenient thing about new people was that I couldn't trust them. Drew might be able to, but I didn't know them. And I'd learned not to trust so easily after all this time.

I cleaned up my breakfast and finished my coffee and just left the dishes in the sink. I looked through my closet to decide what to wear. In all honesty, I can be a bit of a picky dresser. I settled for a collared shirt and khakis—nothing too formal but nothing too greasy. I didn't want to impress anyone, but I didn't want to look lazy, like I didn't want to be there.

I stood out on the front steps, got comfortable, had a cigarette, and waited. I didn't even know what the guy or the car looked like. I just had to assume the first car that would pull up was my ride. Drew never knew how to be cautious. But I damn well could have asked for these details. So, I guess we were both to blame in some sort of fashion for being a little careless. After doing what we did for so long, you tended to realize that this stuff mattered. I know I say that a lot. But with repetition, you get too comfortable. And when you get too comfortable, you get too vulnerable. Vulnerability would be the death of us. Just you wait and see.

After almost two whole cigarettes, a car pulled up, honked the horn, and rolled down the window. My hand was already on my gun. My phone could have been tapped, and this just might be a trap.

DRIVER. **Carter?**

Way to make a fucking scene, retard. There may have been no one else in the street—no drivers and no one walking. But still, what the fuck, man? I mean, come on. Could you be any more obvious? My position at this point was more like that of a witness in protection, rather than that of a trained killer. I shrugged it off, assumed it was all clear, and went toward the driver.

CARTER. **You realize it's broad daylight, and I'm a wanted man, and you just yelled my name?**

He didn't care. He didn't seem to be in any mood for shit talk or being reamed out. I wasn't gonna go too in depth on him. Maybe I'd just mention the issue to Drew.

DRIVER. **Are you him or not?**

I nodded in frustration and walked around to the passenger side and climbed on in.

CARTER. Take me to Drew.

KYLE. I'm Kyle, by the way. You don't have to be a dickhead with me.

What a weird way to put it. The man didn't even care, did he? I'd be honest with him though, of course.

CARTER. OK, Kyle. Well, I'm just saying, you can't just scream my name in the street. I get a little paranoid all right. I'm a wanted man.

KYLE. Well, I'm sorry, Carter. But all I'm here to do is drive you around.

I swear to God, I almost pulled my gun on him. What kind of a dickhead would say something like that? Annoying. But I could just ignore him for the rest of the drive. It shouldn't be all that bad. A couple minutes went by and he decided to put in a Pet Shop Boys' CD.

My hand was on the gun the whole time.

The drive was nothing but miserable. We went from Pet Shop Boys to Nickelback and then back to Pet Shop Boys,, and if I'm not mistaken there might have been some Michael Jackson somewhere in there too. It was absurd. I couldn't believe Drew hired these kinds of people. Where did he even find someone like this? Just kids off the street trying to do what they saw in action movies and video games. It was ridiculous. Maybe this was why we used to be losing.

Traffic was heavy and I was starting to get light-headed from the god-awful scene in the car. After a while, my anger started to die down when he let me smoke in the car. The drive, however, was a bit too long for my taste. We arrived at the coffee shop around an hour after I got picked up—too long for comfort.

Kyle parked the car, and we both got out at the same time and went on in. The surprising thing was that the coffee shop was open this time. I mean, there were people everywhere. In fact, it just might have been more crowded than the shop across the street. Business was booming, and it was all thanks to me. But even I knew good things didn't last forever. I digress. I continued following Kyle to the back and to the basement door. I was starting to get hungrier and hungrier from the ride and the walk down the stairs. At the foot of the stairs was that same henchman whose face I'd put the grip of my gun into numerous times. He gave me a furious look. Knowing he wouldn't be allowed to touch me probably nearly sent him right over the edge. I gave him a smile and went on my way to Drew's office.

I knocked twice.

DREW. Who is it?

CARTER. It's Carter.

The door was opened by the soldier on the inside. With all this hospitality, I almost gave up a tip. But I had no cash to spare. I took a seat in front of Drew's desk and waited for Drew to issue everyone an order to leave the room.

DREW. Leave us.

And so they did, one by one, even Kyle, until it was just me and Drew.

DREW. So, what did you wanna talk about, Carter?

First things first.

CARTER. You know that Kyle kid who picked me up?

DREW. If you're only here to complain, you can fuck right off.

CARTER. No. It's just, where'd you find him? Smoking pot outside the high school or something?

DREW. I don't need to ask you who can or cannot be recruited, all right.

CARTER. All right, fine. Whatever. It's just the kid's a clueless retard.

DREW. Well that kid is my nephew.

CARTER. Oh, well then, your nephew's a clueless—

I stopped myself.

CARTER. You know what? I apologize. I'm sorry. It's just he's a little new to the game. That's all. No hard feelings.

And another thing. Please don't have him ever pick me up again.

DREW. Can we talk about something else?

CARTER. Of course.

I could have called Kyle all sorts of names, but it just felt wrong. It just felt like he deserved something different. Maybe he was some bright kid with an independent future. Why would I give a fuck? Was I going soft? Hell no. I'd better not be. I'd just push it to the back of my head like all my other thoughts. No worry about regret, just a possible serious brain aneurysm.

> CARTER. I was thinking. What do you have in store for a plan B if yakuza starts getting fidgety with all their guns and no one to use them on?
>
> DREW. What do you mean?
>
> CARTER. I'm just saying, what are we gonna do if they betray us?
>
> DREW. And you're thinking about this now?
>
> CARTER. Well ...

I really had nothing to say. I tried to be open and honest with him. But in reality he was right. I'd really just neglected to plan ahead again. In the end, we could just rat them out to the cops. But that went against the main rule of decorum in the crime business I shamefully loved. No snitches and no pussies. I was thinking of the most radical thing when a solution could damn well be right under me.

> DREW. So you're pretty much saying they really could just fuck us over at any time they like, and you thought to keep quiet about it.
>
> CARTER. To be fair, Drew, you could have thought of something too when I first came through here.
>
> DREW. No. Don't you blame this shit on me. This was all your idea.

He was truly a paranoid maniac. I'd simply mentioned a "what-if," and he was yelling at me like they were right outside our door. What had made this man so unhinged over all these years? The work he did wasn't stressful; he'd probably never even seen a dead body. The man was a nut.

> CARTER. Drew, first off, calm down, all right. I'll figure something out.
>
> DREW. You fucking better. And you can forget about brunch.

I had come to the office to brainstorm with a partner in crime, and he put it all on me and told me to deal with it—as if I was the only one who could do something about a possible scenario. He wanted me to single-handedly fix a problem that might not even occur. I needed to create an exit plan per se. But did I really need it? Why had I even shown up? What did I expect was going to happen? It was Drew. Why the fuck would he remain calm? I just felt frustrated; he wouldn't even help me. Then again, I usually did help myself.

CARTER. **Oh, by the way, Drew, your nephew's a retard.**

I scrammed out of the room before he could throw anything at me. I was only messing around. But genuinely, Drew needed to have some sort of criteria set before he just started hiring relatives. I didn't go around giving bullets to my family and telling them to bring back a stolen car.

I didn't need to think about my family. They didn't need to be affected by what I was doing here. I started to remember that I'd just left them behind to become a criminal. Still, I could see them later. I tried to reassure myself. But when would that be? When could I just sit down and have dinner again. I hadn't even shown up to my own funeral. I figured it was too late now. But maybe I'd just repress these thoughts as well. No need to put myself in a bad mood.

I left the shop and just waited around until I could wave down a taxi. At that point, I felt stupid, knowing I could have just taken Todd's car today. I had thought having Drew send a driver was a friendly gesture. But then again, why did I steal the car if I wasn't going to use it? Maybe it was a good idea to leave all that evidence behind at least for a day.

A cab pulled up, and I got in and told him to just drop me off at a Crown Heights farmers' market. I didn't know him. So, I didn't trust him. So, he didn't need to know my address. The whole while, the driver was just on his phone. But I made sure to watch his every move. No way to tell a stranger's intentions in a time like this, especially for me.

The drive was short, and I was pleased. This man drove all the way through the Holland Tunnel. Just to be nice, I left the man with an awfully generous tip; after all, he left me in a much better mood than the one I'd been in getting in the car. I ended up talking to him a little bit after he got off the phone. He was born around the same part of Missouri I'd washed up in all those years ago.

I was just about to go on my way down the street when, out of nowhere, I got a tap on my shoulder. My day could only get worse. I turned around. Lo and behold, here was the man who would ruin my day, the yakuza courier. I decided to tell him how happy I was to see him.

CARTER. **Buddy, fuck off, or I'll scream rape.**

He seemed confused. But he wasn't going away so easily. Instead, he merely pointed to the open door of the blacked-out SUV on the other side of the street. I really didn't want to. I was still hungry, and it wasn't that good of a mood to ruin.

COURIER. **Please, sir.**

It wasn't the right time. But only in my life could a good day be ruined every single time. From good to bad and bad to worse—that was how the cycle went. I was stressing over something simple again. Last time hadn't been that bad; it had been more of just a friendly chat anyway. There had been no violence, no threats—or at least almost none. That fact was still very curious actually.

CARTER. **What does he want this time?**

He just motioned toward the SUV again.

COURIER. **Please. Mr. Soko does not like to wait on his clients.**

Refusal would only worsen our relationship, and next time they might not be so friendly. So, stubbornly, I accepted. But of course, I would always carry on with my doubts. I followed the courier over to the SUV cautiously. It occurred to me that the very fact they had managed to know exactly where I was the second I'd left the cab was somewhat worrying. They used that worry factor to their advantage. They didn't want me doing anything I might regret. How long had they been following me? I wondered. They probably knew where I lived and might even know about Drew. I was overthinking. Maybe they wanted to talk to thank me for my, so far, job well done. No true way to tell yet.

I did the remembered routine of handing over my gun and being wedged and uncomfortable in the back seat of the full SUV. The drive would be short up to the Bronx or Brooklyn. I couldn't remember. Not to mention the fact that it was a vital part of information to know. It was the main thing I didn't remember. So much for attention to detail. *Pay attention this time around*, I told myself.

The city had increased the number of patrol vehicles around known gang-related areas. So maybe Mr. Soko wasn't too happy on that note. But what did he expect anyway?

Sooner or later, we arrived at the house I never wanted to return to. The driveway wasn't as full as it had been last time. The rest of the cars were just probably hidden somewhere instead, as the outfit was probably not wanting to attract any unwanted attention at this point. We all got out of the car. And just like before, I was followed inside. The doormen were just as polite and helpful as they had been last time, and I still remembered my way around the household. This time, I took in all I could remember—attempting to memorize each foot from the door to the office. I counted all the doorways and rooms I could on the first floor. If things had to go south, I would need to at least understand my fighting grounds.

I went up to the office door. But they didn't want me to knock this time. Instead, the doorman just opened it for me. I found the change in protocol this time around surprising. But then again, these were different circumstances.

Mr. Soko was sitting at his desk and looked somewhat displeased. If I had a smile before, it was no longer there.

MR. SOKO. **Please, come in and have a seat, Mitchell.**

I did as he said and went on to have a seat.

MR. SOKO. **Or is it Stevenson now? I get confused.**

Fear tactics. He just wanted to let me know he knew everything. Intimidation at its finest.

CARTER. **How can I help you, Mr. Soko? I was only a little busy.**

MR. SOKO. **No you weren't.**

Fair enough.

CARTER. **That's true. But still, what is it you need from me now?**

MR. SOKO. **Well, first off, I want to thank you for doing a good job.**

This was the only outcome I wanted. But still, he clearly wanted more. Or did he?

MR. SOKO. **Tell me something, Mitchell. How is your relationship with Sandy these days?**

How fucking dare he? She had nothing to do with this and never would. I was not letting her get fucked over by this too. She didn't deserve any of this; she didn't deserve more pain in her life. I knew her. And maybe protecting her could give me a sort of forgiveness for all my wrongdoings. Maybe it could somehow make up for my treacherous deeds and deceits, all that bloodshed and all the lies told over and over again. I could kill every single person here and just walk away. What the fuck did he want? I cooled myself down the best I could but still you could hear the anger in my voice. He'd better quit while he was ahead.

CARTER. **She has nothing to do with this.**

He smiled. He laughed—right in my face. He took pride in this game. I was about to take his life.

MR. SOKO. **It seems I could not intimidate you into cleaning up this mess quick enough. So, now I have to give leverage to my side.**

CARTER. **What the fuck did you do?**

MR. SOKO. **You kill Anastasia. I will give you the location of little Timmy and Maria.**

I jumped out of the chair and lunged right at him, trying to get over the desk and get my hands around his fucking neck. The men grabbed onto me and held me back. I wasn't willing to rationalize anymore. He had stepped too far. He knew exactly what he was fucking doing. Sandy's kids. How did I get mixed up in all this? It just wasn't fair. None of this was fair, and I wasn't going to pretend anymore like it was. This was the leverage game. I knew I couldn't trust these people. But what fucking choice did I have? I just added another man to my hit list.

CARTER. **You fucking touch them, this whole block goes up in smoke.**

MR. SOKO. **You have one week.**

I calmed down. But still I would love nothing more than to paint the walls with this man. I would watch him suffer as I had. I would watch him bleed like the rest of them. His was a sick and twisted mind, and he deserved nothing but the worst. I should have just joined the air force.

I stubbornly and shamefully walked toward the door after the scumbags let me go, though they remained wary of my anger.

MR. SOKO. As a token of goodwill, I will also throw in the location of Special Agent Colton upon the death of Anastasia.

A token of goodwill? I mapped out scenarios of how to kill this man and escape while still killing everybody else.

There was no point. I didn't have the leverage like he did. I had nothing but my anger. It just wouldn't pan out no matter how much I wanted it to.

CARTER. Mr. Soko, before I leave, I just want you to know, if I had the opportunity, I would kill all your men all over again.

He wasn't fazed by this.

CARTER. So, at any rate, fuck you and your Chinese new year.

MR. SOKO. I'm afraid I'm Japanese Mr. Mitchell.

CARTER. Well, I'm afraid I don't give a shit ... Mr. Soko.

17

The men dropped me off right at my doorstep, just to prove even more they knew too much about me. It was starting to get on my nerves. But if they wanted me to expedite the outcome they had demanded, then sure, I'd fucking expedite things. I could have Anastasia dead whenever I wanted. I just wanted to blow shit up along the way.

First things first. I needed to talk to Drew. And I was damn well sure he was not going to know a goddamn thing. I tell Drew anything and he loses his fucking mind and goes into seclusion. It was something I didn't need. But shit, I had to get him to man up at least a little bit. He needed to cut the shit and grow up. How could I influence him to do the right thing without him pissing his pants before he'd even walked out the front door?

I got out my phone and dialed up Drew.

He didn't pick up.

He was definitely just ignoring my calls. Must not have taken what I'd said about his relative too kindly, I suppose. But I was still fucking right about the whole thing. How could Drew hire a retard like that?

You know what? Never mind. It didn't fucking matter. That wasn't the crux of the current problem at hand. I called Drew again but still no response. I didn't want to have to drive all the way to Jersey City. But fuck, at this point, it didn't matter. Sandy's kids were in danger. Was it even my problem? *No, don't think like that. I have the opportunity to do some good*. And why shouldn't I? if anything, it just might cancel out the bad shit I had done along the way.

I made sure my handgun was on me and I had a fresh pack of smokes, and I went into the garage and started the car up. I had a new license plate and a new enemy. And if they wanted to start shit. I could definitely dish it out. I drove out and headed over to the coffee shop. I continued to try to get a hold of Drew all along the way. Still nothing. It was starting to really piss me off. To think, all these problems I had caused over a stupid fucking jewelry store. Why did it have to happen? Why me?

All along the George Washington Bridge, my stress was starting to get the best of me. Why couldn't I just end it? I could just, at any point, drive into oncoming traffic. I didn't want to, but I just could. I had the power. I'd already had around four cigarettes by the time I got to this point in the drive. My life, if I even had one before, was practically gone. Everything was different. And I was just here to have to accept these changes. It wasn't like I could go back It wasn't like I could be safe. It was just all fucked. I just wanted to go home. Why couldn't I just go home? I needed to get a hold of myself. Only I could solve this problem. And by God, I would.

I arrived downtown. But I knew not to pick the same parking spot as last time. I didn't want to lose the car again, especially just after I had gotten it back. I drove around for a bit more, looking for alleys or dark corners with little sight of law enforcement or curious passersby. After a while, I found a little space on the curb not too far away. I parked it, got out, and made sure I wouldn't get a ticket. No handicap spot and no fire hydrant. The walk to the coffee shop wasn't too far, just a block or two away, and I was in no mood for slowing down or getting distracted.

Some police cars passed, sirens blazing. They were probably on their way to another shooting.

I locked the car and went on my way down the road—furious and ready to snap. I didn't know my plan. But to expedite this killing spree, I'd have to get relentless and reckless. It was time to make all those on my list face judgment for what they'd done. God, I sound like some Jesus freak hell-bent on destruction and self-preservation. Why did I think I was some executioner to punish evil? I was no better. But I always could be. I could prove myself, I thought, and maybe, just maybe, I could live a normal life again.

I walked down the road for a bit until I got back to the coffee shop; it was still crowded as it had been before. As I considered how the I worked to keep Drew and his people ignored by law enforcement, it occurred to me that I hadn't seen any feds in a while. It made me wonder. I took myself down to the basement. I was already becoming a famous face in these parts.

I past more victims of my first visit, with their broken noses and dreadful concussions.

I nodded and smiled, and they just spit on the ground and walked out of sight. I shrugged and continued making my way to Drew's office. I just knocked on the door. He wasn't expecting me of course; the door opened instantly. He clearly wasn't happy to see me.

Drew. Carter, what the fuck are you doing here?

Like I said, I couldn't really tell him the actual reason for my sudden appearance; it would only make everything worse. Maybe it would even end up with my death. Who knew at this point? I was making this shit up as I went along. But I still needed to convince Drew to expedite all of this. To get to Anastasia. To win the war.

Carter. Well, Drew. I'm just gonna be straightforward with you on this one. Can I sit down?

Drew. Carter, I really don't want to hear any more fucking bad news on this one. So, if you got nothing good, then just fuck straight off. I'm doing the right thing here as is.

I couldn't really ease into what I wanted from him, could I? Shouldn't I just spit it out? Fuck it. What was the worst that could happen?

Carter. Do you know that bitch Anastasia?

Drew. Never heard of her.

He wasn't joking. I didn't really expect him to know. But still, in his job, he should at least have an inkling of knowledge of who the fuck he was killing. Hadn't I told him this already? I didn't even know. I couldn't think straight anymore. With all this chaos going on in my head, I just couldn't concentrate. My head was starting to ache, and I had to put my hand to my forehead to see if I could minimize the pain. I shook my head and paid more attention to the conversation.

CARTER. **She is the greasy bitch in charge of Greenwich.**

He thought for a second as if he still knew what I was talking about, but it was obvious he didn't. He was trying hard to follow along but couldn't muster up a helpful thought.

DREW. **OK, sure. Whatever. What about her?**

Yeah, no clue. He was just impatient, and I couldn't blame him. I didn't even wanna hear what I had to say.

CARTER. **We need to kill her, Drew.**

A big step and a big move on our part. He stepped back, acting like I was insane. He wasn't ready and sure as shit wasn't happy.

DREW. **We?**

> **Who's we?**

CARTER. **Don't act fucking stupid, Drew. If you want to make an impact in this, you have to go out for more important figures.**

> **These little fucking goons are expendable. She doesn't care about them. I mean, sure, we're stretching out their resources and decreasing their numbers. But it's all for a main goal. And you have to understand that or this would've all been for nothing.**

> **Where did you think this was gonna end? Just kill a couple guys until they surrender and eventually regrow their numbers until they're fully capable of fighting back?**

> **Drew, I know you're a paranoid kinda guy. But you gotta grow up. You just gotta.**

I sat back down as I'd recently gotten out of my chair to further prove my point with a more intimidating and serious attitude. I didn't even realize I had. There was just so much emotion built up. When would I snap?

DREW. **And how would you suggest we kill her, huh? We just go ask around where she is and put a bullet in her head?**

CARTER. **Basically, yeah. But it would have some more details, you know.**

He didn't like it, and he was starting to not like me. But he knew I was right. I was always right. And judging by his face, he was starting to realize it. He then sat down with his hands in his head and started to sniffle and eventually was tearing up.

I was starting to feel a little uncomfortable, to say the least. I mean this guy was literally crying right in front of me. A grown man was crying right in front of me, and I just kinda sat there twiddling my thumbs. I was even starting to feel a little embarrassed for the guy; it wasn't that big of a deal.

Eventually, after a couple minutes, he got some tissues, cleaned up and came back to his senses. He leaned back in his chair and looked back up at me. But his voice still wasn't all there. It was breaky and shattered—he was a visage of a shattered man with nowhere to go. Finally, he spoke up.

DREW. Higher-ups have been asking questions, and I can't keep them away for much longer.

We both knew what that meant. If the higher-ups found out what was going on here, we were all dead, and plans were over. He was petrified but had good reason to be. I figured all this would be done before it got to that point. But God were we fucked now.

The walls were closing in, so we would have to move quickly if we wanted this to go our way. Some opportunities were lost to time. But then new opportunities always open themselves up. Running wasn't such an easy idea anymore. It was kill or be killed. Die standing or die running.

CARTER. Drew, I need you to listen to me now, and I am not fucking around anymore, all right.

There were still tears in his eyes. He was gonna break down again. But I was here to bring him back to reality.

CARTER. You give me an opportunity, and I can have her dead in two days. Then we can all just run away, Drew. We can get away from this, but I need you to focus. I need you to help me so I can help you.

Have you ever heard of witness protection?

He snapped at me.

DREW. No, Carter. I'm not gonna be a fucking snitch.

CARTER. You knew the fucking risks. But you need to wake up, Drew. You need to realize how many options we have left.

DREW. This is all your fault.

His statement certainly shut me up. He was right to an extent. I shrugged it off and just pushed it to the back of my head again, just like all the regrets before that.

CARTER. Drew, let's fix this together. You want to win and survive, you need to listen.

He was on the verge of hyperventilating; he didn't want me to do all this over again. He wanted to trust me, but deep down, he couldn't. The truth was he had no choice, and everybody knew that.

DREW. What do you want me to do, Carter?

CARTER. I need a capture.

If I could get a hold of someone from Greenwich, I could interrogate our captive, working my way higher and higher up the food chain. It was the only thing that came to mind. But by God was I gonna have to make it work. This whole month was riddled with tragedy, with miserable sleep habits, and with deathly threats and empty magazines. I just needed Drew with me on this. I couldn't have him run off into a corner while I was still fighting.

CARTER. Drew, I can win this. Just get me what I need. Tell me what you know, and I can guarantee your freedom.

He stood silent for a minute, still frustrated at me for all the chaos I had caused and how the worst was yet to come.

DREW. Carter, I just wanna let you know, you've fucked us.

He sighed and made his decision.

DREW. Maybe I can put an order out to have a gangster detained, and then I could have them call you and stand by until you get there.

I could see in his face he was completely distraught. But what could I really do at this point? Apologize? Apologies didn't matter anymore. Where had an apology gotten anyone? Nowhere. Or at least that was the case now.

I'd have to make it up to him somehow. But how would I do it? I could offer him a beer. But last time I'd offered a friend a beer, it had led to losing Todd. I still needed to have a funeral for him. He had no family, no next of kin, and his friends were criminals under constant surveillance. It was like the enemy had no respect for mourning the dead.

CARTER. Drew, I want you to know I'm thankful for everything you've done. It's OK if you don't want to be here anymore. You can go. I won't tell anybody.

DREW. The thing is, Carter, you're the reason I'd have to leave.

I had to snap at him.

CARTER. Drew, I don't give a fuck, OK? Either you stay and die or fight or you run. Those are the only options now. I'm sorry I put you in that position. But that's just life. Maybe you should think about growing up. Send out that order, and I'll have her dead. And you'll be free.

You know what? After you put out the order and put your phone down, you can leave. Don't fuck with me right now. Just listen to what I tell you, and I promise you safety. You just have to fucking trust me, Drew. Can you do that for once—just fucking trust me.

He just stared through me without a response. He was starting to tear up again, but I didn't need to be here to see that again. It wasn't my problem, but it was my choice. I shouldn't think that all of this was my fault. I didn't want to lose all my confidence when I was so close to the end. I couldn't. I needed every bit of me to be somewhat intact for what I had left to do.

I left the room and left him to it. He could cry if he wanted. And to be honest, at this point, he could fucking kill himself. I didn't care. Maybe that was too rough. But like I said, no distractions.

I walked out of the shop and back down the street to my car, just one step after another. It was weird. I felt like breaking down and crying myself—just giving up. I was just tired of all this running and killing. I could've been happier than this. I could have been a lawful citizen with an actual job and maybe a wife and kids. I could have been just another victim of the world. I could be among those cast out of society because who wanted to help out a struggling person? I mean, sure, politicians would say anything to get votes. But they didn't care about the people who actually struggled. Maybe that was why I'd ended up on this path. I just realized we all had our own future. And when no one else helped me, I'd set out to change the world. All I'd ended up changing was death certificates. It was sad.

The car was still warm. That cheered me up in the slightest way—hey, simple pleasures and all that. Everything else was pretty much set in stone at this point. So I guess all there really was left to do was wait. All I had to do was wait. It would be hard. I was too nervous, too fidgety, and too paranoid. A couple drinks should calm me down. First things first. I needed to get back to the city and get drunk there. Another day, another sad adventure.

There were many bars to choose from in the city. Most were packed with lightweights without a tolerance for even a single shot of liquor. These hot spots were out of the question. I didn't need a place brimming with activity. I needed to distract myself. I didn't want to frustrate myself and end up lashing out at some teenager. A quiet place with constant refills and a calm atmosphere was in order.

I drove out to the Rockaways. No one even lived there anyway, so the joints around there should be quiet enough, right? It took a couple red lights, but eventually I found a couple good choices. However, when it came down to it, none of the options really suited my fancy; they were more just not my type of place. Why did I need to be so picky?

Next bar I find, I'm going in, I told myself. The next bar was too crowded. OK, now the next bar would be the ticket. The next bar was a gay bar. I was starting to get frustrated. The last bar, all the way on the corner, was just what I needed. It even had a parking space on the curb out front. Just went to show how desolate and dull the place was.

I parked and strolled on in.

The scene was practically eerie. I didn't think any of the plants in the windows had been even alive in the last month or so. The actual bar just had some old people trying to relive their youth with empty beers in front of them and some baseball game on the TV, played by teams whose names I couldn't care to remember.

I sat down at the bar next to the half-passed out middle-aged man. It was even two o'clock, and the man already looked like he'd had half the barrel from the back. Good for him. Then I called over the bartender.

CARTER. I'll have what he's having.

I pointed to the man who was in the better mood than I was.

BARTENDER. Guinness?

OK. On second thought, he might have just looked the way he did because he'd had the wrong kind of alcohol. It wasn't proof of him having a good time. It was just the sign that his stomach was too twisted to understand what year it even was. No Guinness—not now, not ever. It just wasn't my kind of drink.

CARTER. I'll just have a Coors or something.

BARTENDER. Of course.

He brought the glass bottle over, and I opened it and enjoyed what I could of it. I even indulged in some peanuts. Peanuts were dry and unsalted. No wonder there was practically no one in here. The place was just what I needed though. I wasn't going to complain.

The TV wasn't even in color. Just went to show the budget in this little bar on the far side of town. I sat there, impatient and furious at the events of today. Should I even care about the kids? I mean, I knew it would be fucked not to. But was it my problem? I'd been an asshole all my life. This was the time I changed for the better? I had been given an opportunity to prove myself and help out an almost complete stranger.

I waited at the bar for another hour or so. I had downed at least three or four beers by that time. But it wasn't enough to even give me a decent little buzz. The baseball game on the TV came and went, and so did the man next to me. Some new people showed up and traded time for beers and a good time with their friends. I was definitely the loneliest and saddest person in the whole room.

No one was interested in what was on after the baseball game so the bartender settled for just switching it to the news. I couldn't remember the time. But it must've been around six at least, as the sun had gone and NY1 wanted to tell me the weather for the rest of the week. It was starting to warm up, as April was almost coming to a close. I didn't really care for the winter and cold in all honesty, so it was at least somewhat uplifting to hear this. This part didn't really intrigue me though.

After the weather was an evening special about corruption and state and federal law enforcement—namely the FBI. I knew my shit stirring at the docks had shaken up the state. It was amazing to know how much power a single man determined to rid the world of a nuisance while being just as bad as the forces he was trying to eliminate could have. I might've been selfish. Or maybe I had just gone rogue.

The news presenter was female, but she wasn't that attractive, and it would be another couple beers until I thought otherwise. She spoke about the incident at the docks. So far, twelve federal agents had been fired and were awaiting court dates. Now, this was something to celebrate. I played a dirty trick and ran away. They didn't mention any of the agents' names. Could Colton have been caught already? That would explain their hesitation to come after me. Maybe they didn't want to draw more attention to themselves and get caught. But who fucking knew?

I could always get a newspaper. Maybe they'd mention some of the names. Mr. Soko had mentioned he'd give me Colton's location. But he could just be locked up somewhere. Was it worth killing Colton if he was just gonna rot in prison anyway. The alcohol was starting to cloud my head. Maybe that was enough beer for one day.

I told the bartender I'd had enough and wanted peanuts instead. He agreed.

Some more time had passed, and I had forgotten to stop drinking. But still, I was feeling great. There was no reason to complain.

Drew texted me.

Drew. 88th 72 Myrtle Avenue

I smiled but realized I was drunk. A location meant an opportunity and showed progress.

I tipped the bartender and stumbled out. I started to wonder. Did Drew and I even trust each other? All that had happened had definitely taken a toll on his psyche over these last couple weeks. This could be a trap. No. Drew was just scared. He wasn't a traitor. He wouldn't do that, would he? Only one way to find out. Either I saved the world or I died tonight. Was I ready? Or was I just buzzed? Where the fuck did I park the car?

The car was exactly where I'd left it. I thought. Or at least I was pretty sure. I unlocked the door and started it up. I took a deep breath, trying not to look like a drunken menace on the road. I was definitely sober enough to drive. I just had to keep my drunk fantasies under control. Small world problems like these were common, especially for normal people. Some guys just wanted to have fun.

I started driving, making my way to the location Drew had texted. It wasn't long before I realized I was seeing double, which kind of worried me. I didn't know how much I'd had to drink at this point. It couldn't have been all too much, as I was still somewhat aware of what was going on. I kept all my focus, as best I could, on not looking inebriated and following all traffic laws along the way. I managed to hit only a couple trash cans and traffic cones along the way. I was definitely causing attention. Nevertheless, I was still probably fine.

I showed up at the address around five minutes later than I could've. I'd cut some time in the corners, and I'd thought I was speeding. But somehow, I was still slow overall. I parked close by but not too close or far. I needed to keep my distance. I was still clueless as to what was going on. I got out of the car and noticed all the scratches and dents that hadn't been there a couple minutes ago. It was amazing I'd gotten here without being pulled over. Just went to show the effectiveness of the police. However, I had more fun blaming the mayor instead.

I wasn't too aware of current politics in the city. I had stopped caring about that nonsense a while ago.

I stumbled over to what I thought was the front door and just started banging. I looked over my shoulder all the while, still making sure no one was about to pick me off. I also, of course, stood to the side of the door in case whoever was behind it decided to shoot through it.

After a quick couple seconds, which I should've been timing, a middle-aged man in his pajamas opened the door.

MAN. What do you want? Who are you?

He was also definitely buzzed and somewhat agitated. This was the wrong house. I wasn't exactly sober either. Still, it was just a little fuck-up on my part. I needed to make up some bullshit on the spot. Or I could just tell the truth.

CARTER. Wrong house. My bad.

I turned around, walked down his little steps, and tripped and stumbled on the last one. I turned around to see him staring at me and silently judging. It actually pissed me off. I almost whipped out my gun just to intimidate, but that wouldn't be the smartest decision.

I pretended the whole event had never happened and carried on next door to the neighbor and probably the right house this time as well. I walked over and up the doorsteps to perform the same actions all over.

Knock, move away from the door, and be alert of my surroundings. The door slowly opened. Lo and behold, Kyle was there to greet me.

KYLE. **Carter, come on. Get in here. He's in the basement.**

Seeing him didn't give me the highest hopes for the rest of the night, and my response was even worse.

CARTER. **What the fuck are you doing here?**

I slurred my way throughout the whole sentence, which led Kyle to just look at me and know exactly what was wrong with me. He even paused for a second until I came in and closed the door behind me.

I began to follow him. But wait, I gotta follow this retard into the basement? This shit didn't look suspicious at all. I was so unnerved it almost made me sober. I noticed two other Outlaws in the kitchen ransacking the fridge. What had happened here?

CARTER. **What happened here?**

KYLE. **Well, there's this little bastard we caught trying to plant a fucking tracker on a motorcycle, and we were about to kill him until Drew gave out some stupid order. And yeah, that's basically it.**

This kid must've smartened up, because his answer was straight to the point, clear, and sensible. I didn't even remember why I hated him.

He opened the basement door for me.

KYLE. **Go on down.**

I was shocked. But I wasn't gonna let this retard best me in anything but ass kissing.

CARTER. **No. You go first.**

He was confused for a second. But eventually, he agreed and went down. If this was a trap and bullets started flying, I wasn't gonna let anybody be behind me. At the bottom of the steps, some stupid Greenwich scumbag was tied in a chair and covered in bruises and another Outlaw standing close by.

The Outlaw came around to shake my hand.

SMITH. Carter, right? I'm Smith. I'm excited to work with you

CARTER. Yeah, of course.

I was relieved to understand this wasn't a trap. But then Smith and even the guy in the chair looked up at me, knowing I was drunk. They looked at me like I was a moron.

I changed the subject and moved over to the Greenwich soldier.

CARTER. So, what's up here, fucker? What's your name?

He just looked at me with the same moronic expression. I certainly wasn't making myself look professional, but who gave a fuck honestly?

Smith came over and punched the man right across the jaw.

SMITH. Answer him.

I was flattered, but I could probably handle this bastard. He didn't need to show off to me. But I wasn't really going to stop him yet. Meanwhile, the guy was spitting all his excess spit and blood right onto the floor.

CARTER. Has he told you anything yet, Smith?

That sentence was a rough one to get out, and even I knew it didn't sound intelligible.

SMITH. Say again.

I turned to Kyle.

CARTER. Kyle, go make me some coffee.

He went on his way back upstairs without asking questions. And I turned back to the Greenwich weasel.

I took a deep breath and tried to sound as sober and serious as possible. It actually worked.

CARTER. Dude, I'm not here to fucking kill you, all right. So just tell me your name.

Smith was cracking his knuckles.

CARTER. Smith, don't hit the cocksucker until I do, OK?

He nodded and stepped back so I could deal with it.

The man looked up at me with his eyes almost swollen shut. He couldn't even cry because his tears would just pool up under his eyelids. I almost felt bad. But if this man was going to give me what I wanted, I wasn't going to kill him. Look at that, a new me. Showing mercy and forgiveness. Let's see how long I could manage like this. Until it killed me.

OSCAR. My name is Oscar.

If I was good to him, he'd be good to me and comply. right? Sure.

CARTER. OK, Oscar. I'm gonna be honest with you .I don't want to have to hit you. I just want to …

I was trying to figure out a way to say that I wanted to kill Anastasia in a less blunt way, but I couldn't really figure it out. Then Smith interjected.

SMITH. Enforce!

He was enthusiastic, sure. But he had no idea what I wanted to say.

CARTER. What!? No, what are you talking about? No.

It kind of upset him for me to just shoot him down like that.

CARTER. What I'm trying to say is …

Fuck it. I'd just be blunt. Either way, he wasn't leaving until I got what I wanted. He was my prisoner, and I had all the power.

CARTER. You know what, Oscar. You know Anastasia, right.

He just stared down at the ground and ignored me. I thought he was either dead or sleeping because there was no way he would be this disrespectful. He had just met me, and I was being polite.

CARTER. Oscar, you there, pal?

He looked up at me.

CARTER. Oscar, did you hear what I said?

I didn't expect it. But right then, he spat all his blood and spit right at my shirt.

I recoiled in surprise and anger. My immediate reflex was to slap him across the face—just to show him he was the bitch.

Smith wasn't the brightest. So, he instantly punched him across the jaw again. It wasn't necessary.

CARTER. Fuck's sake, Smith!

SMITH. What?

CARTER. You didn't have to do that, you know.

SMITH. **But you told me to.**

He was right. I just didn't want to kill the guy before he had a chance to speak.

CARTER. **Yeah, OK. You're right. But just don't be so rough. We're trying to interrogate him not torture and kill him.**

This again made him upset. Sure he was maybe six two and built like a fucking boulder. But Smith was being such a whiny baby. Wow, these underclass Outlaws really admired me, didn't they. At this point, Kyle came back down with my coffee. My buzz was starting to wear off, and I didn't really like coffee. But I wasn't just gonna make him make it for nothing. So, I graciously accepted and thanked him.

CARTER. **All right, Oscar. Tell me where Anastasia is. That's all I want to know. That's it. I don't understand what's so hard about that.**

OSCAR. **Get fucked, faggot.**

Now I was going to have some fun.

CARTER. **OK, Oscar. I don't want to have to do this, so I'll ask just one last time. And if you give me some shithead response or spit on me again, I'm just gonna beat the fuck out of you. I'm gonna be honest.**

Everyone stood silent for a second, even Oscar. Until he broke his silence.

OSCAR. **Fuck you.**

I'll be honest, it actually made me happy. I really needed to relieve some stress, and alcohol couldn't always do that. I even smiled and started to laugh. Smith and Kyle thought I was crazy, but Oscar wasn't buying it. And why would he?

I looked around for something that could do some damage.

I walked around, looking through drawers while the others looked at me with curiosity. I opened a door that was like just a closet with a bunch of tools. A garage in the basement was weird, but I was just happy I'd found it. I grabbed the toolbox and went back outside. I walked over to Oscar and dropped it on the ground. It startled him. Just what I wanted.

CARTER. **Oscar, look at me.**

Oscar looked up from the toolbox and right at me.

CARTER. You know I did a tour in Guantanamo way back when marines were still stationed there. Unfortunately, what I did there was classified. But the memory is still implanted in my brain. And let me tell you, Oscar, it's been a while. So, I might be a little rusty.

Oscar was starting to breathe more and more heavily. He was nervous. He was scared. He was terrified. I was about to make him piss blood. I had given him a choice, and I'd offered him a way out. Some part of me hated what I was doing, but it was for a better cause, right? Just when I said I could change, I had to do something like this. I couldn't change until this was over. I hated to admit that, but it was true. I had to fight evil with evil.

And just like that, I moved it to the back of my head as always.

I sifted through all the rusty tools. Some of them already had blood on them. Why the fuck was that a thing?

I turned to Smith and Kyle standing behind me.

CARTER. Did you already use these tools on him?

They both said no. But how could I believe them? It just didn't make sense. I guess someone else was tortured with these tools too. I must not be the only sick bastard working for the Outlaws. Then it made me think. Where the fuck was I? Was this actually an Outlaw safe house or had I just assumed that was the case because I was drunk. So, I stood up and turned to Kyle.

CARTER. Kyle, where are we right now?

He looked at me puzzled; he must've thought I was still drunk.

KYLE. Uh, we're still in Queens.

CARTER. No, Kyle. I mean whose fucking house are we in right now?

I was about to snap at this kid. I should've planned ahead already, but I was too busy trying not to look drunk. This was what I got for trying to relax. I ended up making mistakes. As soon as I asked him, his face went pale. Now, I was fucking pissed. He just realized he'd fucked up.

KYLE. I-I don't know.

This kid just might have fucked everything up.

SMITH. Sir, if I may.

CARTER. Smith, stop talking.

I didn't take my eyes off of Kyle when I said it. I was still staring him down, trying not to kill him. Smith didn't have to stick up for him; he'd fucked up just as much as Kyle had.

CARTER. Kyle, if you don't know, then how did we get here?

Kyle fell silent; he didn't want to be the one to admit it.

SMITH. We tailed him here after we caught him fucking with a soldier's bike.

I turned to Smith. Oh my God, we were fucked. This was a Greenwich safe house, and we were torturing someone in it. That was why there was blood on the tools. It was the blood of Outlaws. I needed to calm down before I did something like lash out at these two retards for unknowingly being the two biggest idiots I'd ever had to work with. But how could I turn this situation around? And what could I take my anger out on?

I turned to Oscar. Now, Oscar was probably hoping backup would arrive before I did whatever came next. But Oscar didn't know how I thought. Oscar had probably tripped an alarm. So, it was likely a backup was on the way. But who knew? We'd have to act quickly either way. If Oscar wanted to win, I would not let him.

I pulled my gun and pointed it directly at Oscar's forehead—as if the room wasn't quiet already.

Oscar started to get real nervous now. He was trying to plead for his amnesty, but all I needed to ask was one question.

CARTER. Oscar, tell me something right now. Or I will kill you just like that.

He just closed his eyes.

CARTER. Oscar, if you know who I am, you must know I'm not joking. So, please, Oscar, for your sake, tell me something important.

He opened his eyes and took a deep breath, trying to talk in between sobbing.

CARTER. Oscar, stop crying and spit it out.

He blurted his next words out in between breaths. He actually gave me something, and now we could finally leave.

Oscar. Anastasia has a safe house in Staten Island. But I don't know where. I swear to God, that's all I know.

It was euphoric in a sense. But still, I was pretty pissed off.

So I shot him in the head.

Kyle and Smith didn't have much to say, but they were satisfied, nonetheless. Or at least smith was. Kyle ended up vomiting nearby. I didn't want to stand by any longer. We all needed to get out of this place.

The two extra Outlaws came running to the basement from upstairs to see what had happened. I didn't acknowledge them directly because they didn't matter to me. Instead, I addressed the whole group of morons.

Carter. Pack your shit. We're leaving.

18

It was me, Kyle, and Smith waiting patiently a block away in Todd's car with all the lights turned off. I told the other two Outlaws to leave, as I didn't want to have to deal with more than two idiots in one day. I didn't need someone else fucking this up.

We were waiting for the Greenwich backup to arrive. They had to at some point. All we had to do was be patient. But Smith's snoring was starting to upset me. I had thought him sleeping would just make him shut up. But of course he just had to snore, didn't he? I had at least made sure to punch the alarm system at the front door a couple times to draw in some wanted attention. The cops hadn't shown up, which only meant it wasn't their jurisdiction—which made me wonder. Where were all the fucking gangsters?

Kyle was quiet. He was still traumatized from what had gone down a mere twenty minutes earlier. Or at least I'd told him to be quiet, but I felt bad for him. Why did I keep forgiving this kid? Why did he have to be here anyway? Had Drew set this up on purpose as some kind of cruel initiation? Or was he just trying to get his nephew all the experience and opportunities available? Maybe it was just dumb luck. Whatever the case, I could see Kyle wasn't meant for this. He didn't have it in him. It was just a family career he was being forced into. Maybe that was why I kept feeling bad for the kid. This wasn't meant for everybody, and I knew that. I should at least try to cheer him up. I needed him focused for later.

CARTER. Kyle.

He jumped a little bit. I'd startled him. And I hadn't even spoken that loudly. He just looked at me and didn't respond.

CARTER. When you were growing up, what did you want to do for a job or something?

KYLE. I don't know?

He was trying to avoid conversation. He was still thinking about the dead man in the basement.

CARTER. You want to know something, Kyle? I hate this job. I'm thinking about retiring.

Because this job isn't meant for everyone. You just have to have the balls to quit.

He was still silent. He was still ignoring me. So, I figured I'd spit it out.

CARTER. You know what I'm trying to say, Kyle?

KYLE, *whimpering softly.* No.

CARTER. I'm trying to tell you you're gonna get yourself killed, and you shouldn't be here by force. And I don't give a shit what Drew says.

He looked up at me, but he didn't say anything. If he wouldn't respond, then maybe at least I had given him something to think about. I started to think about it. And you know what? He and Drew really were alike. They were both fucking pussies who should move on.

I saw the headlights of a car moving down the street. It had to be them. I shook Smith until he woke up.

CARTER. Smith, how good are you with a gun?

SMITH. I, uh, go to the shooting range every Monday.

Probably something I should've asked earlier.

The car stopped in front of the house and two men with guns got out. My time to shine I thought. Kyle was starting to hyperventilate. I knew he didn't want to go in there, and I didn't want him to either.

CARTER. Kyle, stay here.

He sighed with relief as Smith and I got out. I headed to the trunk and opened it. I moved the blanket and grabbed the rifle. At this time of night, I probably wouldn't be noticed walking across the street with a rifle. And even if I was, nobody would care. There had been gunshots earlier, and the police hadn't come. This was gang territory. No law enforcement presence was here—just the way I liked it. Or at least I did right at this moment.

SMITH. What the fuck do you need that for?

Smith was eyeballing my rifle. And damn was it a stupid question. I just had to tell him. And why the fuck was he whispering?

CARTER. Smith, what the fuck do you think in need it for? And why the fuck are you whispering?

He shut his mouth.

The men went inside the house, and I motioned for Smith to follow me from our position at the car. First, we moved directly across the street and inched forward slowly until we got in front of the neighbor's house. Now, it was the time to whisper.

CARTER. Smith, you stay out here and guard my six. Make sure nobody goes in that building. Do you understand?

He nodded, and I moved in and charged my rifle. They'd left the door open ajar. So, I slowly opened it with my rifle up and surveyed the hallway. I peeked the rifle around the corner into the living room. It was never smart to clear a room alone. But seeing as how I had no choice, I pressed on. And besides, I was going up against morons anyway. The lights were off everywhere except the basement doorway. These guys really were stupid. They had gone straight for the basement. I moved further down the hallway and stopped at the basement door. That's when I heard them starting to talk.

GANGSTER. We're too late.

I slowly turned into the doorway and tried to make as little noise as possible. I was trained for this. They were outmatched and outgunned. I knelt down so I could see underneath the railing and into the basement. I could see them at this point. Kill one and maim one I thought. Interrogate at will. Both of them were turned away from me.

I shot once, hitting the man on the left in his upper thigh. At this point, the man on the right turned around. So I shot twice, putting both in his chest and killing him. The man on the left threw his gun as he fell. But he ended up crawling toward it.

I got up and ran down the staircase. I got to it before him, kicked it out of the way, and aimed at his head. He knew not to move. He was breathing heavily. I'd probably hit an artery if I wasn't mistaken. So, either way, this guy was fucked. But I didn't need him for long anyway.

CARTER. How many more do you have coming?

He was still breathing heavily, so I raised my voice.

CARTER. How many?!

GANGSTER. It's just us. We're it.

CARTER. Where is Anastasia?

He shook his head. We both know he'd be killed for it. It was time for the honest truth.

CARTER. Listen, fucker. You're gonna bleed out soon anyway, and I'm not going to save you if you're quiet. But I can still put you in more pain.

He fell silent, and he didn't cry like a bitch. He knew the risks; he just didn't have the training.

CARTER. Tell me.

GANGSTER. She's in Staten Island.

If two people said it before death, then they couldn't be lying.

CARTER. OK. But where?

He fell silent.

I stopped aiming the gun at him and chose a calmer approach. I got down on one knee. I'd tell him what this was really for, try and get him to sympathize with the situation. In his position, slowly dying, he had to understand it was just common sense.

CARTER. Listen, buddy. Two kids' lives are at stake if you don't tell me, and I don't want to see them die. They don't deserve to die, and neither do you. I can still help you.

I was lying to him. But I didn't care. Some things were more important anyway.

He looked up at me and told me.

GANGSTER. Park View, 5th floor, room 12.

This could all finally be over.

I stood up and walked toward the stairs, but I stopped to turn around.

Two more shots in the back.

CARTER. I'm sorry.

I went back up the stairs, almost ashamed of what I had done. Why should I be? I had gotten what I wanted. This life was starting to wear me down, to drive me into darkness. And it was all my fault.

I got up the stairs and down the hallway to the front door. Smith was still in position. I went down the front steps and walked back towards the car.

CARTER. Smith.

SMITH. Yeah, what's up? Is everything all right?

CARTER. Take yourself and Kyle home. I don't need you guys anymore.

SMITH. Well what happened in there? Did you get what you wanted.

CARTER. It doesn't matter. Smith just go, all right. I thank you for your help, but I've gotta go do something.

This again upset him, but he didn't want to argue anymore. He knocked on the window and told Kyle it was time to go. I opened the trunk and put the rifle back. But I didn't forget to say goodbye to Kyle as he was walking away.

CARTER. Hey, Kyle.

He turned back.

CARTER. Get a fucking job.

He turned and walked away with smith. I didn't even know if I was right on that part. I just knew this job wasn't for him. He was gonna get himself killed. At least after tonight, he'd have something to think about.

I went around to the front seat and opened the glove compartment to find something to write on. The first thing I found was the registration. But it didn't really matter. I got a pen from the driver's side door and wrote down the address before I forgot it. Park View apartments, Staten Island, 5th floor, room 12.

If I showed up and it was just a bunch of tourists, I was gonna be really pissed off. I should expect there to be security. So, I'd have to do some recon work first, and they wouldn't expect me to do it at night, now would they? I smiled and turned the car on.

It was gonna be a decently long drive to get to Staten Island. I'd finished my coffee beforehand. So I should be fine. But still, I'd have to stop for gas. And I might as well get refreshments just in case I needed them.

I drove past the whole crime scene and the gangster's car. It wasn't my job to clean this up, so I wasn't going to. The great thing about NYC is, if you know how to read signs and where all the big landmarks are, you don't really have to use a map. Unless you were a tourist, in which case, learn how to read a map. But anyway, I knew how to get to Staten Island from here. It would be just two bridges, and that was it. Instead of taking a detour to fill up, it made more sense to get gas on the way. I did end up passing by maybe three or four gas stations. But they were all full, and I wasn't going to wait. I didn't even manage to find one before I got to the bridge to Manhattan. Very upsetting.

I drove a little bit more through the city and finally found one that seemed just right. I put on my blinker and turned in. I parked next to the pump and walked inside. I perused the snacks and drinks for quite a while, as I tended to be quite picky when it came to this sort of thing. I needed energy. But if I just got an energy drink, I'd look like a douchebag. So, I settled for a sprite instead. I was also not a huge fan of diets and healthy eating. So, I got a box of Oreos. Or at least I thought it was Oreos. But when I got to the counter. I noticed it was just some knockoff brand. But I was too embarrassed to go back.

The cashier scanned my items. I paid for the cookies and sprite for around $4.25, and I put $20 down for pump number 3. The thing was, I only had hundred-dollar bills on me still. So, I got some change back. I can't recall if this bill also had blood on it; it must not have. I went outside with my merchandise, filled up, and went back on my way. It should only be another thirty minutes or so until I got to Staten Island. But I couldn't tell about the traffic. It was around four thirty at this time, so rush hour wouldn't be so kind. And I was aware of this. I sucked it up and drove on anyway.

It took maybe ten minutes or so to cover a mile and a half. So, I was particularly pissed off. I should've gone around Manhattan. For one, I wasn't even paying attention to see if I had been followed since the shooting. I should probably stop drinking on the job. I just got lucky this time around. Also, I should learn from my mistakes. I pushed it to the back of my head and waited patiently in traffic. I was bored. So, I turned on the radio and switched through channels. All this new shit on the radio, I just couldn't really understand it. It was like all you needed to make music nowadays was no talent. I said it. I meant it. I kept scrolling through and settled for the news.

REPORTER. A recent crime spike leveled out this week, with police making several arrests. Police believe the sudden rise in gang shootings can be attributed to disagreements between the Outlaw motorcycle crew and the Greenwich Mafia concerning gun running. Federal agents have put their manpower forth, claiming the recent arrest of several federal agents are connected.

At least they weren't too stupid. They had a decent bit of it right. It didn't matter who got arrested. No one involved in the shootings was aware who I was or that I might be behind it. So at any rate, if anyone was arrested, it wouldn't come back to me—unless the feds were talking. The only person who really knew was maybe Kyle. But he only knew because Drew couldn't keep his mouth shut half the time. The traffic moved slowly, and eventually I was on my way over the Verrazzano Bridge. From Staten Island on, I made my way in the early morning to Park View.

This part of Staten Island was beautiful in all honesty. It was like you forgot you were even in Staten Island. I had nothing against this part of the city. It was just more of a rich area I avoided. There were barely even any jobs. There was no point in visiting. I drove around a bit following the roads and mapping out exit routes. Looking for an ambush. I didn't need to be too eager and go in there without staking the area out a bit first. I drove around a bit more until I was confident.

I finally went out to the apartments. I slowly drove by, gazing at the complex until I almost crashed. Then I just parked up on the curb in front of the place. There was something wrong about this. This bitch had millions in her offshore accounts—undoubtedly hand-me-downs from the older generations. Her bloodline was dying out, and she decided to stay in a shithole like this. This was dangerous even for me.

How could I even decrease the severity of threats in this situation? I needed to get in there but there were just so many windows I couldn't keep an eye on all of them, especially those in the buildings across the street, not to mentions the cars and pedestrians. Everywhere I looked or didn't look, there were too many eyes on me.

Then I had an idea—so long as Pizza Hut was open for delivery at five thirty in the morning. I would just need to find a pay phone. I started the car and started driving down the road. In all honesty, I should've fucking realized pay phones weren't a thing anymore. So, what was the point in looking? I was running out of ideas and starting to get hopeless. I wasn't gonna use my phone to avoid all the risk. And I wasn't gonna use Marvin's; by this time, the service was probably turned off. I parked the car on the curb after covering only a block and a half at most. I was planning.

I looked around a little bit more, trying to grasp an idea. Then I saw a Chinese food place on the corner. Ingenious. I turned off the car and got out. Why a family-owned restaurant was open at around six in the morning was no business of mine, and I wasn't going to complain. I walked in, expecting the place to be crowded with yakuza or something. But then I realized I was being racist again—wrong culture, wrong country. The only person inside was this elderly Asian man standing behind the counter reading the morning newspaper and drinking what I assumed was coffee or some sort of tea. I walked up to him.

CARTER. Can I use your phone?

ASIAN MAN. How much?

CARTER. What?

I was understandably confused.

ASIAN MAN. How much you pay for phone?

I wasn't going to argue. I really wasn't. I didn't need that right now.

CARTER. Uh ... five dollars.

He held out his hand. So, I took out my five and gave it to him. What a dickhead, though. Come on, at six in the morning, you're gonna be an asshole. He took out a landline phone from behind the desk and put it on the counter as he went back to reading through the newspaper and drinking his morning cup of mysterious energy.

I hadn't thought this far ahead up to this point. But I didn't actually know the phone number to Pizza Hut or a place along the lines of that. I took out my phone and looked it up real quick.

Asian Man. Hey, you have a phone. Why use mine?

Carter. Because I'm a paying customer.

He shook his head. He was really starting to piss me off.

I found the number and punched it into the landline. I held it up to my ear and waited. The line was, in fact, ringing. After a minute or so of such impatience, it spoke to me.

Recorded Message. We're sorry—

I instantly hung up. I didn't want to hear what I was already afraid it was going to say. "We're closed."

Then my smile came back as quickly as it faded. I had an even better idea. I attempted to punch in the numbers.

Asian Man. Hey, five dollars per call.

This motherfucker seriously wanted another five. I was frustrated to say the least. Whatever. I checked my wallet, and all I had was tens, twenties, and hundreds.

Carter. Look. Here's the thing. I give you a ten. You give me back the five.

Surely, the man would understand the reason.

Asian Man. OK. Give me the ten.

I handed it over. He must've forgotten to give me back the five.

Carter. Now give me the five.

Asian Man. No. Phone call is now ten.

I wasn't about to rob this man, was I? I took a deep breath and made the call.

I dialed 9-1-1.

It rang for an annoying amount of time. It was almost comical.

Dispatch. 9-1-1. What is your emergency?

Carter. Hi. Good morning. I hear screams coming from my neighbor's apartment, and I think he might have a gun.

I wasn't fucking around anymore. The Asian man slowly looked worried.

Dispatch. OK, sir. What is your location?

CARTER. Well their apartment is Park View apartments, 5th floor, room 12.

DISPATCH. OK.

CARTER. You might want to hurry up. I think he's hitting his wife.

DISPATCH. Sir—

I hung up.

Drastic I know, but I needed to be aware of what was going on here. I looked back at the Asian man, and we had some unusual contact for a couple seconds. He tried to hand back the fifteen dollars, but I declined.

CARTER. Keep the change.

So, I went outside. Back to the car, I looked in the passenger side mirror, taking in the building behind me and waited. I wondered if they had police lines were tapped or something. I would find out now. That was sure. I was thinking of doing the same thing with the pizza guy. Or I could've kicked the delivery driver's ass and stolen the uniform. The cops were plan B.

Two minutes had already passed. So far, no one had left, at least not through the front entrance. So, maybe Anastasia was still in. The response time wasn't looking so good for NYPD. But they couldn't be an advantage for me all the time. I mean, I could hear sirens in the distance. But nowadays all you heard was distant sirens.

After a short time waiting, I heard those sirens came around the corner eventually. I even ducked my head underneath the car window as they drove by, as to further avoid my already alarming suspicion. Was this really the smartest plan to get around this problem? I couldn't remember the last time I'd slept. Maybe this had been a bad idea. I couldn't think straight. I needed sleep. But how could I with the walls closing in so soon already?

If I was a mob boss, would I be hiding in a place like this? I was so impatient. The cop cars pulled into the parking lot, and the officers hauled ass out of the car and into the building. As much as I always seemed to have a disagreement with the law, I had to give them credit for seeing their energy at this hour. Protect and serve, I guess.

I sat there for a couple minutes and got more and more bored. I might as well just investigate, right? Why the fuck should I stay here even if Anastasia was up there. I'd never felt so tired in my life. I was starting to lose my mind. I hated it. Paranoia, stress, exhaustion, fear, and anger were a bad combination. And the mix of them all was coming back to me from the back of my mind. Regret was a big thing at this time. But why was I feeling all this right now? It was almost over, and I was about to have a panic attack. I took a deep breath and stepped outside. I just needed to move and not stop walking. I needed to keep myself awake. And soon the struggle with myself would pass.

I walked through the parking lot, ready to just shoot her on sight. I just wanted all this to be over and done with. *Don't be stupid*, I told myself. *Don't be that killer who lost his mind.* I thought about the ones who had been caught and institutionalized or those who had turned the gun on themselves. Was this a breaking point? What was happening?

Before I even knew it, I was already in the elevator, heading up to the sixth floor. I didn't even realize I had entered the building, much less the elevator. Was I conscious that whole time? *Calm down, calm down.* I took some deep breaths in the elevator to slow my heartbeat.

I was still thinking somewhat clearly. The plan was to go to the sixth floor and go a floor down to avoid the officers and most chances of running into them.

The elevator stopped at the fifth floor. I had instant goosebumps. Anything could come out from behind those lift doors. The officers? The mob? Anastasia? My hand was on my gun, the perfect weapon. The doors opened, and a businessman walked in, smiled, and stood in front of me. I could see past him and down the hallway and saw the two officers knocking on the door. One of them stared right at me but didn't see me as a threat. Did they not recognize me from the news? I was about to throw up. I was so scared I was nauseous. The doors closed.

What if this man was, in fact, my enemy? I had no close-combat weapons on me. I had my fists, but I was too tired to win.

BUSINESSMAN. **Going down?**

I was quiet for a second and didn't make eye contact, even when I replied. I was just looking at his hands, on edge the whole time.

CARTER. **No, up.**

I could tell I was making him nervous. No big deal. There were a lot of weirdos in this city. I was just another one.

If this man was on the fifth floor, why would he go up?

The question made me even more tense. I was overthinking. Maybe it was no big deal.

Was he going down? What button did he press? What did he say? I needed to sleep desperately.

The lift opened at the sixth floor, and I got out. I jutted off into the stairwell directly off to the right of the elevator. I stood in the stairwell and peeked out around the corner to see if anyone was coming after me. I was fine. There was no threat, and the businessman hadn't followed. I turned around and went down the stairs to floor five. As before, I turned back to look for a threat and then curiously peeked my head into the hallway.

The officers were talking to a man in the doorframe, but I couldn't get a good look at him. I couldn't see. It did seem like the officers were at ease. They had their arms crossed and talked to him with a smile. So, the mob had tricked me? Or was the mob tricking the officers. I wanted to get a closer look. But I didn't want the officers to spot me.

The man finally walked out of the room and greeted the officers with a happy and thankful smile. It was a fucking priest!?

He had his neck piece on and everything. He was ready for early Mass or some shit. I put my back to the wall and slammed my head a couple times. How could I be so stupid? But was I? I was following the only lead I had. Those men were begging for their lives. Why would they both tell me this location? Unless it was a ploy to throw me off course. But then, why wouldn't it be a trap? Maybe it was—a trap with a killer priest, someone you'd least expect. Or maybe it was something more sinister.

The cops nodded, and they all walked my way. I ducked and went back up to the sixth floor, where I looked over the railing and watched as the officers and the priest all went downstairs. The officers still must've been very interested in the phone call I made, assuming it was some sort of sick joke. They just let the man go. Amazing what you could do with the power of the church.

I kept following them slowly down the stairs, careful to avoid being seen. I watched as they split up, and the officers went home, and the priest went to work. I was going to follow the priest. If I was wrong in all this, I would be one sick bastard to question a priest like this. But I had no other choice. The priest had his own car, parked not far off from mine. So, I hopped in the Nissan and gave chase as he drove down the street, I assumed toward a fucking church or something.

The drive was short but terrifying, as I nearly fell asleep behind the wheel at least four or five times. It got to a point where I turned up the AC to the max to freeze myself and get more uncomfortable so I wouldn't fall asleep. It actually kind of worked, I'm not gonna lie. A while into the drive, I forgot what early-morning traffic in New York City was really like. It was dog shit. I followed for miles and miles. Eventually the priest stopped in front of a church. I parked a bit behind him on the curb. He walked up the front steps with keys in hand, used them to open the front door, and walked on in.

Holy shit. This really was just a fucking priest. But I really couldn't be sure. I should investigate further. I got out, looked around, and walked on in as well. Now, I was never really the religious type. I never wanted to actually think there would be righteous punishment for the shit I never got caught for.

In the empty church, I saw the priest standing alone right in the middle of all those pews. He stood there and looked right at me. We both stopped right in our tracks and looked each other dead in the eye. We were both shocked. But why was he?

He blurted out.

PRIEST. We're not open!

He didn't want me here. But why? Did he recognize me? Did he know me? Some things started to make sense. But then other things didn't. More questions meant more answers to find. It was weird. And I was even more suspicious. Why would a fucking priest say something like that—especially in such a rude manner too? Something wasn't right, and we both knew it. He started to back up and even just might've looked terrified. I was confused.

CARTER. D-Do you want me to leave, Father?

PRIEST. Yes … uh, I mean please come back later … my son.

What a bad fucking actor. But no matter really. I had a better idea. I slowly backed up right back to the front door. I wasn't taking my eyes off him. I left the church and decided there was something definitely wrong with this whole situation. But what could I really prove right now? He'd left his apartment unattended. It was time to search his shit I guess. At least I now knew this really hadn't been a trick all along. I had to be sure though, and I had no problem with searching a priest's apartment, so long as it benefitted me and my investigation.

I didn't really worry about leaving him all alone. He was a little odd though. Why did he act in such a manner? It was just fucking weird, even suspicious. I was just gonna go back to his apartment and toss all his shit around to find some sort of actual tangible evidence, instead of attacking a priest. I was still on the road of change for the better, and that was too far, maybe even for my old self.

The drive back was a lot shorter, so I wasn't too upset. If anything, I was happy. Or maybe I was just losing my mind. One thing, I didn't think over was, if I did find something in his apartment, wasn't I then going to ask myself why I would just leave him alone in his church when he knew of my presence. My smile faded, and I started speeding. I was already too far away to go back, and the apartment was just around the corner. My heart started racing, and paranoia set in once again. I wanted to scream at myself. I was letting my training slip. I'd noticed it recently. But why? Was it actually time to retire?

Those retirement thoughts were a hope I wanted in my reach. I wanted to leave all this behind. I knew after this it was all over. I was done with this. I had to finish this first.

I drove into a random parking spot and slammed on the brakes just in time. I got out and ran inside and up the stairs because I didn't trust that fucking elevator. I was out of breath before I got to the third floor. I kept pushing myself until I got up to the fifth floor, and then I just jogged down to his door. I rested at the door just to catch my breath so I could break the doorknob off in one kick.

I was lucky. All it took was one well-placed kick right next to the doorknob. That bitch flew right open. I ran in and just started throwing shit everywhere. I was tripping on a bunch of stuff that was on the floor, like cardboard boxes and wires. I would expect a priest to have a clean room, but I guess not. I felt no remorse in tearing the kitchen apart. And after I found nothing, I just moved on to the closets and then to the living room and finally to the bedroom. First I started with the bed itself. I threw up the mattress. Jack shit. I searched the dresser drawer and every sock. At the bottom of the drawer was something sharp. It cut me as I dug deeper. I reached back in slowly and pulled out an FBI badge.

What the fuck?

Next was the closet. I threw open the closet door, and on the floor was a pile of clothes. I rifled through the clothes. And holy fuck.

There was the duffel bag—my duffel bag, filled with the money. At that point, time stopped for me. I just froze. I left that motherfucker all alone in that church. What the fuck was wrong with me? I had searched, and I'd seen enough anyway. I'd gotten what I wanted, and I left. I walked out of the room to see some curious neighbors. My cover here was blown. So, I started running again.

Down the stairs and out into the lobby, outside and over to the car. I threw the duffel bag in the back, and after all, it was mine. I started the car and sped out. The cops were definitely being called. So, I needed to be quick, and maybe I could sleep.

I drove back to the church laughing in anger. And if you didn't think that was possible, it is. It was anguish and fear and frustration with myself that came out as a screaming laugh. I hated today, and I was gonna take my stress out in beating the fuck out of that priest. Out of context, I understand that would be frowned on. But my discovery justified this course of action.

I pulled in front of the church to see a small crowd had gathered outside the front doors. I got out and walked up the stairs to investigate. All these people were clamoring and confused, saying it was weird the doors were closed, as the church should be open at this time.

He was hiding inside. Why didn't he just run? And how was I going to get inside? Genius struck my mind.

CARTER. Clear the way. Clear the way!

Everybody looked at me as I flashed that FBI badge I found earlier. They looked at each other, shocked and asked themselves, "What could our good old priest have done to deserve such a treatment?"

Fuck off. I was too pissed off to even mock these people. I got over to the door. And sure enough, it was, indeed, locked. I really didn't think I was gonna have to kick one door down, let alone two in one day. But it was just the way it had to be. I took a step or two back and gave it a go.

The first kick did dick all, and in all that silence, I was actually pretty embarrassed. I gave it another go. Sure enough, the door wouldn't budge. But I wasn't giving up that easily. At that point, one of the elderly men asked if he could help. I just held up my hand as a sign to just let me do my job. He understood. I gave it a third try, and open sesame.

CARTER. **Everybody go home. It's too dangerous.**

I really hoped the crowd listened to that.

I ran in, gun in hand. I looked around, and he wasn't in any of the pews. And why the fuck would he be? I wasn't too familiar with the actual interior design of a church, but I assumed there were like offices or something in the back. So, that's where I went. I kept my gun close to my chest so I'd be prepared if he came out around any of these corners. I got all the way to the other side and up a stair or two onto the stage. I pulled away the curtain in the back and moved down a hallway, clearing rooms with open doors first until I came across my first closed one.

I stood to the side of the closed door and jiggled the knob a little bit to make sure it wasn't locked. I turned it full cycle and pushed it open. I didn't enter yet. I just waited.

I took a deep breath and turned my body in.

The room was clear.

I moved out and made my way farther down the hallway until I heard footsteps from behind me. I used one of the open doorways of the cleared rooms as cover. Around that corner all the way at the end of the hall, a man jumped out. He was clearly Greenwich, so I put two in his chest, and he fell down. I meant to put another bullet to his head just to make sure, but I missed and only hit his shoulder. I really was tired. My aim was garbage.

All the way at the end of the hall, a door flew open. So, I turned around and aimed at the priest. He had a gun under his chin. More footsteps came from behind me, so I had to turn around again and put one lucky-ass bullet into some poor mobster's head.

I turned back to face the priest. He had tears in eyes, fearing for his own life, which was in his own hands.

PRIEST. She set me up that bitch. Fuck.

He was rambling nonsense. But I knew he would actually do it. He would actually kill himself, but I needed him. I didn't really know exactly what to say.

CARTER. I-I'm here to help all right. I'm with the FBI.

I started moving closer slowly.

PRIEST. Fuck you!

He turned his gun on me now, moving in one fluid and angry motion. He knew I was lying, and it made him furious. So I went back to taking cover, this time behind another open doorway.

PRIEST. You think I'm retarded, Carter, you fucking faggot. I know your shit. Just stay the fuck back.

Yeah, this cocksucker knew exactly what was going on here, but the scene was now so much more tense.

PRIEST. Why me? Why the fuck are you here for me? Why!?

If I knew what he wanted, I could calm him down. But what the fuck did he want. To live I assumed. But I was his killer in his eyes.

CARTER. I'm not gonna kill you man. I'm not. I just want to ask you some questions and shit.

I kept looking behind me, as my ears were tricking me into thinking there were more people coming.

PRIEST. What the fuck do you want?

CARTER. All I want is Anastasia, man. That's it. Were you saying she set you up? I can help you.

He almost looked relieved, but he was skeptical.

I moved closer.

PRIEST. Get the fuck away from me. Stay back.

I was tired. I was fucking exhausted. I was pissed. I was hungry. I just wanted to go home. I hadn't done too well with suicidal suspect training way back when. So I was just not up for it. If anything, I really didn't give a fuck. So, I just shot him in the foot and sprinted toward him before he had a chance to react. He fell to the ground, and I kicked the gun away from him. Under most laws, purposely aiming to maim and injure is immoral and inhumane. But to me, it was nothing but helpful. He was screaming, yelling, and crying like a little bitch. But he would last quite a while without bleeding out. I pulled off his shoes and used his shoelaces to tie his hands together.

I couldn't really shut him up, as he already had a bullet in his foot, and for some people, that might cause a little discomfort. I'd really fucked myself into a bad situation. I had just shot and killed two people and injured one. The Nissan was outside the church, and the cops are definitely on their way.

I would just have to make a run for it—in the middle of the day with all those people watching. I was running on almost forty-eight hours with no sleep. I couldn't interrogate him here. It was time to move. I took off one of his socks, put it in his mouth to shut him up and picked him up, and practically dragged him through the hallway and off the stage and through the church and out through the front door.

Many people were still outside. But this time, they kept their distance, their faces crinkled into worried expressions. They remained unsure of the situation, not knowing what had just happened. I could hear those very distant sirens closing in closer and closer.

Everyone got out of my way quickly enough for me to just drag him down to the car. In all fairness, the way I was treating the suspect was unbecoming of an officer, and people did start harassing me, asking for my badge, my name, and my God. I ignored them. I was in a rush to get the fuck out of there. I opened the trunk and attempted to shove him in until a bystander grabbed my arm. I twisted his arm and shoved him away, no problem. But the scene was not looking good for me. The crowd closed in, so I hurried with getting the priest in the trunk and shut it on him. The protesters started moving in on my car. I didn't have many options left. I pulled my gun and pointed it at the crowd. This was not the way I was gonna go down. I got into the car, started it, and drove like hell.

As I left the curb in the distance, some of the people ran after me for a bit but couldn't keep up. The scariest part of my job was running away from the scene of a crime. Most of the time, luck was a big factor. You didn't know what motherfucker was hanging around that next corner. This particular time was especially unnerving, seeing as though the car had been made. I couldn't drive it anymore. It was a small thing to remember Todd by, and I couldn't be seen in it ever again. God knows those people had called the police, giving the details of the car. I didn't speed. I couldn't get caught and ruin everything now. So, I just drove slowly enough to blend in. My heart was still racing, and I had that sense of paranoia running down my spine. I just kept looking over my shoulder.

I started to doze off, so I attempted to distract myself, playing the radio and then opening the window to have the wind blow on my face and give me a sense of relief. The priest in the back started to bang more and more loudly, so I put my foot down hard on the brakes until I heard a thud from the back. It took about ten seconds before he started banging again, so I just turned up the radio volume and kept going.

The drive back from Staten Island was dangerous. With my level of exhaustion, the smartest thing to do was pull over and sleep somewhere. But obviously that wasn't such a good idea after my recent and current crimes. I was running on over forty-eight hours without sleep, and it was starting to take its toll on my mind. I wasn't happy, and I wasn't having it. Before I knew it, I got over the bridge and into Manhattan.

It was just another five or so minutes until I got to the coffee shop, so I wasn't gonna make a big deal about it or finish strong when it came to speed. *No speeding and no suspicion. Just smooth sailing. Act natural. You got this. You're a professional. Just keep driving at this pace and you'll be fine. Nothing to worry about.* I had to constantly keep calming myself down because I didn't have any experience working this tired. It was like I didn't know what was gonna happen next. My mind was against me.

Eventually, I came around the corner and was flooded with relief to see an empty street. *No witnesses. Good.* I didn't want to park on the street though. I just pulled into that alley right next to the shop. I pulled up all the way to the back and parked. I got out of the car and went back to the trunk and opened it. The priest was ready with his feet to start immediately kicking me. I simply just caught his foot and squeezed. He screamed in agony as I smiled, thinking he was stupid.

He'd spit the sock out on the ride over here, so I threw him out onto the floor as I searched around for it. I even looked under the space for the spare wheel, but it was just lost. I didn't need it anyway. I picked him up and dragged his ass up to the back stairs and through the door. The coffee shop itself was empty, as it was too early for any real customer traffic. I opened the basement door and accidentally dropped him down the flight of stairs. He shouldn't have been struggling; it wasn't my fault.

The bikers at the foot of the stairs stood up, staring up at me and then down at the body. I didn't worry about them interfering, as they knew not to fuck with me. I got down to the bottom and dragged him over to Drew's office, with much kicking and screaming on his part. I didn't have to knock, though, because Drew had already opened the door to see what all the commotion was. We both looked at each other for quite some time until he spoke up.

DREW. Why the fuck is there a priest with bullet hole in his foot in front of my office?

I didn't notice till then, but dragging him had left a small blood trail, which shouldn't be too hard to clear up.

DREW. Carter. are you gonna fucking answer me or not?

I'd forgotten to even say anything until now.

CARTER. Well, Drew, I need this man's wound treated, and he needs to be questioned when I wake up.

Everyone was staring at us, as we were making quite a scene.

DREW. Carter, what the fuck are you talking about?

As everyone was still staring, I just got pissed off.

CARTER. Everyone, get back to work.

And they did not hesitate to do so.

CARTER. So, anyway, Drew, you know how I interrogated those guys, right?

DREW. Yeah sure. Whatever.

CARTER. Well they both gave me the same address. So, I went there to find this guy, the stolen bag of money, and an FBI badge. And I also killed two people and haven't slept in two days. So please just fucking listen to me and get this guy in a closet or something until I wake up.

I was trying his patience. Even I would snap at this point. But what could Drew do except listen? There was no other person to turn to for either of us. This had to be done, and he knew it.

He waved over a couple bikers an instructed them to take the priest away from me. They dragged him down the hallway to a room at the end of the basement. Euphoria at last. Drew silently judged me and slammed the office door in my face. I started to look around. There weren't a whole lot of places to sleep. I went down a couple doors from Drew's office and found a supply closet with plenty of sleeping room. I didn't really give a fuck at this point. So, I made some room, closed the door, laid down, and fell asleep within seconds.

19

I woke up, and my neck was very sore. But I had gotten a good eight hours of sleep, so I laid there for another forty-five minutes or so scrolling through Tinder. I looked around and asked myself what was wrong with me. I'd literally decided to sleep in a janitor's closet. I hadn't even put effort into looking around for a better place. Sometimes, you just get too tired to care though, and at that point, I really didn't. Eventually I got up, stretched, just and went to work.

I opened the door to see many peculiar faces staring me down. I judged them as much as they did me and went on my way. I was starving, and I wanted some water. So, I went to the kitchen before knocking on Drew's door. I walked in to see some people having a friendly chat. They ignored me as I walked past them saying good morning. Disappointing. I opened the fridge to see a Poland spring bottle, which would now be mine, along with someone's lunch that had "Johnson" written on it or something close to that. I put it in the microwave next to the fridge and sat down at a table drinking water and waited.

I almost decided to light a cigarette, but I wasn't really going to be an asshole, so I didn't. Instead, I waited for my stolen food to be done and ate it peacefully with my water. It was a little cold, as I hadn't cooked it right. But when you were hungry, some things were more important than others. I cleaned up washed my hands and went on to what I was supposed to do, which was commit a possibly unforgivable sin in interrogating a priest. But that would just have to be a cover. There was no other way.

I got up and went on my way. I passed by unruly businessmen bumping into me and not apologizing even after I almost got confrontational. What was going on with these people today? Regardless, I went on my way.

I knocked on Drew's door.

DREW. Enter.

I opened the door to see Kyle and Drew looking up at me. I'd obviously interrupted something because already Drew looked pissed, and Kyle got up and squeezed by me and left the room. It was already very awkward, as Drew and I were staring at each other in silence.

Then I spoke up.

CARTER. Good morning.

Me and my smart-ass, shit-eating grin.

DREW. Carter, I don't want to have to talk to you right now. If you want that priest, he's down the hall in the empty office Briggs used to work in.

I was going to pretend I knew who the fuck that was, but I did actually know which office he was talking about.

CARTER. Wasn't Briggs the one who cheated on his wife with his therapist?

DREW. No. That's Livingston. Briggs shot himself in the leg and fell off a building and became paralyzed.

Still didn't ring a bell. But I was still standing there.

DREW. Is there anything you need?

CARTER. Yeah, uh, actually. Why is everyone being an asshole to me today? Did someone get cancer or something?

DREW. Maybe it has to do with the fact that you shot a priest in the foot, pushed him down a flight of stairs, tied his hands behind his back, and plan to interrogate him. I mean, think, Carter. Why wouldn't everyone hate you?

I nodded my head, and it seemed fair enough.

CARTER. All right, well, if you need me I'll be—

DREW. Get out.

I didn't hesitate to leave. I took a deep breath and prepared myself for not fucking around with this guy. I was going to be straightforward and honest. I wasn't gonna let him lie to me, and I was gonna make him tell me what I needed. It was as simple as that—no hassle, no stress. I walked down the hallway, my eyes fixed on the office whose door was guarded by a biker with a shotgun. Had to be the place, I thought. I walked up to him, and he opened the door for me. See, that was the thing with these organizations. They may work together, but these bureaucrats and bikers were so split on everything. One wanted violence, and one wanted business. I never knew where I fit into it all until they gave me a gun. I was that good old local psychopath. How wrong they were. I never lost my mind. I just remembered who I needed to be. And so, I was retiring.

I walked in, and there was the priest, handcuffed to a table with a biker watching him inside. His foot was all bandaged up, and he looked exhausted. I bet he hadn't sleep at all. I told the guard he could leave. He didn't argue. And then it was just me and him face-to-face. No outside interference and no threats in this room, except me if I snapped.

I pulled up a chair that was against the wall and placed it across from him at the table and sat down. He was looking me dead in the eye. He wasn't scared to die, but he knew I could be the one to do it. After an entire minute of me staring him down to try and see how tough this guy really was, I started asking questions.

CARTER. So, tell me, who the fuck are you?

PRIEST. You really don't know?

Entitled little bastard.

CARTER. Either I can beat it out of you, or I can ask you again because I'm not fucking around here, all right. Do you understand what situation you're in right now and how bad this looks for you?

PRIEST. They said you were smart. And looking at you right now, I can tell otherwise.

He was trying my patience, but I was honest with him.

CARTER. Look, man, I can just shoot you in the other foot if you want. I don't care. I'll do it.

He shook his head.

PRIEST. Calm down, all right. I'm Nicolas Paganti.

I looked at him blankly. Still had no clue. He rolled his eyes.

NICOLAS. Anastasia's brother.

I was really fucking surprised by this one, and he could see it in my face. It made no sense. He'd told me like I was an idiot, like I should know. This was all so confusing.

NICOLAS. I thought I could run away, and me being a priest is a cover.

CARTER. Right, well I'll be honest, none of us even knew Anastasia had a brother. So, you're overreacting. But you are in a much worse spot now.

NICOLAS. I don't wanna hear shit from you. You're a lunatic the way you torture and kill people.

CARTER. Oh, so you've heard of me.

I had to admit, the statement fueled my ego quite a bit. But still, I was a changing man, forced to do desperate things.

CARTER. So, I'm not interested in killing you. I couldn't give a fuck about you or what you've done, so long as it hasn't affected me. What I need from you is to tell me where Anastasia is.

He didn't react badly to that; he really just sat there and nodded his head. Finally a breakthrough.

CARTER. She set you up. You know that, right?

I've had to interrogate multiple individuals, torturing them to the culmination of death. And they all gave me your location as where I could find Anastasia.

NICOLAS. Jesus.

CARTER. So, I actually want, first off, for you to tell me what was going on on your side so I can just get both sides together. And don't lie. I don't wanna have to get your robes even bloodier.

He sat there for a second, and I let him think about the predicament he was in. There was no escape, no salvation except in our custody. We weren't going to kill him. We could, if anything, recruit him.

NICOLAS. OK. After all that shit with the cops coming over to the docks and taking our money, thereby making the feds no longer allies, I had to cut and run, you know? The walls were closing in, and I had no other option.

CARTER. Yeah. Sorry about that, by the way.

He didn't like that joke but kept explaining.

NICOLAS. Anastasia shut out our assets. She didn't want me there anyway. She thinks I'm trying to take over the club, but I don't give a shit. So, I got some fake FBI badges made up for me and some soldiers, and we went to the port authority and took the money out of your car.

Sorry about that, by the way.

Little dickhead.

NICOLAS. I knew she would do something like this. She's fucking insane. She's not even blood related. She's like some ... Whatever, I don't care. But know, if you want her, I'll sure as shit fucking help you.

He was too calm. Either he really did have the same interests, or this was a larger scheme to trap me and ambush and kill me.

NICOLAS. I want some assurances though.

I'd play the game. I'd see how far we could take it until I handed him over to the feds.

CARTER. Name them.

NICOLAS. I want guaranteed protection from her. In case you didn't know, she's pissed at what you're doing. She wants your head.

CARTER. OK and?

He shook his head. He didn't like the confidence I was showing. He thought I was too cocky. But I knew exactly what I was going to do. I leaned in.

CARTER. I guarantee security here in this building. You are safe. Now, tell me where this bitch is.

This was a moment of trust and truth. He took a second and looked around before he happily ended it all. Just like me, he wanted her dead, and he wanted to be happy and free. Maybe we'd both get what we wanted. But for now, I needed to get just a little more blood on my hands, and then I was done.

NICOLAS. She still has a real estate operation in Queens over in the old Mafia districts. She's probably protected in the big mansion just off Cambridge road in Jamaica Estates. It's her last option, and I'm done supplying her protection.

Was this all really going to end? Just like that, with this final piece of information? I felt nauseous with anticipation. Nonetheless, I smiled and nodded.

CARTER. Thank you, Nicolas.

I stood up, turned around, and moved toward the door. I needed men and arms and a good plan. This would be the final siege to end a regime and guarantee my escape.

NICOLAS. You're gonna leave just like that?

I looked back at him, pissed off. Like what was he expecting? A fucking kiss goodbye. Nah, fuck this dickhead. So I smiled again.

CARTER. Sorry about the foot. I should've aimed for the pussy.

Piece of shit.

The interrogation gone about as well as expected. I just wasn't too used to communicating with crooks. I was more about interrogations with criminals—and not peaceful ones either.

DREW. Carter!

Drew was coming up on my back, probably coming from some unnecessary meeting about how fucking stupid the Outlaws were.

DREW. What happened there?

I smiled at him. I was in such a good mood today. I knew tonight was the night. I wanted to remember his reaction and his everlasting thankfulness to me for following through on my promises.

CARTER. We will kill her tonight. But I need some men and guns and explosives. And for cops to turn a blind eye is necessary.

DREW. About fucking time.

And he walked off back to his office, so I followed him.

CARTER. Drew, come on. At least be fucking thankful.

DREW. Thankful? I have you putting everyone looking down the other end of a gun every other day. Just fucking end this so I can run the fuck away from Outlaw leadership before we all get fucked.

It killed my mood, but he was right.

CARTER. Can you support this or not?

DREW. I'll give you five guys to scope the place out before you hit it. It could still be a trap.

CARTER. I'm not planning on scoping anything out. I'm planning on killing her.

He looked at me wide-eyed.

DREW. You must've lost your mind. You have no idea if the information you got from the guy you shot in the foot is actually true or not. You have nothing. How can you trust that priest?

CARTER. I don't want you to trust the priest. I want you to trust me.

DREW. That's just what I want to hear. More trust. Have I not trusted you enough? And you've brought me nothing but more bloodshed and bodies. You know, ever since you showed up, you have fucked over each and every person you've come in contact with.

And Todd wou—

I snapped and violently slammed the door behind me as I charged in.

CARTER. Don't you fucking say another word. I did my fucking job. and I'm avenging him. Don't you want that for him too?

DREW. You think you're hot shit because you're some fucking army specialty guy with all you're fucking training. If you're so fucking good, why did they kick you out?

CARTER. I don't have to put up with your shit, Drew. I'm gonna go get my shit. Take your men. Go to one of the armories we have in the Bronx, and I'm gonna do your fucking job for you. And you know what? Yeah, I am hot shit. I am a badass. I may be selfish in saying it, but at least I know what the fuck I'm doing. I don't need your men. They'll only get in the way. I'm gonna go there and finish what I started.

I turned away to leave. He yelled at me and ordered me to come back. but I was done. He wanted his safety and freedom. I would guarantee both. I still loved the man. He was just stressed. The dogs were at every corner, closing in on us. It was one of those situations where you have so many enemies it's hard to know if the few friends you do have will stick with you to the end or betray you.

I was about to go up the stairs, until an idea sparked in my mind. It was something so cruel and evil I just had to try it. And why not? It would work either way. I turned back and went to the interrogation room. There was still a guard out front. He let me right in without any hesitation. It was respect that let me walk in there, and it would be others' fear that would let me walk out.

The guard standing inside was watching Nicolas eat his lunch. We all looked at each other, and Nicolas stopped eating; he was terrified of what was to come. *Why is he back?* he must've thought.

I looked back at the guard with a smile.

CARTER. Uncuff him.

Everyone was surprised by this.

GUARD. I can't do that.

My smile dimmed into a look of confusion.

CARTER. Why not?

GUARD. Boss's orders.

CARTER. Drew?

He nodded.

When did this happen? I'd only just left the room not ten minutes ago. Must've said some shit when I was asleep. No matter. I was leaving with this prisoner whether they liked it or not. So I pulled my gun and aimed it at the guard—a shock to everybody.

GUARD. What the fuck are you doing, man?

CARTER. Uncuff him.

I was calm in my speech, but my actions reflected my true feelings.

GUARD. Look. You don't have to do this.

CARTER. Uncuff him.

GUARD. I—

Fuck this.

The guard pulled out his handcuff keys and did as I said. I would've uncuffed him if I hadn't left my set of keys at home, which made this process so much more annoying. The benefits weren't as obvious as I wanted them to be, however.

GUARD. You are fucked in the head. You know that, right?

I just smiled at him as he shoved Nicolas over to me. I pushed him out the door while still making eye contact with the guard. He didn't move, but I needed some seconds to prepare myself. I would have to be quick. Yes, very quick. No mistakes. Ready? Go.

I put away the gun, went out the door, and shoved Nicolas in the direction of the staircase. Every few steps or so, I looked back to see what the consequences of my actions could be. The guard didn't even leave the room. He was probably still shaking from the whole scene. I didn't blame him.

I continued on, pushing Nicolas up the stairs and eventually slamming the door behind me at the top of the staircase. I couldn't really block it or stall them. Maybe I didn't even realize what I had just done, at least not yet. Why? Heat of the moment? Of course. Justifiable? Perhaps. Keep moving. Nicolas wouldn't run away. At least in the coffee shop, he would be in a bad spot to do that. But it didn't matter. He'd be dead soon anyway. As the old saying goes, burn a town, save a city. Sometimes you have to make sacrifices in order to prevent bigger catastrophes.

I was still pushing Nicolas around, and he started to get snippy with me. When he turned to glare at me with an angry face, I could see he was definitely still in pain from the hole I'd put in him earlier. We kept moving. I'd turned all my friends against me for the greater good. For the preservation of my sanity? Or was it something more sinister? I still didn't know. After a while, pushing everything to the back of your head takes a toll. You start to forget who you are—or at least who you were before. Was I really in the military? Was this just a nightmare? *Ignore these terrible thoughts and focus on the goal at hand*, I told myself.

We rushed over to the car, but he didn't need to go in the trunk this time. I just had to show him I could be intimidating while driving. I unlocked the car using the fob and shoved him in the passenger side. He hit his head on the frame, and I actually felt bad. But that simple emotion passed in a split second. I got in the driver's side. I took a quick glance at him. He must've had so many questions he was just too scared to ask.

I pulled out my gun and put it on my lap. He knew I wasn't fucking around. He wasn't gonna try anything on me again. We both knew what I was capable of. I started the car and drove off at high speed. It was only a thirty-minute drive to one of our weapons apartments just above a safe house. There would probably be Outlaws on guard. Who knew if they would already be aware of my insubordination? I'd just have to be ready.

NICOLAS. Where are you taking me?

His voice was shaky and nervous.

I didn't respond.

I just kept driving.

The traffic was light, and I had enough energy to get me through at least forty-eight hours of high-amped violence with little rest. So, why not see it to the end? Who knew if I would actually survive tonight? But no matter what, I wouldn't go down without a good damn fight.

I was almost excited to strap explosives to Nicolas and make him march into a gang of Anastasia's own security. It was evil. It was wrong. It was immoral if anything. But it certainly wouldn't be regrettable. I was desperate. So a little mass killing of my own orchestration was really no big deal. I would sometimes sit back and ask myself, How the fuck did my life choices lead me to a place where I had to make these decisions?

I could really go for a cigarette at this point.

I searched my pockets and found my pack. I pulled it out and opened it up to find my darts had been crushed—most likely from me sleeping on them. They were now useless. There was more silence after that. But I could feel Nicolas's eyes prodding me. I could sense it. He wanted to say something but couldn't. Him just staring with nothing to say started to annoy me—until the point where I snapped.

I whipped my head in his direction.

CARTER. What?!

This startled him, but it got him talking.

NICOLAS. D-do you want … a cigarette?

He reached in his pants pocket to pull out a pack of Marb lights. Pussy blend. I couldn't possibly trust my prisoner's gift. After all, I was going to kill him. So in an act of defiance, I snatched the pack from

THE KILLER WHO LOST HIS MIND | 217

his hand, opened up the window and tossed it, and rolled the window back up again.

Nicolas let out one sniffle.

I looked at him in confusion and then shook my head.

If all mob bosses acted like such pussies under tense conditions, then these motherfuckers really must've died out after Giuliani. What kind of breed had I taken advantage of this time?

The safe house was mere minutes away by the time I got over the bridge into Queens. At this point, traffic had died down considerably. No more harsh words directed at student drivers and jaywalkers. This was a calm before the inevitable storm.

I was rambling nonsense and bullshit. It was so fucking annoying.

I pulled down Myrtle Avenue and headed toward 89th street. I was thankful to have such a magnificent weapons depot so close to Jamaica Estates. The only thing that could ruin this was Outlaws on sentry duty and, of course, the armory not having what I want. What did I need? A small application of high explosives.

I drove past the apartment to see an Outlaw standing guard. I kept the same normal speed as to not further arouse suspicion. Fuck. Such bullshit. I could still make do. It would be good to mention the only reason I could tell this guy was gang was because this retard was just standing on the front steps smoking a cigarette with the holster of his silver gun jutting out a little bit from his waistline and behind his open jacket. I drove a little bit farther down the road. I was struggling to find a spot at first. However, I just needed to be patient. I found one a mere block away.

I parked the car and momentarily considered what to do with poor old Nicolas here. I figured I'd just have to take him with me. So, I got out and went to the trunk. I opened it up and pulled out my rifle—not, of course, before looking around first. I checked the chamber, checked the sights and ammo. It was all good to go. I looked down at it to see my reflection in the eye side of the scope. It changed me for that brief moment. Outlaws weren't even my enemies. I was just going out of my way to help them, and I was deciding to drop a couple of their bodies? I tossed the gun back in the trunk and went to the passenger side door to open it up.

CARTER. Get out and follow me.

He was reluctant to get out at first. So, I had to take a more physical approach. I grabbed him by his collar and hoisted him out with force. He was very easy to scare. It was amazing how he'd managed to have such power in the criminal underworld. Then again, he had just been born into it.

CARTER. If you run or you say dumb shit, I'll put the next bullet in your head.

His foot still hurt. I could tell. But there wasn't much I could do to help. I still didn't even know what my plan was. I was just here. There was one thing I thought of, which was stupid but—fuck it—better than nothing. I had Nicolas put his arm around my shoulder. I called over to one of the Outlaws around five apartments down.

CARTER. Hey, I need help over here.

He heard me clearly, and we made eye contact. It was a staring contest for a few seconds. He turned around and called someone from inside to run out and help. This just might work out. He had recognized me as well. Good luck on this day. I saw the help was on the way, running down the sidewalk. They must've recognized me. But they clearly had no idea I had just kidnapped a prisoner a mere twenty minutes ago. That meant I still had a little bit of time.

I let the helpful biker take a hold of the "priest" as I let him go. We would have to be quick. There was no need to stall. Just get him inside, you fool. Get us moving. And get me to the armory.

CARTER. Get him inside.

BIKER. What happened?

CARTER. Greenwich.

He nodded. The war was still raging, and blood soaked the streets. The fear in the biker's eyes showed he knew this as well. His age wouldn't show, but you could tell he was young. I walked beside him the whole way, watching him carry my prisoner. It was times like these that my sympathy came into play. I didn't want to see young men die in fights they shouldn't belong to. Too old to cry but not too old to die. The simple truth always haunted me.

We came up to the front steps of the building as the guard was looking around our shoulders and down either road from left to right, hoping to not spot a witness or two. He let us in and promised we'd not start a ruckus. Places like these weren't necessarily equipped with medical facilities—an issue that came down to budget. I was to make all this sacrifice, with the end result being me either retired or dead. I didn't want to live a life like this anymore. I was in the middle of change.

We took Nicolas down to the armory for a biker to Attend to his medical needs, while I perused the goodies. The place had everything from rifles to snipers to pistols and shotguns. Thanks to Cuomo, all of this was possible. And after the great purge of the eighties and the fall of the mob, everyone sat quietly building an empire back up from the dust. I wasn't into the beliefs of their system. I just killed. That was it. No fancy suits or politics. Blood for money.

I peeked across the room at the explosives cabinet—which was exactly what I had come for. The most dangerous game was about to begin. I first went through the cabinet to grab an extra handgun. I was getting bored of the old one. I put some ammunition that I would need for it on the table and switched out my current sidearm. First, I had to put a silencer on it and put it back in my inside coat pocket. I went over to the explosives cabinet and grabbed what I assumed was remote detonated charges. But I was certainly no expert when it came to stuff like that. So, I took a fair guess, assuming I was right.

I didn't need much. Just enough to cause a panic. I grabbed three explosives and three detonators and put them on the table. That was when the guard noticed.

BIKER. **The fuck you need all that for?**

I kinda stopped and looked at him for a second, not really knowing what to say. A simple joke? A lie? Shoot him?

CARTER. **Uh ... don't worry about it.**

He looked confused but slowly went back to tending to Nicolas.

I had what I needed now to just tie up some loose ends, if that was what I should call it. I armed one of the explosives and put it on top of the table. I didn't want anybody to be around for it. No more unnecessary casualties.

CARTER. **Hey, take him back up and outside. I got a guy down in Brooklyn who can take care of him.**

He was hesitant, as I was loading up a duffel bag filled with more guns and ammunition.

OUTLAW. Are you sure? I know a guy three blocks from here who can patch him up.

I shook my head and ignored any further arguing as I pushed both of them out the door and took back control of Nicolas.

CARTER. Thank you for your hospitality and all—very truly appreciated. But I got what I came here for. So I'll just be leaving. Thank you.

It was a shady and quick response—definitely enough to raise some eyebrows.

I ushered Nicolas up the stairs as fast as he could go. But in the end, his foot was still not in the best shape. He winced at every step. But then the curious Outlaw started following me. It was not the time for this. I had gotten him to the hallway when the Outlaw started yelling after me. *Not now*, I thought, *not here*. I don't want to have to do anything right now. I was too quick for them, though. I pushed through a couple bikers to get to the door. I got to the sidewalk.

One of the Outlaws chased after me.

BIKER. Hey.

I stopped not twenty feet from the car. I turned around to face him, slowly reaching for the detonator in my pocket.

BIKER. I just got off the phone with Drew.

My heart sank. The relationship was really through. I had gone too far. If only they knew I was saving everyone from further conflict. I was a goddamn hero by my own standards. That had to mean something, didn't it?

BIKER. He wants to talk with you.

I was ready to blow the whole fucking armory away. But I just waited. I gave the man a chance.

BIKER. I got a car down there. I can drive you. He says it's urgent.

CARTER. I'm telling you right now that I'm not going with you. And I don't want to hurt you. I'm telling you to just walk away right now. That's the only thing I'll say to you.

A staring contest ensued—a real Mexican standoff. I looked at the

Outlaw to see the outline of his gun in his waist. I knew, if his hands moved, I would be ready. It seemed like minutes rolled by. He didn't know how to respond to such a threat. He could only show a physical reaction, and so he reached for his gun. But I was trained, and I was quicker.

I pulled out the detonator and set it off while the gun was in his hand. The less guns on the street, the better for everybody anyway

The whole building blew out, with glass and debris flying onto the street. Giant flames and black smoke billowed out the windows and doors. For a moment, the Outlaws had no idea what the fuck had just hit them. The biker had no choice but to turn around to witness the tragedy. I, for one, was surprised that shit had actually worked. Not to say I wasn't confident; if anything, I was maybe a little arrogant. I couldn't believe it was that easy. The confrontational Outlaw focused back on me, but my gun was already drawn.

One to the stomach and one to the chest—it was self-defense. And I wished it had gone down in a different way.

I ran myself and Nicolas back to the car in the height of the confusion and panic. I unlocked the car and threw him in the passenger seat and ran to the driver's side. The faster I get out of here, the better. People would've heard that explosion a mile away. The cops were closing in, no doubt. But of course, I had to obey the rules of the road. I pulled out and drove off with a smile on my face.

I could feel Nicolas staring at me with a sense of fear. I was capable of so much, yet I grabbed a gun and joined the mob. It was selfish and poor tactic I continued to regret.

The first police car I saw had sirens blaring and was racing toward the scene. It made me nervous, but I had no trouble just passing through. Several more patrol cars flew past with ambulances and fire engines on their tail. The Outlaws wouldn't snitch me out; it was against their code. However, cameras in the vicinity would not be so friendly. Besides, the police would be more interested in the contents of the building than they would the culprit—at least for the first couple hours maybe.

The rest of the drive up to Jamaica Estates seemed peaceful. I focused on developing more of a plan, rather than running in with explosives strapped to my chest and hoping a stray bullet wouldn't set them off. All the while, the news played on the radio, reporters making exclamations about the rising crime rate and gas prices. There was only a brief mention of a mysterious explosion that had rocked Myrtle Avenue earlier in the afternoon, as not much was known ten to fifteen minutes after the incident.

As we grew closer and closer to Jamaica, I grew more and more worried and paranoid. I was constantly checking my mirrors and finding it increasingly likely I'd see a familiar face or, God forbid, either I or the car would be recognized. Nicolas felt this way as well.

I drove slowly up an incline and into the cul-de-sac, passing by mansion after mansion of the esteemed New York wealthy class. This place was a refuge for politicians and mobsters, who lived side by side as neighbors. Why was I getting political about this? This didn't matter. All that mattered was finishing the job. I turned to Nicolas for guidance.

CARTER. Any of these houses look familiar to you?

He sat quietly for a moment with a pale and horrified face. He still didn't know the plan or what his outcome would be, and neither did I for that matter. At this point, it was just blind rage fueling me, and I had nothing to do except kill. The future and its mysteries started to fog my head with delusions and bad thoughts. But I shook it off as if it was nothing.

NICOLAS. There. That's the one.

His voice was shaky and soft. His nervousness made me more on edge, and I didn't know why. He also didn't have any reason to lie anymore. Judging from his fear, he thought his honesty could save him. I trusted him in this, which was wild. But after all, a wild night was about to ensue. I didn't believe all that much in religion, but I was sure as shit about to pray I'd get out of this one alive.

I wasn't ready for this, though. I wanted the sun to be down at least. So, I Looked for a place to pull over somewhere for a little bit to get out of the way. Obviously, I didn't want to sit on their front curb waiting for an opportune moment to strike. That would be flat-out stupid. I ended up pulling into the driveway of some house going up for sale. It wasn't that far away either, and I wouldn't have trouble from anybody coming home, as the place was vacant. I contemplated getting out and taking down the sign. But I felt that would be too much. I would just hide in plain sight, no need for extra precautions. So we sat there and we waited—patiently.

20

After much patience and paranoia, the sun slowly set. And still there was no movement of any vehicles. However, by this time, the number of guards on the outside increased, and most of the lights were still on inside the mansion. Obviously, she wasn't going anywhere. That would make this so much harder. We hadn't been noticed thankfully, so there was still an upside. I still had the element of surprise up my sleeve.

We sat in silence, but Nicolas got curious.

NICOLAS. I read your record, you know.

CARTER. Good for you.

I wasn't in the mood for talking, but I could do with a little distraction.

NICOLAS. A lot of missing pieces.

CARTER. Missing pieces like what?

NICOLAS. Well, first off, like everything. It's like you never existed until you were twenty-five. And there's only a little bit about you being in the military. That's it.

Was it really time to tell the truth? To expose it all? I didn't need to lie to myself. Yes, training had taught me secrecy. But why was I still holding onto that? In order to let go of the past, I had to be honest, right?

CARTER. Do you really want to know?

NICOLAS. I was just curious. That's all.

I took a moment before deciding it was time to get all of it off my chest.

224

CARTER. I was a marine.

I was an operator.

He looked confused because he didn't know the term.

CARTER. I was Special Forces.

He didn't really know what to say, as my record didn't say any of that. It was all blank, all a mystery. Older files shed more light. But then again, those files didn't match up with the new ones—made it confusing.

NICOLAS. I know, yeah. But there's something more about you that isn't there. Your file is blank from the point you enlisted until the point you showed up in Missouri under a fake name.

CARTER. We did this operation back in Iran in 2013.

I took a deep breath. Nicolas stared at me, curious to learn more. The truth couldn't hurt me anymore.

CARTER. Me and five other guys were dropped into this village a couple miles from the shore. Our task was to capture a Russian arms dealer supplying weapons to the Taliban. We didn't know how the fuck they knew first, but they did. They knew when we would get there and what we were there for. Half the fucking village lit us up with machine-gun fire from all directions. We had the advantage with NVGs. But still, it was a losing battle?

NICOLAS. NVGs?

CARTER. Night vision goggles—the cheapest ones the American military could afford too.

We had to shoot women and children who were firing at us. I tried not to count how many I killed. It just made me sick.

NICOLAS. Jesus.

I started to tear up, but I soldiered on into the story.

CARTER. After hours of fighting, we ran for a mile or so into the woods until we found a clearing to exfil. One marine and two SEALs died that day. And at one point, we even got within shooting range with a pistol of that Russian cocksucker. But there was no chance.

I stopped for a moment to take another deep breath.

CARTER. The next week, an American convoy drove over mines in the road. We managed to link it to him, and that fucker killed nineteen marines that day.

CARTER. The Iranians had cameras and shit and got all our faces. They wanted us all dead after that. They put out bounties and everything. They wouldn't let me go on anymore missions after that.

The car was silent for ages. He didn't know what to say. He couldn't imagine what it was like to have been through that.

NICOLAS. I'm sorry.

That was what everybody said, even the fucking officers. But what did they do? They let the bastard go on some prisoner transfer or some shit. Politics in the military was too fucked for my understanding. But my God, was there more to say.

CARTER. That shit wouldn't be on my record, I hope you know. They didn't trust that information being out there for obvious reasons. And instead of putting all that down, they wrote out some bullshit story about PTSD or dishonorable discharge, whatever the fuck it is now.

They would have written down something better. But then something else happened—the reason I got kicked out.

I started to raise my voice. I was obviously emotional the whole time. I had damn good to reason to be. And shit was it good to say it out loud.

NICOLAS. Well ... Why'd you get kicked out then?

I took one last deep breath.

CARTER. A year or two after that operation they let me have a desk job in Sigonella, Italy. I got bored after a while and got nosy and did some digging in the area.

I uncovered a prostitution ring that involved high-ranking military leaders, including admirals and generals and all that sort of shit. After I had enough evidence, I brought it up to a trusted friend, who was a colonel.

I trusted him, and he sold me out. It turned out he was in on it too. But no one else would believe me. So next time

I did a piss test, I magically popped for opioids. I fought that case. Believe me I fought it—until they had ripped that staff sergeant patch right off my sleeve.

They discharged me for that. And since I knew about special operations, they had to fuck up my record even more and dropped me off in Missouri. The worst part was, not three months later, they all get arrested and charged for that prostitution ring. And I stood alone and forgotten in the middle of fucking nowhere.

My heart was racing, and I could tell the veins on my forehead were showing. I was fucking furious. But I needed to calm down. Going into a fight with anger leads to mistakes. *Calm down*, Tristan. *Just calm down.*

NICOLAS. That's awful. I am truly sorry. No matter who the fuck you are, that's just, well, fucked.

It felt like we were starting to build a friendship. Odd how that happens. The only relationship we had was our shared hatred of Anastasia. Man was too old to fight, though, and had no experience. I didn't need a partner, just a scapegoat.

NICOLAS. You're not going to kill me. Are you?

Changing the subject so soon? Made a little sense, but the topic we had been discussing was still running around in my mind.

CARTER. I never planned on it, Nicolas.

NICOLAS. Then why am I here right now? What are you going to do?

I checked my watch and smiled. It was finally time. I turned to face him.

CARTER. You are gonna go in there.

NICOLAS. Oh. No fucking way. They'll kill me if I step one foot on their lawn.

CARTER. Well, actually, they're probably not gonna kill you outside. They'll at least wait till you get in the house.

NICOLAS. You can't actually be serious right now, can you?

He looked at my face, and the expression did not change a single bit. I was not kidding. I then reached for the duffel bag that had the explosives. I took out the other explosive as well. I needed to inspect them so I could tell which detonator went to which bomb. Once I'd determined that, I placed the other one on the floor behind me. I sure as shit wasn't going in there with my last explosive. I needed it for Mr. Soko. I then showed it to my prisoner.

NICOLAS. Is that a fucking bomb?

CARTER. Nicolas, you're gonna have to trust me on this OK?

NICOLAS. What? Fucking no!

CARTER. I'm gonna give this to you.

NICOLAS. What? So you can blow me up like some fucking suicide bomber. I'm not fucking doing it.

He was starting to interrupt me.

CARTER. Nicolas, you keep interrupting me, then you *are* gonna be a suicide bomber.

He stopped arguing instantly.

CARTER. I'm gonna give you this, and I'm gonna give you the detonator. You're the one who decides when to blow it up.

NICOLAS. This still seems like a very bad idea.

CARTER. Well you wanna fucking go in without the bomb? Either way, you're going in first.

He knew he didn't have any other choice; it was just a matter of him accepting it.

NICOLAS. Well, what the fuck are you gonna do?

CARTER. I'm not gonna tell you specifics. But I can guarantee you, as soon as that thing goes off, my ass in charging in there to kill Anastasia.

He sat there staring at the explosives and detonator in my hand. He really didn't want to do this, and I didn't blame him. It was a stupid idea. But while he went into the front, I would go in through the back.

NICOLAS. But if I blow it up, it'll still be, like, in my pocket and shit.

CARTER. Well, obviously, don't blow it up while it is still in your pocket. What you do with it is up to you. Just try to enjoy some revenge while you're in there, OK?

NICOLAS. You really are fucking crazy.

CARTER. Well, you know what they say. You can take a man out of the marines, but you can't take the marine out of a man.

I smiled. He frowned and took the explosives from my hand and then opened the car door.

CARTER. **Oh and, Nicolas.**

He turned back to me.

CARTER. **Good luck.**

He gave me this sort of sarcastic smile and closed the door.

The plan was in motion now. I waited for Nicolas to slowly walk across the road and down the sidewalk. All the while, I was talking to myself. *Don't turn around. Don't turn around.* Eventually, he came up to the house and stopped. I held my breath. He limped up the yard, still wincing. I *had* put a bullet in his foot. I really hoped I'd just given him the right detonator.

Nah, should be fine. I turned the car on and turned right down the road, just as the guards drew their weapons.

I took another left turn at the first stop sign, and after the next stop sign, I took another. My goal was to end up behind the mansion. Unfortunately, there was a dead end. I would have to go on foot. I put the car in park and grabbed the duffel bags filled with extra weapons. It was, of course, a little heavy, considering I had a lot of shit in there. But I could manage. I trekked into the woods and tried to be as quiet as possible but still be a little quick. I didn't want to miss an opportunity.

I had to go through another hundred feet of trees and bushes before I saw the clearing. I was on the other side of the mansion now. In the back windows, I saw guards patrolling hallways. Now, all I had to do was wait. I went into the duffel bag to get an M500 shotgun—a classic and familiar favorite. I had even worked alongside her often at the range back in the service. She was very powerful; very fun; and, of course, very deadly. I even made sure to bring a sling, just in case I lost my grip. Now I was slinged up, and the bag was considerably lighter. The sling was practically a bandolier, with many spaces for extra ammunition.

I waited.

And waited.

And waited.

The minutes rolled by, and I was starting to think the man had gotten himself killed.

All of sudden, the ground shook as the explosive ripped out the right side of the house. Debris flew into and smashed the neighbors' windows and damaged their shingles. Some guards were thrown by the force, and others stood staring, shocked at what had just happened. I took a second to catch my breath and then took the shotgun off safety. They'd never forget me after this.

I leaped over bushes and logs and climbed over the fence before they set their sights on me. Three armed men were in the back. I crouched down and fired one shot, hitting one in the chest and another in his shoulder, as they didn't know anything about spacing. The other started to fire at me. I was quick enough to chamber another shell and hit him square in the forehead.

The last injured man grabbed for his gun as I ran up toward the back door. Another shell to the chest, and he was done. I took the wall next to the back door as cover and reloaded the three shells I had just spent. No one was coming around the left or right side of the house, so I busted through the door and checked my corners instantly.

I was in this long hallway with corners on either side. I decided to go left, as it didn't really matter where I went. I had a gun drawn high while I moved through the hallway, occasionally stopping for cover to check behind me. They still might not even know I was here. I continued on and took the corner almost too wide, exposing myself before the gun. One guard was running toward me to ascertain the situation. He didn't know what hit him. Well, actually a buckshot hit him in the chest. But it wasn't the time for jokes I suppose.

Another man came out of a door to the right, and he got hit in the chest as well. I moved up to the open door to see it was a staircase. That seemed like a fair route. Two men appeared at the top of the stairs to fire down at me. I hit one in the shoulder before I had to take cover. I used the time to reload and check my surroundings. A man ran out from the side of the hallway I had come from. He almost got me, but his aim was terrible. He took one to the heart, and then I reloaded again.

The gunman on the stairs stopped to reload, and I jumped out and put one in his head. I was getting low on ammo for my shotgun. I might have to change soon. I passed the man on the stairs with the injured shoulder, and he begged me not to shoot. I kicked his gun away, along with his partner's and came to a corner of the balcony overlooking the main entrance. This was the busiest area of the house. Multiple men seemed to be streaming out from fucking everywhere.

I crouched down to become a smaller target. I took a man out on the left and one on the right before I started taking shots from the main entrance. At that moment, a bullet flew, and I took it into my left shoulder. I thought it was all over. I got up to the wall and slouched down. They couldn't hit me from there, but that bullet had knocked the wind clean out of me. Those bastards had actually managed to hit me for once in their lives. I just sat there thinking about how I had gotten to this moment. I smiled. And then I laughed. I was not gonna die in this shithole.

I took out another man who scared me coming from the right. I slowly stood up until I had my sights on someone on the ground floor. One to the head. I circled back over to the staircase, as they would definitely be coming. And sure enough, four oblivious men with no sense of sight or direction got mowed down like cattle. I was down to my last round on the shotgun and realized I needed to move a little more quickly now, as the police would soon arrive. *Don't panic. Please continue.*

I took out the bastard who'd shot me on the ground floor and then defiantly chucked the shotgun down and got out my rifle with the sling. My arm was in excruciating pain, but the sling made it a lot easier. I made it a little farther before I came on another staircase in front of me. Two men with automatic rifles sprayed down at me. I hit one in the chest and ducked for cover.

I took yet another look at my surroundings. It was starting to quiet down on the back end. I must've killed most of the men on the first two floors. I had just the last floor to go. I shot back out and hit the last man in the chest and head. I ran up the stairs to see five men shooting at me. This was not what I wanted to fucking see at all. I managed to find some cover on the corner of the wall in the nick of time.

I don't normally condone switching your gun to automatic, as it is not only a waste of ammo but also very inaccurate. I'd never actually done it though, so it was now or never. I peeked my head out for a split second to see where they were. And of course, if there's automatic fire spewing at you, the last thing you wanna do is poke your head out. So, at least I had that going for me.

I ran out and held the trigger down. As I'd predicted, they all ducked. But it was not so effective to duck behind a wooden dresser or box, as bullets tended to go through that sort of thing.

I took out one and then two and then three. The gun clicked, as I had spent all my rounds. I noticed this, and so did they. I quickly switched to my pistol, still in my jacket. The curious gangster took two to the chest. The last man stood up and threw his gun on the ground.

GANGSTER. **Hey, don't kill me. I quit OK. She's down there. Just let me go.**

At least I knew I was right.

CARTER. **Well then go.**

He ran past me and down the stairs, pleading his thanks to me.

I took off the silencer, as I didn't need it and just tossed it aside. I moved on to the room at the end of the corridor. My breath was heavy, and my shoulder was still bleeding. I got up to the door. I then heard sirens in the distance. Shit. It was now.

I kicked open the door, went in blind and found myself in sight of two men. And of course, Anastasia was right in the fucking middle.

I hit one man in the head and the other in the chest. And that bitch—that rotten bitch—got me in the leg. But I then got her in the shoulder. She fell back onto her office chair. I quickly stood up as best I could. She attempted to shoot again, and I put one in her hand.

We were both breathing very heavily. Each of us had taken two shots. But I was still standing.

She looked up at me.

CARTER. **Long time no see, huh?**

She was silent and in disbelief.

ANASTASIA. **How?**

CARTER. **How what?**

ANASTASIA. **How did you not die after all of this?**

CARTER. **It's called training. And if you're men had that, they wouldn't be dead right now.**

ANASTASIA. Why did you have to do all this? We could've been peaceful.

CARTER. You killed my best friend—my best fucking friend—and you expect peace? No. You just didn't expect it to go this way. I gave you a chance, and you didn't take it.

The sirens were getting closer. I needed to wrap this up. I could only kill her once.

ANASTASIA. I'm sorry.

It was too late for that. I remembered I had Marvin's phone still on me. One last joke before she went. I pulled it out and threw it on her desk.

CARTER. That's Marvin's phone. That's how I found the pier. The best part was he didn't have a good password on it. What a retard.

One to the head.

She was done, and that nightmare was over. But there was still a lot more to do. I whipped out my phone and took a photo as proof for the yakuza and then turned around and limped out. I let go of the duffle bag and rifle, as it was too much weight, and I didn't need it anymore. As I limped down the staircase, the sirens got closer and closer. I limped across the balcony and the second flight of stairs. I was actually gonna make it through with enough time.

Down through the hallway and out the back door I went, slowly but surely, bleeding and in pain. I couldn't go to a hospital, and I surely couldn't go to Drew. I'd really fucked that one up, indeed. I didn't care, though. It was the right thing to do, and Drew knew it.

I had a lot of trouble climbing over the fence. But in the end, I got it and was in a lot more pain from having done so. I limped through the trees. I could see the lights of the cop cars over on the road, speeding toward the house in the dozens. Shots fired at a mob house? Send in the cavalry of course. It made me laugh, but even that hurt.

I managed to get up to the car—to see Nicolas standing there waiting for me. He'd actually managed to survive. He noticed I was shot but didn't say anything. He probably didn't care or thought it was some karma bullshit. I used my keys to unlock the door and climbed in or, at least, struggled to. He kept staring at me. And it was starting to piss me off.

CARTER. What? What is it? What do you want?

NICOLAS. Well now what?

CARTER. She's dead. And you're free to go

NICOLAS. Where am I supposed to go?

I shook my head, as I was applying a rudimentary tourniquet.

CARTER. I don't fucking know. That's up to you now.

NICOLAS. Well aren't you going to drive me?

I flipped him off through the window as I drove off. I didn't like him, but I no longer wanted him dead. He was now a stranger to me. His future was up to him. He'd probably end up behind bars, though, which wasn't really my problem. Right now, my problem was that I was bleeding out, and I was in pain. That was the number one priority. But where the fuck could I go? I had burned all my bridges.

I drove down a side road to avoid driving past the police and continued on. I should get to my apartment perhaps. If I operated on myself, I'd surely go into shock. I was running out of time.

Sandy.

No, I couldn't go to her now. On one hand, she was a nurse. On the other, I was responsible for getting her kids kidnapped. She didn't know that, though. And besides, I had literally nowhere left to go. It seemed wrong. But then again, like I said, I had no other option.

I started speeding away faster and faster. I didn't give a fuck about the traffic laws anymore. They didn't apply here. I was dying, and I didn't want to. I made a beeline for the Bronx as fast as I could. I ran stop signs and red lights for a while until I got close enough, where I could calm down a little bit. The police wouldn't even know I was here. And for her sake, I hoped that remains so. That way, she wouldn't get that whole harboring a fugitive charge.

I came up to the apartment building. But instead of parking on the sidewalk, I left it in an alley so it wouldn't be as easily spotted. I parked, got out, and limped toward the front door. I got up the steps and started to feel light-headed. *No. Not now.*

I soldiered on past the front desk without getting noticed, as the woman there was asleep. Lazy as hell. Good for me though. I got over to call the elevator and waited. Eventually, I got in and took it up to my floor. I was praying I would not pass out in this elevator. I needed to be conscious.

The elevator door opened, and I stumbled out and saw there was no one in sight. I limped over to her door. I banged and banged. *Please open the door*, I thought.

The door swung open, and we locked eyes. I was bleeding all over her doormat. She was, without a doubt, shocked.

CARTER. **Hey.**

I mean, what the fuck else do you say in a situation like that? Well maybe help or something. But it was already out.

SANDY. **Oh my God. I'm gonna call an ambulance.**

CARTER. **No, no, no. Wait.**

She stopped.

CARTER. **I need your help, please.**

At that moment, she knew I didn't work at the police academy and that I sure as shit was on the run. She didn't say anything for a second. I needed her help, and she was saying nothing.

CARTER. **Please.**

I was actually begging now. Had my soul shattered tonight? Had I lost a piece of myself? What was happening?

She then put the phone away and put her arm around my shoulders and carried me to a chair in the living room. The door closed by itself. She set me down gently on the chair.

CARTER. **I've been shot once in my left shoulder and once in my right thigh. No arteries hit.**

SANDY. **I can see that, yeah. What the fuck happened to you?**

I couldn't tell her. We had been on like three fucking dates. It wasn't much of a relationship. But I was glad she cared enough to do this. I still couldn't tell her though, could I? Would she understand? Even I didn't understand sometimes.

SANDY. **Carter, I need you to tell me what happened and why I can't call the police.**

Shit. If it meant my survival, then so be it.

CARTER. I killed like twenty fucking mobsters over in Jamaica.

She stopped. She stared up at me. It wasn't hard to tell that I was being honest. However, she continued on. She went and got scissors from the kitchen to cut off my clothes. At this point, I could see the wound, and it upset my stomach for sure. She then poured alcohol on the wound on my leg.

Sheer fucking pain. I recoiled in agony.

SANDY. There's no bullet in your leg I don't think. It went straight through. You'll be fine.

That was somewhat a relief I thought. I let her continue on as I clenched my teeth and tried not to scream.

SANDY. Why did you kill all those people, Carter? Why?

CARTER. Because they killed my friend.

I could only muster short responses in between heavy breaths.

SANDY. Why couldn't you just go to the police?

CARTER. Because I'm working against them. I was in a rival outfit.

She hesitated.

SANDY. I shouldn't be doing this right now. I should call the police.

CARTER. Sandy, please. I know we didn't get to know each other that well. And I'm sorry I'm putting you in this situation. You are not in danger. And if you don't help me, they will kill me.

SANDY. Who's they?

CARTER. The Mafia, the yakuza, the bikers, the feds—anyone of them.

Do you remember that stuff on TV about the mob and the FBI working together on some gun-running thing? That was me. I called that in.

What I'm doing right now and what I've been doing is for the betterment of everybody. I'm not in the military anymore. But that doesn't mean I can't do a better job than the police. And for God's sake, I actually do.

If you call the police, they'll hand me over to the feds, and then they'll kill me. I am begging you to do the best you can here.

I have nowhere left to turn to, Sandy. Please.

She didn't know what to say. But maybe God was looking down on me that day and decided what I was doing was right—how I was changing myself into a better person. She put the phone down.

SANDY. **Do you know where my children are?**

Please don't make me say it, Sandy. Please don't.

CARTER. **Sandy.**

SANDY. **Do you know where my children are?**

I'm so sorry.

CARTER. **No.**

She continued working on my wounds as if nothing had happened. It was quiet though. She stopped now and then began to quietly sob. What had I done? I didn't want to be the bad guy. But it had come down to that, and that was exactly the opposite of what I needed. I couldn't plan for this. No one could.

Time rolled by, and before I knew it, she was close to finishing up. The sooner I got out of her hair, the better for both of us. It was still bizarre how she continued to care for me even after all of this. Eventually, she stood up after my arm was in a sling and my thigh was wrapped in bandages. She didn't tell me I would need antibiotics, but I knew I did. All she said was the last thing I could have imagined.

SANDY. **Tell Drew I quit**

Her voice was a quiet yet powerful whimper. She had been an Outlaw the whole time, and I would have never known it. Yet another bridge burned. It was so sad. I was coming back into the realization that my actions had consequences. I slowly stood up, still in pain.

SANDY. **If you ever come here again, I'll shoot you myself.**

I couldn't even say sorry. It would never matter. All there was left to do was end the rest of this awful nightmare. I had to leave this place and never return. It was a great idea indeed. I limped toward the door, and she held back tears. She was waiting for me to leave, and so I did. I closed the door behind me, and I could hear her sobbing on the other side.

I went into my apartment to get a change of clothes, which were very hard to get into, and an empty backpack for later use. I also stuffed the backpack with the bloody and torn clothes I had just gotten out of.

I limped down the hallway. I hate to admit that a man such as myself could cry. But I had no backbone left after that. I was the villain, after all.

I made my way over to the elevator and took it down to the ground floor. I then limped back across the lobby to see the receptionist had woken up. She looked up at me but didn't care much. She just smiled. If only she knew.

I limped out the door and down the stairs. I looked both ways before crossing and went across the street to the alley where my car was. I unlocked it and got in the driver's side.

A man stepped out in front of my car with a flashlight blaring in my eyes. The jig was up. He put the flashlight down, and my eyes needed to adjust. It was that motherfucking yakuza courier.

He motioned for me to get in an SUV across the street. I knew the drill. I reached my arm into the back seat to get the last explosive and shoved it to the bottom of the backpack. Then I got out and closed the door.

COURIER. You are injured?

CARTER. No shit.

I obviously wasn't in the mood.

COURIER. Come. We can help.

Sure, fuck it. Why not? I thought.

I limped along past him.

COURIER. I can carry your bag. What's in it?

CARTER. My bloody clothes from tonight. I want it disposed of properly.

COURIER. Oh OK.

Thankfully he was taking the bag with us.

I limped back across the street and into the SUV. I expected a blindfold this time, but it never came. They didn't even search me for my gun. It was obviously an urgent meeting.

The drive down was calm and soothing. The seats were comfortable, and I almost wanted to take a nap. But I was still on edge—still racing from the events of this eventful day.

The radio played news of the explosion earlier today, labeling it a "gang attack" and noting the explosion at Jamaica Estates was a sign that the war was over. For me, it wasn't. Mr. Soko and Colton had to die; they were too dangerous and too corrupt to live. They were a stain on the city that, if not removed, would cause more harm, and this terrible cycle would undoubtedly repeat itself with another poor victim taking my place as some sort of scapegoat.

I was still thinking about how much pain I'd caused Sandy tonight. It almost made me tear up again. I could cry later. Now was the moment of execution.

It was late at night when we arrived at the house—around 11:00 p.m. I'd say. It was definitely past my bedtime for sure. The car stopped and everybody got out. I took the opportunity to grab my backpack from the front seat. If I was trusted enough to not be searched, then surely I was trusted with explosives.

I limped up the lawn. The yakuza tried to help me time and time again, but I insisted on going in on my own, no matter how painful it was. The doorman opened the door for me, and I strolled in and headed for Mr. Sokos's office. The two men guarding it knocked on the door and waited for permission to enter. I was then granted entry.

MR. SOKO. Tristan!

I didn't say anything. But I put my backpack on the table.

MR. SOKO. What's this?

CARTER. They're my clothes from a few hours ago. They're bloody, and I want them destroyed properly.

MR. SOKO. Yeah, yeah. No problem. I want to congratulate you on a job well done.

CARTER. Thanks.

I wasn't enthusiastic about this at all.

CARTER. Where are the children?

MR. SOKO. They are safe as promised. In fact, they were dropped off at a fire station a mere twenty minutes ago.

CARTER. Can you prove that?

MR. SOKO. Well, if they don't show up, you'll know where to find me.

I had to take his word for it. Did it even matter now?

CARTER. What about Colton's location?

He handed me a slip of paper. On it was an address.

MR. SOKO. Very eager to leave. And you only just arrived.

CARTER. I'm just tired.

MR. SOKO. I can understand that. I'm sorry.

He was joyful tonight. I could understand as well.

MR. SOKO. Tristan, I want someone with your talents working for me for the betterment of this city.

CARTER. Let me sleep on it. As you can tell, I'm in not that good of working condition.

MR. SOKO. If you ever change your mind, if you ever have a problem, just call.

He handed over his card with numbers and an address. Odd thing for a mob boss to have.

CARTER. Well, Mr. Soko, it's been a pleasure. And I'm off to say goodnight and sweet dreams.

MR. SOKO. I hope to see you again soon, Tristan.

CARTER. Likewise.

He held out his hand, and I shook it with a fat grin. I turned around and limped out the door. I limped down the hallway and limped out the front door. I limped down the lawn and back into the SUV.

At this point because of my hasty retreat, there was only a passenger and the driver. I was ready to end another nightmare. I waited for them to start the car and hoped I was still in range. And a couple seconds later, I pressed the detonator.

I heard the explosion behind me, and I didn't flinch. I didn't even look. I was quick to pull out my gun and shoot behind the seat at the passenger and driver. If I shot their heads, there'd be blood on the windows—not a good look When driving around. I quickly got out of the car and tossed out the driver's body.

At that point, I looked back to see what kind of damage I had done this one last time. The office has been completely incinerated, and there was a gaping hole in the side of the house. *Another one bites the dust,* I thought.

I took control of the wheel and headed straight for Colton. Up next, the last showdown, the last step, the last bullet.

21

I waited patiently in a chair behind a desk Colton had at his little safe house. I was still in pain and sore from the events of the night, I wondered about infection. Were nurses even qualified to treat bullet wounds? I was just glad they were both through and through. Otherwise, I'd be in a lot more pain than I currently was. I still had to worry about getting my hands on antibiotics, however. I would have to find another time to worry about that.

Colton's apartment was bigger than mine and a lot nicer. His desk sat in the corner of the living room, giving him a clear view of the door at the back of the room. I always liked to be dramatic. It wasn't so much that I wanted some sort of confession. More or less, I wanted his acceptance. I wanted him to understand his wrongdoings and for me to understand mine. I wanted him to admit his defeat, and I would go on my way somewhere. I couldn't stay in the city anymore. That ship had most certainly sailed long ago. It was just me, him, and the gun. I wondered how many people in law enforcement or federal agencies were looking for me now. How many people in the Outlaws wanted me dead?

An escape after tonight wasn't planned. I had been careless these last few hours with the excitement of finishing it all. Were Sandy's children even safe? Had I gotten her killed after bombing Soko? What did the future have in store for me? Should I just turn myself in with no evidence and have this cycle repeat itself? Was I some vigilante? What had all this been for anyway? So many questions had raced back and forth since day one. I'd thought I was a hot shit with everything I'd done. But in the end, I had come to realize I was only human. I had been shot twice and had barely made it out of that mansion.

I was just lucky. Was God a factor in all this? I should've been dead long ago. *No*, I told myself. *Don't bring religion into this.* Just be glad to end this.

And to think, all these organizations pitted against each other, and I had been placed in the middle with an expected outcome of, who knows what? I had come so far and lost everything in order to secure my own safety. I almost felt selfish. Todd was dead. Sandy despised me. And maybe a hundred more could've survived if these events hadn't happened. I never liked thinking about those things. Maybe it was because I wasn't willing to face the truth. I was the bad guy. I did realize something like that a bit ago. Saying I could change myself while simultaneously killing all these people in a rage unlike anything this city had ever seen did seem to make the point.

Did the good outweigh the bad in all of this? Had I saved more lives than were lost? I wanted to know the answer, but there was no way of telling what would've happened if I hadn't intervene—if I hadn't caused all this chaos and killed all these people. I told myself it was self-defense. It was me or them. But did it have to be any of us? Fuck that hippy shit. I was no pacifist in the end, and I couldn't act like it ever again. Nothing could take away what I'd done—repair the lives I'd ruined, restore the families I'd destroyed, bring back the people who no longer lived. I was going in circles with the same thing over and over again. But once you get locked into a deadly battle, your sanity is at stake.

The time had come. I heard keys on the other side of the door. I had been ready for this since day one. I had the element of surprise. Now was just the right moment to strike. Here in this dark room, I hoped I wouldn't be spotted until after he closed the door behind him.

The door opened, and it got tense.

Colton showed up in the doorway, oblivious to my existence.

He closed the door behind him.

He turned on the lights and spotted me, with my gun aimed in his direction.

He froze. He was shocked. No words could possibly describe the fear in his face. But he snapped back to reality. He just might have been willing to accept his fate.

We didn't say much for a moment or two. Needless to say, even my younger self was paralyzed. I had planned for this. But did I really expect this plan to follow through?

CARTER. **Surprised?**

He refused to speak.

CARTER. **I know your gun's in the shoulder holster. So, first take off your jacket so I can see.**

He hesitated and shook his head in disbelief. He did so at an aggressive pace, which made me uneasy.

CARTER. **Slowly, Colton. Don't do anything that'll get you shot right now.**

He paused to hear what I was saying and began to remove his jacket slowly. He then slammed his suit jacket on the ground in one agitated motion.

CARTER. **Now, slowly remove your gun from the holster and put it on the ground.**

He knew what I was capable of. So, he didn't try anything, no matter how much he wanted to. He knew the risk and didn't attempt to provoke any reckless action. He slowly removed the gun from his shoulder holster with two fingers and gently placed it on the ground. Cooperation would make him live longer. I hoped he knew that.

CARTER. **Now, come over and have a seat.**

He slowly shuffled over to have a seat at the chair in front of the desk. But I couldn't see his hands that well. He tried to put them in his pockets.

CARTER. Come on, Colton. Make your hands visible. Don't be stupid.

He showed his hands as he continued on slowly toward his final resting place. The last place he would live would be his own wooden chair.

He sat down calmly.

CARTER. Both hands on the desk.

He looked at me angrily but did as I asked anyway.

We sat there for another moment. I was smiling, and he was not. He had no reason to be happy. He'd lost the upper hand, and he never even knew when.

He finally broke his silence.

COLTON. Do you know how much shit you caused in this city, Tristan?

Damn right I did.

COLTON. I've been watching the news, and we know it was you. We have video evidence of you bombing out an Outlaw hideout. We have witness testimonies. We have physical evidence. We have everything we need

It's over, Carter. We're closing in.

I didn't care anymore. My job was nearly done.

CARTER. They can have me, Colton. But you can't. And I hope you understand that now.

COLTON. It doesn't matter about me, Carter. It was always about you. You are a menace to society. You kill without reason or mercy for your own self-interest.

CARTER. Oh, and you don't?

COLTON. I was taking down criminals—actually fugitives. Don't try and make me look like you.

CARTER. You gave weapons to Greenwich for them to continue what they were doing. They tortured innocent men and had them killed for just being in a different outfit.

COLTON. We we're pitting the mobs against each other. We were taking them both out.

CARTER. Then why did I have to be a part of all of this?

COLTON. You should have never been there, Carter. That was never planned.

CARTER. Yet you tried to kill me anyway.

COLTON. Like I said, you shouldn't have been there.

CARTER. I had everything taken away from me in this. Everything I had left was taken from me—my jobs, my friends, my safety, and my own sanity. I did not deserve this.

COLTON. Oh don't be dumb, Carter. Let's face it. You're a criminal as much as any of the other people you killed. It's just you didn't die. That's it. You have this giant superiority complex; you think you're some fucking savior of the people because you were in the marines.

CARTER. Do you wanna know why my record was so shady?

COLTON. Frankly, Carter, I don't really give a shit.
Before Missouri, you were a marine. Now you're a gangster.

CARTER. If anything, Colton, I did your job for you. I killed off the yakuza and Greenwich, and it'll be quite some time before they can build themselves up again.

COLTON. You didn't do anything, Carter. Someone will come along to replace those you took out anyway. They're just pawns in it all. You don't think it ends with them, do you?

CARTER. I do, Colton. Yes.

COLTON. You're so naïve. Why can't you get this through your head? Everyone knows who you are now. You're no longer some cretin off the street with a gun and some bullets. You're a wanted man now. The FBI wants you, and so does the rest of the city. You are no better than them.

Was he right? Or was he putting all this stuff in my head to confuse me? He wanted me to turn myself in. He was lying to me. It was a dirty trick. He did bring up some valid points. However, my goal was never to rid the world of tyranny in any way, shape, or form. I just wanted to leave. But I had been stopped and pursued. I had defended myself. There was nothing more to it.

COLTON. You know what they'll do to you if they find you, Carter? They'll do to you what you did to them. They will make you suffer.

CARTER. I won't listen to you, Colton. I will never understand what you do and why you do it. You sell guns to people and destroy lives. You destroy families and overrun cities. We had to deal with someone like that in the military once, and I let him get away from me. And in return, he killed nineteen service members. I can never let that happen again.

You are no better than a killer, Colton. That's exactly what you are—a murderous monster who is only fueled by innocent blood. You think I'm the one who's crazy? No. I was a goddamn hero once. I might not be now. But I certainly didn't lose my mind like you. You are nothing but a killer.

COLTON. You are beneath me.

CARTER. Really?

COLTON. Yeah.

CARTER. I don't think so—because, from now on, you'll always be six feet under.

One to the head.

Relief and peace swept over me—a wave of bliss.

I left the gun on the desk and stood up. Using a rudimentary crutch I had shaped out of a lamp from the corner an hour or so earlier, I strutted over to the door and took one last look at the room. *I won*, I thought to myself. *I won.*

The loose ends were tied.

But I still went back to Sandy's to drop off half of the cash I had stolen from Greenwich nearly a month ago. She needed it more than me anyway. She should never have been involved in any of this. I couldn't take back what had happened to her. And God knows what they did to her kids. I felt awful about the whole thing. To imagine the thoughts that had gone through her head the last week or two; the whole ordeal must've been horrifying.

I could finally admit that it was my fault. I couldn't run from that anymore. Hopefully, as time went by, she would be happier than I had ever been. All I could give her now was almost a hundred grand and a happy reunion. Our time together had been short. It could've been something more, but it was just never meant to be.

I took the rest of the money for myself, not in any selfish or egotistical way. It was just I needed a fresh start. I couldn't live somewhere and show up with empty pockets. I never even got to set up Todd's funeral. My rage and hatred blinded me from that. For that, I hope he knows I'm sorry and that I miss him. The city would have probably done something anyway. I think he had a cousin in Albany who would be there for his passing. But I couldn't go back there—not ever again.

After a few days, the news reported on what had happened over the last few weeks. They called it the last gang war. Why? I don't know. Probably some publicity thing.

When all was said and done, they claimed to not know who had done all the killings. Or at least it looked like Greenwich and yakuza had killed each other. Maybe I was off the hook. Maybe Colton had actually been lying. Even if he was, it would be best to get as far away as possible.

I called Drew later on down the endless highway toward Nebraska to find him actually happy to hear from me. Another lucky instance, I suppose. He informed me that Kyle had ended up leaving the Outlaws and getting a job at a lumber business so he could save up enough money to go to college. I was glad he'd listened to me. He was a smart kid after all.

Drew ended up going into witness protection. He sold out everybody. The last big gang was taken out by his own hand. He would die in the other case of continuing his work. Leadership did not like my plan. He didn't tell me where he would be heading though. It was best if neither of us knew our futures anyway. It was best that we left it all behind us.

As for me, Nevada seemed like a decent enough place to start off. Maybe I'd work in real estate or something along the lines of carpentry. That had always seemed interesting to me. Tom Stevenson, although a terrible fake name, was not wanted by either federal or state law enforcement, and the gangs wouldn't stretch out their last bit of operations far enough into the desert to take me out.

What was next though? Back to Missouri? Overseas? My home state of Illinois to be with my parents?

I was happy driving down this empty highway. I was finally free. I had escaped by the skin of my teeth. My wounds still needed to be fixed in a more professional way. But right now at this moment, I had survived. And I was happy.

Somewhere along the highway in Pennsylvania, I threw my gun out the window. I didn't need it anymore. I'd even stopped smoking the other day. Just another bad habit to bury with the rest of these memories I had to let go. In the end, I was a good person turned bad, and then I was in some limbo for a long time, and now I was the good guy again—just like how I was when I served. That's just one of the many lenses my life and choices can be perceived through.

However, if you're still reading this, Sandy, perception didn't always have to be reality.

Matthew A. Knorpp is an active duty United States sailor. He was born in the outskirts of Chester County, New York, and raised in North Conway, New Hampshire. From an early age he always had a fascination with writing.

Made in the USA
Middletown, DE
16 May 2024

54456888R00151